THE LANGUAGE OF MURDER

Shelaeva elbowed the militia photographer out of the way and presented the contents of the car boot with an indifferent wave of her rubber-gloved hand. By contrast with the man in the passenger seat, the occupant of the Volga's boot could not have looked more dead. Bound hand and foot, and doubled up like the occupant of some ancient burial pit, it was difficult to say much about him save that he had been shot several times through a length of sticking plaster that covered his mouth.

Grushko sucked his cigarette as if reminding himself that he still had a mouth, tipped his head to one side the better to see the dead man's face and then uttered what sounded like a grunt of affirmation. But it was Nikolai who offered the explanation.

"Looks like Mafia Morse code, sir," he said.

DEAD MEAT

PHILIP KERR

SEAL BOOKS
McClelland-Bantam, Inc. • Toronto

This edition contains the complete text
of the original hardcover edition.
NOT ONE WORD HAS BEEN OMITTED.

DEAD MEAT
A Seal Book / published in association with Doubleday Canada Limited.

PUBLISHING HISTORY

Doubleday Canada Edition published in 1993
Seal edition/March 1996

CIP: 94-930568-5
All rights reserved.
Copyright © 1993 by Philip Kerr.
Cover art copyright © 1996 by Douglas Fraser.
The use of any part of this publication, reproduced, transmitted in any
form or by any means, electronic, mechanical, photocopying, recording,
or otherwise, or stored in a retrieval system, without the prior written
consent of the publisher—or, in case of photocopying of other
reprographic copying, a licence from Canadian Reprography
Collective—is an infringement of the copyright law.

For information address:
Doubleday Canada Limited
105 Bond Street
Toronto, Ontario
M5B 1Y3
ISBN 0-770-42704-9

PRINTED IN CANADA
UNI 0 9 8 7 6 5 4 3 2 1

For Jane

ACKNOWLEDGMENTS

★ This novel would not have been possible without the help of St. Petersburg's Central Board of Internal Affairs. In particular, there were three senior policemen, General Arkady Kramarev, Colonel Nikolai Gorbachevski and Lieutenant-Colonel Eugene Ygetin, who ensured that almost every door was open to me. I was given a police pass, which enabled me to go in and out of the Big House (as they called their headquarters) as I pleased. A police car with a driver and telephone were made available to me on a twenty-four-hour basis and this meant that I was able to take part in several of their operations against the Mafia. At the same time several detectives and investigators took the trouble to describe to me many real cases with which they had been involved, as well as inviting me to their homes and extending to me a hospitality that I often found hard to let myself accept. In short, I was presented with a unique opportunity to observe the men of Russia's anti-Mafia squad and their methods at considerable length.

As well as the men of the Central Investigating Board, thanks are also due in Russia to Alla Shelaeva, Nina Petrovna, Stella Starkova and, for her unfailing patience and honesty, Elena Khristotonova. Thanks are due in London to Nicky Lund, Mark Forstater, Nick Marston, Caradoc King, Allison Lumb, Peter Cregeen, Jonathan Powell and Jonathan Burnham.

Naturally I read a great many books about Russia. Especially helpful have been *Special Correspondent* and *Dateline Freedom*, both by Vitali Vitaliev, *Moscow! Moscow!* by Christopher Hope, *Russian Voices* by Tony Parker, *The New Russians* by Hedrick Smith, *Out of Red Darkness* by Trevor Fishlock, *The Hard Road to Market* by Roger Boyes, and *Epics of Everyday Life* by Susan Richards.

"Hm, so you want some bread?" Ivan Ivanovich will ask.

"What's wrong with that, sir? I could eat a *horse*!"

"Hm. I suppose you want some meat as well?"

"I'll be pleased with anything you're kind enough to give me."

"Hm, so meat's better than bread, is it?"

"You just can't be fussy when you're hungry. Anything's welcome.

From "How Ivan Ivanovich Quarrelled with Ivan Nikiforovich," by Nikolia Gogol, Translated by Ronald Wilks (Penguin Books, 1972)

CHAPTER

ONE

★ A Russian can never resist stories, even the ones he tells to himself.

Lone travellers on the night sleeper from St. Petersburg will be well aware of the hazards of sharing a two-berth compartment with a stranger. The Red Express is often filled several weeks in advance and the railway booking office takes little account of the sexes of those whom fate has decided to throw together for eight hours or more. My own travelling companion, a handsome-looking woman with beautiful, muscular legs, must have thought me a very dull fellow. During the first part of our journey her efforts to engineer a conversation were almost unflagging, and in this respect she seemed to have more gambits than Gary Kasparov: spiralling inflation, ethnic conflict, increased crime, the Kuril Islands, the price of bread, even—I think this is right—some nonsense about how placentas from Russian abortions were used to make expensive face creams for Western women. She tried everything to get me to talk short of using a cosh and a bright light.

Most men would have given their thumbs for such an attractive and well connected travelling companion as I had, especially one so obviously keen to talk. Good-looking women are usually cold and distant when you are lucky enough to meet them alone on a train in a two-berth compartment. But my replies were monosyllabic to say the least. Not that I am usually the uncommunicative type; however on this occasion my mind was elsewhere. Sometimes it was racing through the mid-summer's air and over the flat countryside that lay spread like a vast counterpane outside the window of our carriage. But mostly it was back in St. Petersburg with Yevgeni Ivanovich Grushko and the men of the Central Board.

Chekhov says that a storyteller should show life neither as it is nor as it ought to be, but as we see it in our dreams. Dozing in my warm berth that was indeed how it all seemed to me now, for in a sense my story had started on this very train when, several weeks before I had travelled in the opposite direction, on a temporary attachment to St. Petersburg's Central Investigating Board at the orders of my superiors in Moscow. It was hoped that I might improve my knowledge of how the Mafia worked.

Not that Moscow's underworld is any less in evidence these days. Far from it. No, it was just that the St. Petersburg Central Board; and in particular its most senior detective, Yevgeni Ivanovich Grushko, seemed better able to deal with the Mafia than we were in Moscow. The figures would speak for themselves if I had them to hand. Every man has his own special subject. The shepherd knows more about sheep than the most dedicated of scholars. Grushko knew more about the Mafia than any other policeman in the new Commonwealth of Independent States. But there is a saying that ought to have warned me to be careful of him: beware of a man of one book.

Not that there was much that would have made you immediately wary of him. His face, like his manner, was open and friendly. He wasn't particularly tall, although he looked fit enough. He wore his gray hair long on top of his head, like the young Elvis Presley, and, when I had known him long enough to become aware of his habits and saw that he combed it very often, I recognized that this was his only personal vanity. Nor was Grushko·an unlettered man, as I discovered within a few minutes of shaking his sandpaper-hard hand that first morning we met, on the platform at Petersburg's Moscow Station.

"Did you have a good journey?" he asked, picking my bags off the station platform.

I explained how I had been obliged to share the compartment with an extremely smelly *babushka* who had snored like a saw for almost the entire journey.

"Have you been in St. Petersburg before?"

"Not since I was a schoolboy."

That seemed so long ago, in those early Sputnik-Gagarin days, when it seemed that the Soviet Union was the most impregnable nation on earth. For a moment I was transported back to the same railway-station platform, I was holding my mother's hand and listening to her explain how we would see the most fabulous palaces in the world, while my father unloaded our bags from the carriage. I did not hear much of what Grushko said for at least a minute or two. When I came out of my reverie he was quoting what Dostoevsky had said about St. Petersburg.

" 'This is the most abstract and intentional city in the whole world,' " he said, without a hint of self-consciousness and led me out of the station on to Nevsky Prospekt, where he had parked his Zhiguli.

I said that I had always wondered what Dostoevsky had meant by that particular remark about Leningrad.

"St. Petersburg—it's an ideal," he explained. "The product of one man's will. By the way, never ever call it Leningrad, except in retrospect. That's all finished now."

I looked along the length of the broad thoroughfare. It was a warm June day and things could not have looked less abstract. There is an impressive solidity about St. Petersburg.

"Of course, you wouldn't think it now," he said taking a deep, euphoric breath of the early morning air, "but this really is a very stupid place for anyone to have built a city. Ice-bound for half the year, although there are some people who say our northern frost is very good for the health. Little more than a swamp when Peter the Great first came. All the stone had to be brought in specially. Thousands of the poor serfs died. That's why they say St. Petersburg is built on bones."

He opened the boot of the Zhiguli and then squashed my luggage underneath the lid as if he had been crushing the body of one of those poor serfs.

"Perhaps that's why there's so much crime here in Peter," he said, offering me a cigarette. "All that blood."

I thought of what the poet Anna Akhmatova had said about how it loves blood, the Russian earth, and for a brief moment I was tempted to offer some intellectual credentials of my own. Instead I said something more banal, about there being crime everywhere these days.

"Ah, but not like here," he said, opening the car door for me.

I had the impression that he was reminding me of the purpose of my visit. After all, I had been sent from Moscow to learn how they dealt with the Mafia in St. Petersburg. But what he said next seemed to contradict this thought.

"Not like in Peter. After all, this is where crime got started. There aren't many places where there are as many gloomy, harsh and strange influences on the soul of man as there are in St. Petersburg. Here, I'll show you. It's only a little way out of our way."

He climbed in beside me and started the engine. We drove west along Nevsky for a short distance. The pavements were crammed with people who seemed rather scruffier than their Moscow counterparts, but perhaps that was only because the buildings were more beautiful. We turned north along one of the city's canals and then he stopped and pointed at the top floors of a yellowing tenement.

"Up there," he said. "On the fourth floor. That's where the student Raskolnikov killed the old woman and her sister."

He spoke as if this were one of the more celebrated cases of the day. I looked at the building and found to my surprise that it was too easy to recall the scene from Dostoevsky's novel as something that had actually taken place. An axe-murder. There was nothing Russians loved to read about in their newspapers more than a good axe-murder. Especially if the murderer happened also to dismember his victims and eat them. It just wasn't a proper murder without blood. Lots of it.

"Looks like it might have happened yesterday," I observed.

"Things are a bit like that in Peter. Nothing much has changed since Dostoevsky's day. The Mafia have taken over from the nihilists. They believe in nothing except themselves and their ability to inflict pain and hardship on others in the name of one false god or another."

"There's only one false god today that commands any real devotion," I said. "And that's money."

"Not that the students have been entirely forgotten," Grushko added. "Believe it or not we arrested a student just the other day. A medical student from the Pavlov. You know how he's putting himself through med school? As a hired assassin for the Mob. He got himself interested in guns while he was doing his national service in Afghanistan. Became a marksman. We reckon he's murdered at least ten people." He shook his head. "Compared to the likes of him, Raskolnikov was a puppy."

A *babushka* emerged from the courtyard at the back of the tenement building. A small, dried-up woman of about sixty wearing a threadbare raincoat. To my surprise she was carrying a small strongbox under her arm. Her sharp eyes fixed on our car and she stared at us with hostile suspicion. She might have been the actual moneylender whom Raskolnikov had killed. Grushko noticed her too and nodded.

"A ghost," he said quietly. "Peter's full of them."

He glanced in the mirror and quickly ran a comb through his well-oiled hair. When he had finished it looked exactly the same. I noticed a strong smell of mothballs on the sleeve of his dark grey jacket.

"Before we go to the Big House," he said, "I wanted to get something clear between us."

I shrugged. "Go ahead," I said.

He fixed me with a penetrating stare.

"I've been told you're here because Moscow thinks we have a good record against the Mafia: that you want to look at the way we do things in Peter."

"That's right. It's an intercity liaison thing. An exchange of ideas, if you like."

"Yes," he said, "I read General Kornilov's memo explaining your visit. Sounded like bureaucratic shit to me."

I shifted uncomfortably in my seat.

"What's wrong with exchanging a few ideas?"

"Peter's a smaller place than Moscow. Rather more provincial, too. Everyone knows everyone else. It's harder to lose yourself here than it is in Moscow. What would you say if I told you it was as simple as that?"

"Well, I, er ... I'd suggest you were being modest. Look, I'm not here to patronise you. We can learn from each other, surely."

Grushko nodded, measuring his next remark.

"Let me be frank with you," he said. "If you're here to investigate me and my men, you won't find anything. I can't speak for the rest, but there's no corruption in my department. We're clean. Have you got that?"

"I'm not here to investigate you," I said coolly.

"I don't like spies any more than I like policemen who are getting their paws stroked."

"That leaves me out then."

"Give me your hand."

I held out my hand thinking that he wanted to shake it. Instead he turned it over and stared closely at my palm as if intending to read it.

"You're not serious," I said.

"Be quiet," he growled.

I shook my head and smiled. Grushko scrutinised my hand for almost a minute and then he nodded sagely.

"Can you really read palms?"

"Of course."

"So what do you see?"

"It's not a bad hand," he said. "All the same, your head line seems to be nearly split in two parallel lines."

"And what does that tell you?"

"This reading is for my benefit, not yours."

I drew my hand away and grinned uncomfortably.

"That's some forensic method you have there. Does it work with the Mafiosi?"

"Sometimes. Most of them are pretty superstitious." He took a last drag at his cigarette and grinned. "You wanted to find out how we do things in Peter. Well, now you know."

"Great. Now I can get back on the train and go straight back to Moscow to make my report. Grushko's a great detective because he can read palms. They'll love that. What do you do for an encore: a little levitation, maybe? Hows about I ask you to find some water round here?"

"That's easy."

Grushko wound down the window and threw his cigarette into the canal. I was soon to learn this particular waterway was called the Griboyedev Canal. Maybe he could sense something in the future at that. How else can one explain the fact that in only a few hours we would be back at that same tenement to investigate the murder of one of Russia's best-known journalists?

TWO

★ I am a lawyer by training. This is common enough among investigators. The job requires a knowledge of criminal evidence and procedure that distinguishes if from that of the detective. It may sound typically pedantic, but as a lawyer I think that in order to understand this story you must have some understanding of the background—the Big House, the Department of Internal Affairs and its various departments and, of course, the Mafia.

Most of what I now know about the Mafia I know from Yevgeni Ivanovich Grushko. Perhaps the origins and *modus operandi* of the Mafia as described by him were not quite so dry as they appear here, but I have had to paraphrase the contents of many separate conversations that took place over a period of several weeks. Most of what I know about the departments that are included in Internal Affairs is written from an investigator's perspective and it is perhaps worth noting that a detective could and probably would explain things rather differently.

Every Commonwealth city has its Big House—a building the sight of which encourages people to quicken their step, for it is here that the militia and the KGB have their headquarters. But since this story began almost as soon as I arrived in St. Petersburg it seems only right that I should

Near the top of Liteiny Prospekt and close by the south
bank of the River Neva, Peter's Big House is an enormous
six-storey building that occupies the whole block between
Vionova Street and Kalajeva Street. Presumably there must
have been an architect although, as with most of the modern buildings in this country, it is difficult to see how.
Imagine two huge squares of cheese (and in Moscow these
days, imagining cheese is as near as one actually gets to
it), one red, one yellow, lay the first on top of the second
and you have an idea of what it looks like. Something forbidden and inhuman anyway, and that I suppose was the
whole of the architect's idea: to render the individual in-
significant. This was an impression enhanced by the size
and weight of the front door: as tall as a tram and almost
as heavy, it would have been hard to enter the Big House
without being overawed by the power of the State and
those who, theoretically anyway, enforced its laws.

We flashed our identity cards to the militiaman on
guard inside the door, ignored the empty cloakroom and
crossed an entrance hall that looked as if it belonged to a
public swimming bath.

At the top of the first flight of stairs Felix Dzerzhin-
sky's head occupied a plinth on his own personal mezza-
nine. If ever a man was destined for bronze it was Iron
Felix who, in 1917 at Lenin's request, organized the
Cheka. In 1923 this became the OGPU that, in 1934 became the NKVD that was the forerunner of the KGB,
which will now be disbanded and called something else
again. (If this country leads the world in any kind of man-
ufacturing it is surely in the production of abbreviations
and acronyms.) Until the Second Russian Revolution of
August 1991 there were statues of Iron Felix all over the
USSR. Now the only place you were likely still to find

be a little older before I was ready to dwell on the various injuries that had been inflicted on the body of a seventeen-year-old prostitute as a precursor to her being drowned in a bucket of water. Perhaps if I had slept better on the overnight train from Moscow I could have put up more of a show of interest. As it was I glanced through the photographs, nodded quietly and then returned them without a word.

"Just one of the cases we're dealing with at the moment," Grushko said with a shrug. "We know who did it: an Armenian they call the Barrel. He's an old customer." He tapped the window-pane with his fingernail. "One of the frozen-minded. Oh, you'll get to meet them all, my friend."

I took out my cigarettes and came across the parquet floor to the dirty window with its cheap yellow curtains to offer him one. He took one into his thin lips and lit us both with a handsome gold lighter.

"That's rather elegant," I said, wondering how a policeman on Grushko's salary could afford such a luxurious-looking object.

"From the Swiss police. We get all sorts of delegations coming to see us from Interpol nowadays. Tourists mostly, like all the rest of them. They come to spend their dollars and make sympathetic noises and then they go home again. Funny thing, though, wherever they're from, they always buy me a gold lighter as a thank you. Must be something about cops the world over. Mind you, it's just as well. I'm always losing them."

The phone rang and while he was answering it I looked out of the window at the street below. Housewives were heading to the shops, crowding onto an already over-crowded trolley bus. They were none too gentle about it and for a moment I entertained myself with the thought of my ex-wife doing the very same thing somewhere in east Moscow.

I turned away and looked back at the room: Grushko's desk with its self-important array of telephones; on the wall, the huge map of St. Petersburg with all twenty-two districts neatly marked out like cuts of meat; in the corner the huge safe containing Grushko's files and papers and, standing on top of this, a cheap plaster statue of Lenin, like the one I had left in my own office in Moscow; the line of chairs neatly ranged against the far wall; the fitted cupboard with its own wash-hand basin and coat hook; and the colour television set on which a girl was performing gymnastic exercises. I didn't know it then, but the story had already started.

Grushko replaced the receiver and, as he took a super-human drag of his cigarette, closed one eye while fixing me with the other.

"I think this will interest you," he said. "Come on."

I followed him into the corridor that was busy with other detectives and investigators. He barked at two of them to come with us. On the way down to the car he introduced them as Major Nikolai Vladimirovich Vladimirov and Captain Alexander Skorobogatych and added that they were the best men he had.

Nikolai Vladimirov was a big, heavy man, with a pugnacious little boy's face, his green eyes set rather too closely together and his mouth almost permanently puckered, as if he was about to kiss someone. He wore a black sweatshirt with a Bugs Bunny motif. Alexander "Sasha" Skorobogatych was a fair-haired, Nordic-looking man, his features long and lugubrious and his voice a whispering, sandy sort of rasp, as if he had spent the previous afternoon shouting at a football match. They made an odd trio, I thought. Nikolai and Sasha were each taller than Grushko by a head, and yet they were as careful of him as if he had been their own father; and although Grushko wasn't quite old enough—I guessed him to be in his mid-forties—it wasn't so very far from the truth either:

Grushko was an old-fashioned sort of policeman and very paternal with all his men.

The car headed south along the banks of the Fontanka Canal. It seemed very beautiful and, but for speed of Grushko's erratic driving, I might have been able to enjoy it. Almost to take my mind off the journey, I found myself quizzing Grushko about the Mob and how it got started in Russia.

"You know, I've often thought that we simply swapped the Party for the Mob," I said.

Grushko shook his head firmly.

"Whatever gave you that idea?" he said.

I was just starting to explain when he cut me short.

"No, no," he said. "The Mob is the product of our own Soviet greenhouse effect." The car swerved one way and then the other along the road as he lifted one hand from the steering wheel to light another cigarette.

"It came out of a black market which was allowed to flourish under Brezhnev. A black market was only ever a back-hander away from active encouragement, as the main operators were allowed to buy themselves legal immunity. So then, in order that they could offer larger bribes to more important Party officials ... Well, you're an intelligent sort of fellow, for a Muscovite: work it out."

"They got themselves organised," I said.

"Then, after Brezhnev, organised crime received a bonus in the person of Mikhail Gorbachev ..."

"I don't see how we can hold him to account for the Mob as well as everything else."

Grushko chuckled. "Oh, I'm not saying that Gorbachev was some kind of Godfather. But it was his endorsement of the cooperative movement that gave the green light to people to start their own business. What he failed to realize was that operating a private business obliged all these would-be capitalists to break the law in a number of small ways. Well, that left them vulnerable to the Mob and its demands for protection. So you see, it was the Party which created the atmosphere that helped the Mob to grow."

"The Soviet greenhouse effect you were talking about."

"Precisely. But like everything built in the Soviet Union, the Party was poorly constructed and, as it became weaker, the Mob spread its roots and grew strong. Soon it was so tall that it pushed through those gaps in the roof that Gorbachev had made and, rather than perishing in the cold light of *glasnost*, the Mob thrived. By the time the Party collapsed, the Mob no longer needed it to survive."

"And now that the Party is outlawed?"

Grushko shrugged.

"What remains of it has tried to ally itself with the Mob. After all, it's in both their interests to ensure the failure of everything from the free-market reforms to food aid from the West. Half the new cooperatives in Peter are a front for the Party. A useful way of laundering all the money they got away with after the coup failed. Party money or Mob money, it makes no difference to us. For most people in Peter the whole cooperative movement is synonymous with the Mafia."

"It's the same in Moscow," I said. "Where the businesses are legitimate they're a target for the racketeers."

"The cooperative restaurants and cafés are especially vulnerable," said Grushko. "Not only are they obliged by the nature of their business to operate in public, but also they rely on illegal supplies in order to be able to serve food in any reasonable quantities, as well as to justify the high prices they charge for it. A good dinner in one of the better cooperatives costs ... how much would you say, Nikolai?"

The big man stirred out of the reverie he was sunk in. Grushko's erratic driving didn't seem to bother him much.

"More than you and I could earn in a week, sir," he growled.

"Apart from the tourists, the only people who can afford to eat in such places are those Russians who have access to hard currency; and the crooks."

"In my book, they're one and the same," said Nikolai.

"Most of the cooperative restaurants in Peter are paying protection," said Grushko. "It's usually a fixed percentage of the takings."

"But hôw do the Mafia know how much that is?" I asked.

Nikolai and Sasha exchanged a look. Grushko smiled drily as he answered:

"The restaurants are obliged to tell the city council so that they can pay their taxes. In confidence, of course. But for a small fee the Mafia can learn the precise figure. Which is why most of the restaurants fiddle their books in the first place. Then they pay less when eventually they get squeezed. Even so, it can be as much as a thing a day that they're paying these *churkis*. That's a thousand roubles to you and me. But before you can take that kind of burky off them, you've got to squeeze them hard. You're about to see just how hard that can be."

He steered off the road and into a small parking lot next to a white-fronted building. I lurched forward in my seat as Grushko hit the brake. I got out of the car unsteadily and followed the others up to a heavy wooden door.

The Pushkin Restaurant on the Fontanka Canal was relatively new to the cooperative-restaurant scene. No expense had been spared with the decoration that, I discovered later, was a reproduction of the Green Dining-Room in the Catherine Palace at Pushkin. The walls were light green with white bas-relief ornamentation depicting a selection of scenes from Greek mythology. Two green marble pedestals, each displaying a small imitation jade urn, stood on either side of a white plaster fireplace. On the mantelpiece was a large gilt clock. And in the arched windows curtains of shiny green satin obscured the view of the Fontanka. All the windows except one, that is. This was broken and blackened from the Molotov cocktail that had been thrown through it the previous evening.

Things could have been worse. None of the Pushkin's staff or privileged patrons had been injured: for once, the fire extinguishers had performed as they were supposed to. Apart from the window and a couple of well-scorched dining tables there was little other damage. But for one of the customers reporting the arson attack to the local militia, Grushko's department might never have heard about it.

Grushko sniffed at the blackened tables like an inquisitive cat.

"Well, they knew what they were doing," he said finally. "They didn't leave out the oil. Amateurs usually forget it and just use gasoline. But it's the oil that makes a good Molotov. Makes the flame stick more."

The owner-manager, a Mr. Chazov, did his best to play down the incident.

"I don't think there's any reason for you people from Internal Affairs to become involved in something like this," he said hopefully. "It was nothing. Just a bunch of kids probably. Nobody's been injured, so can't we forget about it?"

"And the men who did this?" Grushko replied obstinately. "Do you think they'll forget about it?"

"Like I said, it was most probably a bunch of kids."

"You got a look at them, did you?"

"Not as such," said Chazov. "No, what I mean to say is, I heard them—laughing."

"It's true, a grown man doesn't find much to amuse him these days," said Grushko. "But to be sure that these were kids just from their laughter, well, that's impressive."

He smiled and wandered round the restaurant nodding appreciatively at the decoration. I saw him catch Nikolai's eye and jerk his head meaningfully. Nikolai nodded curtly and went through to the kitchens.

"Of course, the criminals are getting younger and younger," Grushko continued. "Although it's equally possible that I'm just getting older and older. Either way they're vicious bastards and don't mind who they injure. But that's the carelessness of youth, I suppose. Wouldn't you say so, Mr. Chazov?"

Chazov sat down heavily at one of the tables and dropped his head into his hands. He swept his lank brown hair back across his sweating head and then rubbed his unshaven jaw with the desperate air of a man who needed a drink.

"Look," he gulped, "I can't tell you anything."

"I don't know that I've really asked you anything yet," said Grushko. "What I do know is that these men—these kids—they'll be back. And they'll keep coming back unless you help me. Next time someone might be seriously injured. Or worse."

"Please, Colonel, I have a family, you know?" There was a tremor in his voice.

"Maybe I should ask them who did this."

Nikolai reappeared in the doorway, almost filling it, like a toy bear in its box. He called to Grushko.

A cockroach scuttled out of our way as we followed the big man through the kitchen door. Dirty saucepans and unwashed dishes lay everywhere inside. Crates of vegetables stood on a greasy linoleum floor next to an open bag of foul-smelling garbage. Several flies performed slow aerobatics within easy range of a large slab of chocolate cake. My eyes fell upon a collection of tiny bottles that were gathered in a plastic bag that had been placed on top of a box of apples. For a moment I thought they were phials of drugs, but on looking more closely I realized that each bottle contained a tiny fragment of human stool.

Chazov noted my wrinkled nose and shrugged.

"Department of Health wanted some samples from the staff," he said. "We had a small outbreak of salmonella just after we opened."

"You don't have to leave them lying around in here, do you?" I said.

"No, I guess not." Chazov collected the bag of samples and walked out of the kitchen. I wondered where he was planning to put them this time.

Nikolai hauled open the door to a large walk-in fridge-freezer and Grushko touched his hairline with his eyebrows. There were cartons of meat stacked almost as high as the ceiling. For a moment we just stood there sniffing excitedly at the sour, fleshy air like a pack of hungry dogs.

"Did you ever see so much meat, sir?"

Nikolai touched a piece of frozen beef that lay partly chopped on a butcher's block almost reverently, as if it had been a relic of St. Stephen of Perm.

"I'd almost forgotten what the stuff looked like," Grushko said quietly.

"Hard to remember on a militiaman's salary," observed Nikolai.

"Do you think it might be stolen?" I heard myself say.

Both men turned and looked at me with quiet amusement.

"Well, I don't imagine he bought it in the state meat market," said Grushko. "No, these co-ops rely on illegal sources of supply. That's another reason why they're vulnerable to the squeeze." He looked back at the meat for a second. "I bet that's why he didn't want the militia involved in the first place."

Nikolai fed a cigarette between his lips and closed the fridge door behind them.

"Want me to sweat Chazov about it?" he said. "It might help him to recall who tossed the vodka martini through the window."

"Good idea. Ask him—better still, tell him, to come and explain it to us at the Big House tomorrow. That should give him something to think about this evening."

Nikolai chuckled and lit his cigarette. The match dropping from his thick sausagey fingers stayed alight on the greasy linoleum. Grushko regarded it with friendly disapproval.

"Maybe you're planning to sell them some fire insurance yourself."

Nikolai grinned sheepishly and extinguished the small flame with the toe of his trainer.

Outside the Pushkin on Fontanka, Sasha was speaking on Grushko's car phone. Seeing Grushko he waved the handset at him and then stepped away from the open passenger door.

"It's General Kornilov," he whispered.

Grushko took the call and gradually his wide, peasant face grew more sombre. By the time he had finished listening to what the general had to say he was frowning so hard his brow looked as if it had been clawed by a bear. Sighing deeply he handed Sasha the phone and walked to the railing beside the canal, where he flicked his cigarette butt into the still brown water. I looked at Sasha who shrugged and shook his head. When Nikolai finally emerged from the restaurant I wandered over to where Grushko was standing.

"You see that building?"

I followed his eyes across the canal to an old grey palace.

"That's the House of Friendship and Peace. Well, there's precious little of that about, I can tell you. Not these days." He lit another cigarette and waved Nikolai and Sasha towards him.

"I take it you've all heard of Mikhail Milyukin?"

The three of us said we had. There wasn't anyone who watched television or was a fan of the two most popular magazines of the day, *Ogonyok* and *Krokodil*, who hadn't heard of Mikhail Milyukin. As the old Soviet Union's first investigative reporter he was virtually a national institution.

"He's been murdered," said Grushko. "And it's on our sheet."

"We usually leave the murder inquiries to the State Prosecutor's Office, don't we, sir?" said Nikolai.

"Kornilov says that they want us to handle it." Grushko shook his head vaguely. "Apparently there are certain circumstances which make them think that it might be our flock of sheep."

"What sort of circumstances?" said Nikolai.

Grushko propelled himself off the railing and walked purposefully towards his car.

"That's what we're going to find out."

CHAPTER

THREE

★ Zelenogorski lies about forty kilometres northwest of St. Petersburg along the M10 which, some 150 kilometres farther on, reaches all the way to the Finnish border. It wasn't much to look at. By the time I had realised that it was a town we had passed it by and were heading out into the country again, along a smaller A road that lies along the shores of the Gulf of Finland. Several minutes later we turned off this road and drove for a short way until we came upon a militia van parked at the edge of the forest. Grushko drew up beside the van and asked one of the militiamen waiting there for directions to the scene of the crime and the rest of their colleagues. Then we were off again. Uncomfortably fast, Grushko's small, strong hands a blur of opposite lock and gear changing, as if he had been a driver in some kind of car rally. But the drive along the forest track seemed to cheer him up a little and when finally he caught sight of the other militia vans and brought the car to a slithering halt, he grinned sadistically at me. I wondered if he still thought I was there to spy on his department.

We got out and walked down a gentle slope toward a small clearing in the trees. The vans were parked around a black Volga that was the subject of attention for ten or fifteen experts and militiamen. A stout, red-haired woman wearing the uniform of a colonel of militia and who seemed to be in charge walked towards us. Grushko quickened his pace to greet her.

"It's Iron Lenya," Nikolai murmured. "And I'm not wearing a tie."

"You don't even have a uniform, if I remember right," said Sasha. "You sold it to a Japanese tourist for 200 roubles." Sasha chuckled and found a cigarette from his jacket pocket. He tossed it expertly into his mouth and lit a match with the flick of a thumbnail.

The head of the Department of Scientific Experts, Colonel Lenya Shelaeva, greeted Grushko coolly and ignored the rest of us altogether. In the weeks that followed I got to know her well enough to respect and even to like her. But she was particular about smartness among her own staff and while she and Grushko exchanged a few preliminary remarks, Sasha told me that Lenya had once sent a man home because he wasn't wearing a tie. Having had little sleep on the overnight train I wasn't exactly looking my best and I was glad that Grushko didn't bother to introduce us.

We followed her to the passenger door of the Volga. Inside the car a man lay slumped forward in his seat, his forehead resting on the blood-encrusted dashboard. There wasn't much that would have detained the average teleologist, assuming that there were still people who placed much credence in this kind of Marxian working method. The copeck-sized hole in the back of his head indicated the way in which he had met his end clearly enough. He stared at us with grey-green eyes out of a waxy, pale and overweight face. He was dead as mutton but the more I looked at him, the more I had the impression that but for a decent-sized sticking-plaster to cover the bullet's exit wound, the man would have sat up and offered me a cigarette from the packet of Risk he still held in his podgy hand.

Grushko crossed himself and then sighed.

"Mikhail Mikhailovich," he said sadly. "That's too bad."

"Did you know him?" Shelaeva sounded surprised.

Grushko nodded and for a moment I thought he was going to cry. His upper lip inflated as he struggled to bring himself under control. He cleared his throat several times before answering her.

"Ever since the Openness," he said, "when Mikhail first started writing about the Mafia. That was when the government still denied that such a thing as a Soviet Mafia even existed. You could say that my own department owes its very existence to Mikhail Milyukin." He sniffed loudly and then lit a cigarette with clumsy fingers. "He helped us with a number of cases. Got us started with a few of them, too."

Shelaeva turned her own mouth into a tight, thin slit of disapproval.

"I always thought him a bit of a troublemaker myself," she said crisply. "Well, then, here you are: he's got you started on another case, hasn't he? All you have to do is find out who sat behind him in this car, sometime between twelve and two this morning, and blew his brains out. But let's not forget our small friend in the boot, shall we?"

She moved round to the back of the car, brushing past me as she came. Her tone had been so harsh and unsympathetic that I wasn't at all surprised to discover that she was wearing the same scent as my ex-wife. Shelaeva elbowed the militia photographer out of the way and presented the contents of the car boot with an indifferent wave of her rubber-gloved hand.

By contrast with the man in the passenger seat, the occupant of the Volga's boot could not have looked more dead. Bound hand and foot, and doubled up like the occupant of some ancient burial pit, it was difficult to say much about him save that he had been shot several times through a length of sticking plaster that covered his mouth.

Grushko sucked his cigarette as if reminding himself that he still had a mouth, tipped his head to one side the better to see the dead man's face and then uttered what sounded like a grunt of affirmation. But it was Nikolai who offered the explanation.

"Looks like Mafia Morse code, sir," he said.

"That is what it looks like," agreed Grushko. "Maintain radio silence."

Sasha detached himself from our group and went over to speak to one of the militiamen. Having no particular taste for cadavers myself I was half inclined to join him, but then I was supposed to be gathering in these same small nuggets of Grushko's esoteric knowledge, so stayed put.

"Well," said Shelaeva, "I guess it's details like that which made the State Prosecutor think this might be your case, Yevgeni Ivanovich."

Grushko gave her a quizzical glance, no doubt wondering, as I was, if she had meant to be sarcastic or merely pedantic. I decided it was the last.

She took up the position of an imaginary gunman, her arms extended in front of her as if she had been addressing a golf ball. It wasn't a bad stance. And she had the build to be a hard-hitter.

"Your gunman stood here when he fired his shots," she said. "I guess only his mother could have missed him."

She dropped down onto her haunches and pointed out several cartridges that were lying on the ground and which were indicated by small paper flags.

"He used an automatic, I'd say. Something heavy: 10 millimetre, or .45 calibre. And with a high-magazine capacity too, judging from the amount of brass he left behind him. It looks as if he was enjoying himself when he pulled the trigger."

Grushko bent forward to inspect them. At the same time he picked up a small flat stone that he used to stub out his cigarette before carefully putting it away in his pocket so as not to litter the scene of the crime. Then he placed the stone back where he had found it.

"That's quite a lot of noise," he said and looked speculatively about him as if searching for a sign that someone might have heard the shots above the sound of the sea lapping on the shingle beach and the wind coursing through the fir trees.

"Maybe," she said. "But I don't think he was in much of a hurry. He was smoking when he pulled the trigger. There was a cigarette end among all those empty cartridges."

Shelaeva led us a short distance from the car, to where a trestle-table had been erected. The various pieces of evidence that were collected on it looked like a secondhand stall on the Arbat. She selected something in a plastic bag.

"And it looks like he prefers American," she said.

"Don't we all," murmured Nikolai, regarding his own choice of smoke with distaste.

"We found this on the back seat."

Shelaeva handed Grushko the plastic bag containing the empty packet of Winstons. He was about to return it to the table when Nikolai checked him.

"Let's see that," he said, taking the evidence bag from Grushko. "It's been opened upside down."

"He's a careless bastard," said Grushko. "What does that prove?"

"Well, it could mean that he's an ex-soldier."

"And how do you work that out?"

"It's an old army trick I learned in Afghanistan," he said, and glanced uncomfortably at Colonel Shelaeva.

"So, what's the trick?" Grushko sighed impatiently.

"If you open the cigarette packet the wrong way up, your dirty fingers don't touch the filters—you know, the end you put in your mouth."

"You know, for the last twenty years, I've been wondering what those things were," said Grushko.

"I never knew soldiers were so fastidious," said Shelaeva with raised eyebrows.

"You do tend to be when there's no lavatory paper about," said Nikolai, colouring.

"Ah, I see." Grushko chuckled quietly. "Well, no need to be so bashful, Nikolai. These days we all know what that's like."

This was undoubtedly true. For several weeks now there had been a deficit of lavatory paper in all the state shops. A day of so before leaving Moscow I had seen someone on the Rozhdestvenska Street market offering toilet rolls at fifty roubles each. Fifty roubles. That was my mother's weekly pension.

Grushko picked up a passport from the table. He turned the pages with the lugubrious air of an immigration official.

"Belongs to the man in the boot," said Shelaeva.

Grushko nodded absently and then turned his attention to where one of her men was photographing an area of ground not far behind the Volga.

"What's happening over there?"

"Some tyre tracks," she said. "There's not much tread on them, as you might expect, so don't even hope that we can make some kind of identification. And a couple of sets of footprints going between the two cars. My guess is that whoever shot Milyukin was already sitting in the back seat of the Volga when it arrived. He shot Milyukin and then he and the driver got out, shot the second man, and then walked back to the other car."

Grushko wandered over to look at the car tracks.

"Took their time leaving as well," he said. "Nothing

panicky about these tyre tracks. These boys knew what they were about."

Sasha had the rest of what was known from the local militia.

"A local angler found the bodies at around seven o'clock this morning—"

Grushko grimaced. "I don't know that I would want to fish in these waters," he said.

A keen angler myself, I said that I had been thinking that it looked like a pretty good spot. Grushko shook his head vigorously and pointed south at the horizon.

"You can't see it from here, but on the other side of the bay, that's Sosnovy Bor."

"The nuclear reactor?"

He nodded. "You wouldn't catch me fishing in these waters," he said ominously. "No telling what's been dumped here over the years." He looked at Sasha, who continued with his information.

"According to the local boys, the area is very popular with hunters," he said. "If anyone did hear those shots, I doubt they'd have thought it at all unusual."

"Yes," agreed Grushko. "There's elk round here, isn't there?"

Sasha shook his head and shrugged.

"They've checked with the GAI, and apparently the car is registered to—" Sasha consulted his notebook and turned the page—"to Vaja Ordzhonikidze."

"Ordzhonikidze?" said Nikolai. "That name hits a thumb. Isn't he one of the Georgian team leaders?"

Grushko glanced at the passport he was still holding.

"Not anymore he isn't." Catching my eye, Grushko added: "A year or so ago, we tried to sew a number on his jacket for racketeering. Only he had sharp scissors. And a lawyer by the name of Luzhin. That's a name you'll get to know. He only works for Mafia clients."

"What do you think, sir?" asked Nikolai. "The Georgian, giving Milyukin a story?"

"Well, that's what it looks like," Grushko admitted. "Sasha, have the relatives been informed yet?"

"No, sir."

"Then that's our next job." He looked at me again and shrugged. "You'd better come along. If you're going to find out about the Mafia, you need to study the science of bad news."

CHAPTER

FOUR

★ We returned to St. Petersburg and left Nikolai and Sasha to go in search of the Georgian's nearest friend or relative. Grushko and I drove back to the Griboyedev Canal where, just a few hours earlier, he had pointed out the scene of Raskolnikov's crime. He made no mention of this coincidence although from the expression on his face I had half an idea that he was thinking about it.

The Milyukins' flat was in a dilapidated, pre-Revolutionary building on the opposite side of the canal from the mosaic front of a church that stood a little farther north. Grushko parked the Zhiguli, thoughtfully removed the windscreen-wiper blades, which he tossed onto the floor of the car, and then led the way into the backyard. By a cheap, unpainted wooden door was a push-button combination lock; the sequence of numbers was not hard to work out thanks to the forgetful, or possibly mischievous, soul who had scratched it onto the adjacent brickwork.

"It's no wonder that there are so many burglaries," Grushko observed. He pressed the keys and, as he opened the door and mounted the narrow staircase, something scuttled away into the darkness. The steps were quite worn down as in some ancient Egyptian mausoleum and the dirty brown walls were daubed with appropriately primitive sentiments.

We climbed to the fourth floor, collected our breath with a quick cigarette and then rang the antiquated bell-pull. Somewhere the bell tolled as if from a distant church tower and for a moment I had a vision of myself as that hungry, Napoleon-fixated student, preparing to commit one murder in the delusion that a hundred others might be saved. The hunger was easy enough to imagine: since the previous night I hadn't eaten much more than a piece of bread and a slice of cold meat. From the speed of my heartbeat you might have thought I was actually planning to go through with it.

After a minute or so we heard a key turn in the lock and the door opened as far as the sturdy chain would allow. The woman appearing in the gap was in her thirties, fair-haired and good-looking in a clever sort of way and wearing an expression that was worth a whole fistful of worry beads. Grushko flipped open his identity card.

"Mrs. Milyukin?"

"It's about my husband, isn't it?"

"Can we come in please?"

She closed the door, drew the chain and opened it once again, ushering us into the cluttered hallway of her communal apartment and then beyond, into the one large room that she and the man in the forest had called their home.

It was about nine square metres of space, with a double-size sofa bed, folded away, a shelving unit occupying one whole wall, a small coffee table, two armchairs and an enormous wardrobe. On the shelves was a large television set, a VCR and lots of books and videotapes, while on the table were the remains of a frugal meal. It was not a bad room by the average standards of Russian accommodation but at that particular moment I wished I could have been anywhere else. Mrs. Milyukin folded her arms and braced herself to hear what she already knew in her bones.

"I'm afraid I have bad news for you," Grushko said evenly. "Mikhail Mikhailovich Milyukin is dead."

The dead man's widow, whose name was Nina Romanovna, twitched convulsively and let out a deep sigh, like one who has died herself.

Instinctively I turned away. Drawing back the curtain for a moment I looked out of the window. Across the canal the sun touched the church's highest cupola and turned this golden sphere into an imitation of itself that was almost too bright to look at directly. Probably Grushko could have endured the sight of it without flinching. By then he had already held the widow's bitter eyes for what seemed like an eternity.

"Well," she said finally, "that's that."

"Not quite," said Grushko. "I regret to have to tell you that he was murdered. This officer and I have just come from the scene of the crime. There will have to be a formal identification, I'm afraid, but there's no doubt that it's him. And I will have to ask you some questions, Mrs. Milyukin. It may seem insensitive—obviously you want to be alone right now—but the sooner I'm able to establish what were Mikhail Mikhailovich's last movements, the sooner I'll catch whoever is responsible."

He spoke with a stiff formality as if he were trying to distance himself emotionally from what had happened. The widow nodded stiffly and found a handkerchief in the sleeve of her blue acrylic sweater.

"Yes, or course," she said, wiping her eyes roughly and then blowing her nose. A cigarette seemed to help her to get a grip of herself. She snatched a couple of quick drags and nodded that she was ready.

"When did you last see your husband?"

"It must have been around seven o'clock last night," she said unsteadily. "He went out somewhere, to see a contact he said, for some article he was preparing."

Grushko thought of several questions at once.

"Did he say who this contact was? Where they were meeting? When he would be back?"

"No," she said and turned away to tap her ash into the bottom half of a matrushka doll. "Mikhail never discussed his work with me. He said that it was better that way—so that I wouldn't worry about him. Usually I had to read *Ogonyok* or watch television to find out what he had been up to. Well, I dare say you're both familiar with Mikhail's work. He was always sticking his nose in where it wasn't wanted. He used to say that if the Soviet Union was a can of worms then he was the can opener. The only trouble was—" She paused and Grushko finished what she had been going to say.

"—He left a lot of sharp edges." Grushko shrugged. "Yes, I see." He paused for a moment. "Well, I suppose the country's first investigative journalist was bound to make a few enemies."

Nina Milyukin uttered a bitter, smoky laugh.

"A few?" she said with derision. "I think you'd better take a look for yourself."

She went to the wardrobe door and drew the door open. Reaching inside she switched on a light to reveal a tiny office. A bare bulb hung from the top of the wardrobe over a small square desk and a battered old typewriter.

"As you can see, we have a very small apartment," she explained and started to select some box-files from a large recessed set of shelves. "The sacrifice you make for living in a place with a bit of character. This was Mikhail's office."

I was trying to see how the wardrobe seemed larger inside than outside when suddenly I understood the ingenuity of the arrangement. Lacking a back panel the wardrobe had been placed in front of a built-in cupboard that contained the dead man's extensive library. When Nina Milyukin stepped out of the makeshift study bearing several of the box-files I went inside and looked about more carefully.

Some of the books had only recently been made available. Quite a few would have been almost impossible to get hold of at any price. Books printed in English and German occupied a whole shelf of their own. It was the kind of library I had always dreamed of having myself.

On the desk was a Filofax that I opened and looked up the previous day's date; no entry had been made. I turned a few pages forward. The handwriting was long and girlish. It seemed hardly suitable for a journalist. Above the desk was a felt-covered pinboard, and on it were some postcards of London and the Pyramids, a membership card of the Felis Cat-Lover's Club and, in pride of place, a photograph of a smiling Milyukin shaking hands with Margaret Thatcher. But it was not this that interested me so much as the photographs of Nina Milyukin, for in one of them she was naked. It had been taken in some other apartment, in a pose more provocative than artistic: wearing only a pair of stockings she stood facing the camera, her hands clasped behind her back, her head lowered almost penitently, as if she had done something of which she was slightly ashamed. Perhaps the taking of the picture itself had been sufficient embarrassment.

"These letters were forwarded by *Krokodil* and *Ogonyok*," she was explaining to Grushko. "They're mostly all like that one. Hate mail is the only kind of letter that never gets lost by the Post Office. He tried to keep those hidden from me, but there's not much a man can keep hidden from his wife in an apartment this size."

When I stepped out of the wardrobe, bringing the Filofax with me, Grushko handed me the letter he had been reading and shook his head despairingly.

"Comrade Milyukin," it read. "Your article in *Krokodil* on the Leningrad black market made us all laugh so much. Your suggestion, that it is only when people are able to resist this kind of consumerism that the country will be able to rebuild itself, is absurd. Why should they when there's nothing in the shops but empty shelves and excuses. It's bastards like you who try and spoil it for everyone. I hope that one of the prostitutes you are always writing about—no doubt from your own personal experience— gives you AIDS. I hope you pass it on to your wife and that she passes it on to the man she is probably screwing. Yours, a well-wisher."

The thought of her screwing another man reminded me of the photograph in the wardrobe and I was tempted to go and take another look at it.

"Are they all like this?" I asked.

"There are plenty worse than that," she said, extinguishing her cigarette and lighting another.

"When we still discussed his work, Mikhail used to quote a poem by Pasternak, about how poetry is murderous. 'If I had known that this is what happens, when I at first stood up and read; that poetry is murderous, will strangle you and leave you dead I would—' "

Grushko interrupted her, completing the quotation. " 'I would have decided not to play games—with reality,' " he said.

At first I was impressed that Grushko had been able to quote Pasternak with such ease; and then I found myself wondering about the pregnant pause he had brought to the line of poetry. I asked myself if he might have intended some criticism of Nina Milyukin, or indeed of Milyukin himself?

"Mikhail said that the same had become true of journalism." She spoke with uncertainty, as if she too had detected some sarcasm.

"Yes," said Grushko, looking over another one of the letters, "I heard him say that."

"You knew my husband?"

"Oh, yes."

"He never mentioned you, Colonel Grushko."

"No, well, I dare say he had no wish to worry you. Mikhail Mikhailovich put a number of cases our way. Cases which involved the Mafia. You can be proud of him. He was a fine man."

Nina Milyukin blinked sadly and nodded without enthusiasm, as if not much encouraged by what Grushko had said. She coloured visibly.

"He was a fine man," she repeated. "A real hero."

It was evident that she was on the verge of saying something that she might have come to regret.

"These threats," said Grushko. "Were there any he took especially seriously?"

"He took them all seriously. You understand, I'm guessing—he tried to avoid talking about this sort of thing—"

"So as not to worry you, yes, you said—"

"But in the last few months, I think some of it really got to him. He started to have nightmares. And he was drinking quite heavily."

Grushko frowned and shook his head.

"And he never explained what was troubling him? He never once tried to share his worries? I find that hard to believe. Oh, I'm not suggesting you're lying or anything, Mrs. Milyukin. No, I'm just puzzled as to your relationship with him. You'll forgive me for asking—I'm afraid I have to ask these questions sometimes—but how were things between the two of you?"

Nina Milyukin reached for the handkerchief again.

"We were quite happy, thank you," she said. "There were no problems. At least no problems that anyone else—"

"Those are the sort of problems I'm talking about," Grushko persisted. "The usual ones."

She shook her head firmly.

"We were quite happy, thank you," she repeated coolly.

For a moment she was silent, and then she added: "You must understand, Mikhail was a very traditional kind of man. Perhaps you know how the poem goes on: 'When the feeling dictates your lines, you step out like a slave, to pace the stage, and here art stops, and earth and fate breathe in your face.' Mikhail set great store by fate, Colonel."

"Fate comes to us all," he murmured and then waved vaguely at the boxes of letters. "I shall have to borrow these for a while," he said. "As well as any diaries, notebooks, address-books and video-tapes he may have kept. I don't doubt that this death will be connected with something he had written or said."

"I suppose it can't harm him now," said Nina Milyukin. "Yes. Take anything you want." She bent down to retrieve an Aeroflot bag from behind the sofa bed and handed it to Grushko.

"Here," she said. "You can use this to carry it all in."

We left her sitting in an armchair on the verge of some serious crying. Grushko closed the door carefully behind us as we made our way into the dilapidated hallway that led to the kitchen and bathroom that the Milyukins shared with the other people who lived in the apartment. A couple of bicycles and several pairs of skis rested against a damp-stained wall and behind these articles were standing an old gentleman, tall and silver-haired, with glasses and a Trotsky-style beard and moustache, and a woman wearing a blue silk head-scarf, whom I took to be his wife. The old gentleman cleared his throat and addressed us respectfully.

"We were very sorry to hear about Mr. Milyukin, Comrade Colonel," he said and, noticing the question that rose in Grushko's eyes, he shrugged apologetically. "The walls in this place—they're not much better than cardboard."

Grushko nodded sternly. "Tell me, Mr.—?"

"Poliakov. Rodion Romanovich Poliakov. And this is my wife, Avdotya Iosefovna."

"Have you noticed any strangers hanging around this building recently?"

"We've lived in this apartment since Stalin's time," replied the old gentleman. "A long time ago we realised that life is a lot safer if one never sees anything. Oh, I know things are a lot different these days, Comrade Colonel—"

"Just Colonel," said Grushko. "You can forget the Comrade now."

Poliakov nodded politely.

"There was nothing unusual you noticed lately, Mr. Poliakov?"

Before her husband could answer, Mrs. Poliakov had spoken: "Mikhail Milyukin was stealing food from our fridge," she said bitterly. "That's what we noticed, Colonel."

Grushko raised his eyebrows and sighed wearily. This was trivial stuff. There was hardly anyone living in a communal apartment who did not sometimes have an argument about food with whomever they were sharing. I remembered once coming to blows with a fellow tenant about the ownership of a bottle of pickles.

"Advotya, please," scolded the old man. "What does that matter now? The man is dead. Try to show a little respect." His wife turned her head into his bony shoulder and began to weep. Poliakov took hold of his beard and, holding his chin close to his breast, he peered over the top of his glasses at Grushko.

"I must apologize for my wife, Colonel," he said. "She's not been well. If there's anything I can do—?"

Grushko opened the heavily reinforced door.

"Just keep an eye on Mrs. Milyukin, will you?"

"Yes, of course, Comrade Colonel."

Grushko hesitated to correct him again.

"If you do remember something," he said after a moment or two, "something important that is—" he glanced meaningfully at Mrs. Poliakov—"call me at the Big House on Liteiny Prospekt. That's where you'll usually find me. At least, that's where my wife is sending my laundry these days."

We went back down the evil-smelling stairs to the yard. Grushko tossed Milyukin's Aeroflot bag into the car boot and shook his head with frustration.

"You can't teach these old dogs new tricks," I offered.

"No, it's not that," he said. "It's Mrs. Milyukin. How can she know so little about her husband's affairs? Did she never hear him on the telephone? Did she never read something he left lying around their room?"

"That's not so hard to believe," I said. "I didn't know that my wife was screwing my daughter's music teacher. She'd been screwing him for two years and I hadn't a clue. And me an investigator. You'd think I might have noticed something, wouldn't you? But no. Not a bit of it. Bad enough to lose my wife. But it looked as if I'm not very good at my job, either. I mean, I ought to have been suspicious . . ."

"So how did you find out?"

"My daughter's piano-playing," I said. "After two years of music lessons, you'd expect anyone to improve a little. But my daughter seemed to be playing as badly as when she started. Then I found out that she was having only one lesson a month and not the two I was paying for. The other lesson was for my wife. Imagine that. Paying someone to screw your wife." I allowed myself a smile. I was past being upset about it.

Grushko smiled back uncertainly.

"Myself," he said, "I have absolutely no ear for music. But I can still recognize a false note when I hear one. And I tell you, there's something about that woman."

I recalled the picture on the pinboard, the large, almost flawless breasts, the curving belly and the squirrel's tail of hair.

"There certainly is."

CHAPTER

FIVE

★ My own office was located in a building that adjoined the back of the Big House. To go from one to the other required that you walk along the street. Nothing to it in summer I thought, but I didn't imagine that it would be much fun in the middle of winter. The entrance was on Kalayeva Street, where Grushko had parked his car. Kalayeva was one of those women who had helped to assassinate Tsar Alexander II in 1881. The Soviets called Kalayeva a heroine. These days we would have called her a terrorist.

Grushko led the way through an anonymous-looking door that gave onto a small seating area where, under the bored eye of a young militiaman, witnesses in a whole variety of cases waited to be examined on their statements by investigators. We showed our passes, easily recognizable in their cheap red plastic folders, and went upstairs. The walls of the stairwell were being painted.

"Why does it always have to be green?" Grushko complained loudly. "Every public building I go in these days—someone's painting it that awful bird-shit green. Why couldn't we have something else, like red for instance?"

The painter took the cigarette out of her mouth slowly.

Like most Russian workers she didn't look as if she ever did anything quickly.

"Red's finished," she said. "Green is all there is."

Grushko grunted and walked on.

"If you've got a problem with that," she yelled after him, "then take it up with my supervisor. But don't complain to me. I just work here."

The curtains were drawn in the small shabby office that was to be mine, although they did little to hinder the passage of the sharp northern light. I took a look out of the window and decided to leave them the way they were. Weeks later I heard someone ascribe the drawn curtains to my sensitive eyes—a not unreasonable hypothesis since I already wore tinted glasses—but really it was only because I preferred not to have to stare out of a window that hadn't been cleaned in ten years.

"Mikoyan's the chief of the State Investigating Agency in Peter," Grushko explained. "Only he won't be here to welcome you." His short snout wrinkled with disapproval. "Right now he's in Moscow, explaining his part in last summer's coup. I could be wrong, but I don't think he'll be back. So until a new chief is appointed you should report straight to Kornilov. But if you need anything—" he looked around the office and shrugged—"apart from anything that costs money that is, then just pick up the phone and speak to me." He waved his hand at the battery of telephones that sat on my desk like the keys of a typewriter.

"Which one?"

He picked up one of the two enormous black Bakelites. "Internal," he said. "Six lines apiece." He dropped the ancient telephone back onto its bunk-sized cradle and selected one of the more modern phones. "The ones that look like toys are your outside lines." Grushko glanced at his watch.

"Come to my office just before four," he said. "I'm

seeing Kornilov then. I'll introduce you." He walked to the door. "One more thing. The canteen here is disgusting. If you must eat, bring something. That is, always supposing you can find something. By the way, where are you staying?"

"With my brother-in-law Porfiry. Or rather, my ex-brother-in-law. I'd better give him a ring and let him know I've arrived."

"Well, there's always a sofa at my place if he's forgotten about you."

"Thanks," I said, "but Porfiry's not the kind to extend an invitation lightly. Especially since he's charging me fifty roubles a week."

"The sentimental sort, eh?"

"That's right."

"All happy families are the same," he chuckled on his way out of the door.

When Grushko had gone I called Porfiry at his office and told him I was in St. Petersburg.

"Whereabouts?" he asked.

"At the Big House. On Liteiny Prospekt."

"Jesus," he laughed, "what did you do? Want me to pick you up on my way home tonight?"

"That'd be nice, except that I'm not sure what time I'll be through here."

"Got you working on a case already, have they?"

"Two, as a matter of fact. I might even be late."

"Don't worry. It's not like Katerina's cooking anything special." He chuckled. "Same as any other night, really. Have you got the address?"

"Yes. I picked it out of the Good Hotel Guide."

"You and the rats, I guess. See you tonight."

I sat down at my desk and lit a cigarette. It's surprising the amount of nourishment you can find in a cigarette these days. This one filled me up nicely. Then I went through my drawers checking that I had a good supply of the protocols that constitute an important part of the investigator's job: search protocols, identity protocols, arrest protocols, interrogation protocols, confiscation protocols and advocate protocols. There was an ample supply of all relevant paperwork as well as a few little luxury items like desk-fluff, a broken rubber band, a plastic clothespeg, an empty box of matches, a handful of paper-clips and a solitary diarrhoea tablet.

After eating the diarrhoea tablet, which tasted better than I had expected, I set about preparing my "chess-board"—a large sheet of paper squared off into sections that was supposed to help me keep track of progress in the many cases I would be investigating. In the first square of the first column I wrote "Chazov: firebomb" and then underneath this "Milyukin & Ordzhonikidze: Murders." After that, I called the State Prosecutor's Office to introduce myself and made an appointment there for nine o'clock the following morning.

By now I was ready for a drink of something and a brief search of the filing-cabinet turned up a heating element and an earthenware jug. I had brought my own tin of coffee. I went to the lavatory to get some water and found it as unpleasant a place as I could have expected, being several millimeters deep in water and urine. I filled the jug from the one dripping tap and walked gingerly back to my office, leaving a trail of wet footprints behind me.

While the water for my coffee boiled I set about clearing my walls of newspaper cuttings and pin-ups. With more than a little self-consciousness I removed the large portrait of Lenin that hung behind my chair and placed it behind my filing-cabinet. The Party might have been outlawed but there were still plenty of people who looked on Vladimir Ilyich as a national hero. At the same time as I was busy doing all of this, I learned something of the previous occupant of my office. He had left the Central Board to join the State Prosecutor's Office, a not uncommon career path. The photograph of the underground artist Kirill Miller pointed to a man with a sense of humour at least, while a communication from something called the Gulliver Club seemed to indicate someone who was very tall. But I still wondered how he could have afford 80 roubles for the empty packet of German chocolate biscuits I found in the wastepaper bin. A present from some foreigner, perhaps. I took out my notebook and made a note of that.

At ten minutes to four I returned to the Big House, where I found Nikolai and Sasha typing up their reports, and they told me what had happened when they visited the dead Georgian's apartment.

★ ★ ★

Vaja Ordzhonikidze had lived on the seventeenth floor of a block of flats in an enormous housing estate across the Neva, to the northwest of Peter, on Vasilyevsky Island. Seen from the sea, these high-rise buildings presented an unbroken line of grey stone that resembled nothing so much as a range of sheer and unscalable cliffs. This impression of inaccessibility was uncomfortably reinforced for the two detectives by a creaking laundry-basket of a lift that broke down while they were in it, leaving them in complete darkness between the ninth and tenth floors. Or they thought it had broken down until, two or three minutes after coming to an almost complete halt—there was some movement on the cable that supported the platform—the doors opened a crack and a small boy's face appeared near the lift cabin's ceiling.

"Hoi, mister," he said. "how much to switch the power back on?"

Nikolai Vladimirivich, uncomfortable in confined spaces at the best of times, spoke angrily:

"You'll be in trouble if you don't," he barked.

Being rather more pragmatic than his larger colleague,

Sasha took out his wallet and thumbed out a small bank note.

"How about five roubles?'' he said, holding the money up to the urchin's face.

"Ain't you got no hard currency?" the boy asked disappointedly. "No dollars, no deutschmarks?"

"I'll give you hard currency," snarled Nikolai. "You don't know how hard. When I've paid you, you won't sit down for a week."

Sasha took out his cigarettes and added two to the offer ransom.

"Five woods and a couple of chalks, you little—"

"Done," said the boy. "Shove 'em through.''

The doors closed behind the price extorted, returning the lift cabin once again to darkness.

"Didn't they teach you anything at the Pushkin Police Academy?" said Nikolai. "You should never give in to blackmail."

At which point the light flickered on and the lift assumed its rusty, shuddering ascent.

When they rang the Georgian's bell the door was answered by a heavily made-up girl of about twenty wearing a black silk dressing-gown and an equally dark scowl. She looked like the sort who could have smelled hard currency inside a bottle of aniseed. A whore who knew these men were militia from nothing more than the squeak of their shoe-rubber.

"He's not here," she said, gathering the gown over her generous chest and chewing her gum defiantly.

"That much we know already," said Nikolai and pushing her aside he ambled into the apartment.

The furnishings were expensively gaudy, with an abundance of electrical equipment, some of it still in the boxes.

"Oh yes," said Nikolai with obvious admiration, "very comfortable indeed."

Sasha went over to the window. A large telescope mounted on a wooden tripod was pointed out to sea.

"Check the view," he said and ducked down to try the telescope. Nikolai joined him at the window. "Panoramic, or what?"

The girl finished lighting her cigarette and snatched it angrily from her crimson-coloured mouth.

"Have you got a search protocol?"

"To look out the window?" said Nikolai. "I hardly think so."

"So what's this all about, eh?"

She sat down on an imitation leather sofa that creaked like the sound of falling timber. Her dressing-gown slipped away to reveal a long white thigh but she made no move to cover herself. The girl knew that militiamen were easier to handle when they had something to distract their eyes. She shifted her bottom and let some more of the gown slide away until she was satisfied that they could see her flimsy underwear.

"Are you Vaja's girlfriend?" Nikolai squatted down in front of a compact-disc player and began to amuse himself by pushing the automatic disc drawer in and out. "Or just his business associate?"

"Could be I'm his bloody astrologer," she sneered. "But what's it to you?"

Nikolai turned away from the disc player and looked with undisguised discrimination at the girl's crotch.

"You should have been keeping a closer eye on his chart, sweetheart," he said. "Your Georgian friend's planetary aspect just took off for another galaxy."

The girl frowned and, sensing that something was wrong, started to cover herself.

"Look, is Vaja in trouble or something?" she said.

"Not with us, he isn't," said Sasha and went into the kitchen.

"I'm afraid he's dead, love," said Nikolai.

She let out a sigh and then crossed herself. Nikolai picked up a bottle of vodka from the drinks trolley and waved it in front of her face. The girl nodded. He poured one into a square-shaped tumbler and handed it to her.

In the kitchen Sasha found a short length of washing-line hanging above the sink. On it were pegged three condoms, washed and hung out to dry like odd socks. They were recognisably foreign, of a quality unattainable in their Russian counterparts—colloquially known as galoshes—and therefore worth the trouble of recycling. An expensive leather handbag lay open on the kitchen table. Sasha rummaged through it and found the girl's identity card. When he returned to the other room he handed it to Nikolai and looked quizzically at the girl.

"Those rubbers in the kitchen," he said. "You on the game or something?"

"Get stuffed," she snarled, on the edge of tears.

"Now, now," said Nikolai, "no need for that." He glanced at the girl's ID. "Galina Petrovna Zosimov," he said. "Galina. That's my mother's name."

"How would you know that?" said Galina.

Nikolai grinned patiently. "Say what you like, if it makes you feel better," he said.

She swallowed some more of her drink and stared back at him.

"So what's the story?" she said.

"The story? Well, Galina Petrovna, to tell the truth, we're not exactly sure. But the Zelenogorski Militia found him down in the woods early this morning. He'd been picnicking with some mean little teddy bears who tried to make him catch some bullets with his teeth. You know the kind of thing—like maybe they thought he was an informer." He paused for effect. "That sort of behaviour is standard practice among a certain rougher section of our society."

Galina tossed the rest of the vodka back.

"That's the girl," said Nikolai. "Takes the edge off the grief a bit, doesn't it?" She held up her glass and let Nikolai pour her another. He checked the label. It was good stuff, not the kind you needed to sprinkle pepper in to take care of the impurities. "I'd join you myself, only I make a point of never drinking good vodka these days. I might acquire a taste for it again, and then my wife would have nothing to trade."

He pulled up a stool and sat down opposite her, so close that he might have slipped the mule off her little foot and smothered it with kisses.

"So where was I? Ah yes, I was suggesting that Vaja might have been a pincher."

Galina shook her head firmly. "Leave it out. That wasn't his style at all. He was a lock, a top man." She snorted contemptuously. "I think you'd better point your cheap suits in some other direction."

"Someone thought he was pinching," said Nikolai. "The guy who shot him wasn't trying to drum up business for dentists, I'll tell you that much."

"Did he have any enemies among the Georgians that you know about?" said Sasha.

Galina lit another cigarette. She took a hard drag with narrowed eyes and shook her head.

"Maybe Vaja was giving it to one of his pals' wives," Nikolai suggested. "Well, you know what these Georgians are like. They're always chasing pussy. Or some old family feud maybe. Bad blood lasts a long time with these Georgian boys. How about it?"

"No," said Galina.

"When was the last time you saw him?"

"Last night." She shrugged. "Around seven. Just before I went out."

"Where did you go?" said Sasha.

"Out. To meet a friend." She swallowed some more of her drink and grimaced. "I don't know why I'm drinking this. I don't even like vodka." She put the glass down. "There was a phone call from some guy he knew. Don't ask me his name because he didn't say. Whoever it was said he'd washed this fancy watch off some Jap tourist's arm and did Vaja want to buy it?"

"And did he?"

"Are you kidding? These Georgians are like magpies. They love the flashy stuff. Gold, diamonds, silver—can't wear enough of it. Worse than Jews, so they are. Anyway, he arranged a meet."

"Did he say when, or where?"

Galina shook her head.

"Sounds to me like he was this city's first fashion victim," said Nikolai.

Galina grinned mockingly. "Yeah, well, I can't ever see you making best-dressed detective of the year, Fatso. Vaja was a smart-looking guy."

"Not when I last saw him," said Nikolai.

"Did you ever hear him mention the name of Mikhail Milyukin at all?" Sasha asked quickly.

"The journalist? The one that writes for *Krokodil*? Where does he fit in?"

"He's not writing Vaja's obituary," said Nikolai. "He and Vaja caught the same flight north."

"Yeah? You don't say. That's too bad. I liked his stuff."

"How about Vaja?" said Sasha. "Was he a fan?"

She gave him a look of pity.

"Vaja? He was a nice guy, but he was no reader. Take a look around. The only magazines he liked were the ones for the home gynaecologist."

"And the rest of Rustaveli Avenue?" said Nikolai, referring to the main street in Tbilisi, the capital of Georgia. "Where can we find them?"

"Usually you'll find the whole raspberry round the corner," said Galina, jerking her head at the window. "At the Pribaltskaya Hotel. In the afternoon they like to make muscles of themselves in the gym. And in the evening they get mumbling drunk in the restaurant."

Nikolai stood up. "That thief," he said, "the one that stole the watch. If you do remember the guy's name—"

"Sure," said Galina, standing up beside him. She came halfway up his chest. "I'll send you a carrier-pigeon."

She followed them to the door and opened it.

"Hey, promise me you'll catch the bastards who did it and I'll give you some really useful information."

"We'll catch them all right," declared Sasha.

"Do you promise?"

"Promise."

"Take the stairs." And with that she kicked the door shut in their faces.

★ ★ ★

General Kornilov's office was through a double door at the end of the corridor. Although bigger than Grushko's office it was also gloomier, with only a small desk lamp to lighten the almost sepulchral darkness.

A smart fountain-pen in his bony hand, Kornilov sat behind a big leather-topped desk. Another desk has been set at right angles to Kornilov's, making a T shape, and it was here we seated ourselves while the general finished writing the memo in his best copperplate.

In his late fifties, Kornilov was a stern-looking figure with cold, fossilised eyes and a hard, expressionless face like some long-lost funerary mask of beaten bronze. Looking at him it was hard to believe Grushko's assertion that the general had been a committed democrat long before the overthrow of the Party. Kornilov seemed to have been pressed from the same mould that Stalin had used to manufacture murderers like Yezhov, Yagoda, and Laventri Beria. Perhaps it was just because I had known him a little while longer, but while he introduced me, Grushko became an altogether warmer, more human figure than his gnomic boss. The general nodded sombrely and shook my hand.

"Glad to have you aboard," he said with a voice that matched his office. "It's a pretty good team you'll be working with. And you can bet you'll be busy. Right now there are over two hundred armed Mafia gangs operating in this city. Organised crime constitutes the biggest single threat to this country's democratic future."

It sounded like something he had been rehearsing for the television cameras, only there was no complementary smile such as might have pleased some public relations man. Kornilov blinked slowly and lit a hand-rolled cigarette.

"Yevgeni," he said, "at this moment, about how many cases are you investigating?"

"About thirty, sir."

"I'm not suggesting for a moment that you drop any of them. But you'd better make solving Milyukin's murder your number-one priority. He had a lot of friends in the Western press and naturally his death will be reported there. It would look good if we could clear this matter up as quickly as possible."

"Yes, sir," Grushko fumbled a cigarette out of his own pocket.

"I've been speaking to Georgi Zverkov," said Kornilov.

"That vulture," muttered Grushko.

"Nevertheless, quite a useful one when it results in us receiving some information from the public. I want you to go on his television show and talk about Milyukin's murder. Appeal for information. I'm sure you know the drill. Just don't let him make a quilt with you."

Grushko nodded uncomfortably.

"So what do you know about this Georgian?"

"He was from Svaneti," said Grushko. "It's a mountainous part of Georgia and the people there are pretty primitive. But tough too. Vaja's hometown, Ushghooli, means "heart without fear." I rang the head of Criminal Service in Tbilisi but you know what they're like, sir. They're not much inclined to be helpful these days, so it's hard to say what Vaja got up to when he stayed at home."

"Georgians." Kornilov shook his head and muttered a curse. "Too busy killing each other, I suppose."

"Looks like it, sir," said Grushko. "Here Vaja had a number of convictions for theft and assault. Small stuff, really, and all of it quite a few years ago. We knew he was one of the Georgian team leaders but we were never able to sew a case on him. I've spoken to my usual informers but there's not much that's coming down about this one." He lit the cigarette and left it hanging on his lip. "I dunno. Maybe his Mafia pals thought he was planning to sell Milyukin a story."

Kornilov's brow wrinkled as he considered Grushko's suggestion.

"That's what someone wants us to think anyway," added Grushko. "Or else why the dental work? It could be that this was just some bad blood and that Milyukin was in the wrong place at the wrong time. Stranger things have happened, sir."

"All right, Yevgeni," said Kornilov. "But just suppose for one minute that it wasn't the Georgians. Who would you want to consider?"

Grushko's speculation began with a shrug. "The Abkhazians maybe. Not that they're very well-organised at the moment, not since we cracked that taxi-driver racket. Then there's the Chechens. Nobody hates the Georgians more than their Muslim neighbours. This could be the start of another Mafia war."

"Let's hope not. But assuming that the Chechens wouldn't need much of a reason to kill a Georgian, what could they have against Mikhail Milyukin?"

Grushko opened the file he had brought with him and took out some papers and a photograph.

"I had a look through my files for people who might have a grudge against Milyukin, and oddly enough this character here's a Chechen." He handed Kornilov the picture.

"His name is Sultan Khadziyev. About five years ago, before the Organized Crime Unit even existed, Sultan was controlling most of the prostitution north of the River Neva. Representing himself as a puppeteer—how about that?—he obtained permission to go to Hungary with five female assistants. Only they were hard-currency prostitutes who thought their pimp was taking them for a well-earned holiday. When they arrived in Budapest, Sultan got himself a flat and put the girls to work.

"But the profits weren't as good as he had hoped for and so after a couple of months Sultan sold the girls and the flat to the Hungarian Mafia and came home. Well, I don't know what kind of girls they were, but the Hungarians couldn't make a go of them either and so they took the girls to Bucharest and sold them to the Romanian Mafia.

"Finally the girls saved enough money to escape back to Peter when they took their story to Mikhail Milyukin. He did a big article about them in *Ogonyok* and persuaded the girls to speak to us, and give evidence against Sultan. Along the way Sultan kidnapped one of the girls and half-buried her alive to stop her talking, but Milyukin managed to get the rest of the girls to stand firm."

"A real citizen, this animal," said Kornilov, looking at the photograph.

"We fixed him a holiday of his own," said Grushko. "A ten-year stretch in Perm."

"A spell in a labour camp would be enough reason to kill a man. But if this character's still in the zone as you say . . ."

"These Chechens stick pretty close, sir," Grushko explained. "Maybe one of Sultan's friends killed Milyukin.

Maybe they wrote him a fan letter as well. You know, from what I've seen the man got more hate mail than Rasputin."

"Look on the bright side, Yevgeni," said Kornilov. "Food may be in short supply. But at least you'll have no shortage of suspects."

CHAPTER
SIX

★ I spent the evening at the Big House, reading Milyukin's hate mail with Grushko and Nikolai. Having divided the pile of letters into three we sat around Grushko's desk and, fortified by a steady supply of coffee, cigarettes and a considerable quantity of dried bread crusts which Grushko kept in his cupboard, we applied ourselves to this distasteful task. Mostly we read in silence but occasionally one of us would read aloud from some particularly venomous letter. In truth there were none of them that threw up any definite leads. But by the end of that night I think we all found that our admiration of Mikhail Milyukin had grown considerably and, as a corollary, this increased our determination to catch his killers. None more so than Grushko himself. I don't recall every letter that Grushko or Nikolai chose to quote from. However, the following five seemed to me to be typically unpleasant as well as indicative of the lamentable state in which the country found itself.

Dear Mikhail Mikhailovich,

Your patronymic would seem to indicate that you knew who your father was, although I find that very hard to believe, you intellectual bastard. You write about a drug problem among young people today as if there was someone forcing us to sit on a needle. But this is nonsense. Like most of my friends I enjoy swallowing a rope. Heroin, methadone, wheels, hot-water bottle—it's all the same to us what we use. Frankly, we don't much care as long as we can blow our minds free of all that shit we learned in school. You ask what we can possibly believe in. Psychobilly music, that's what. It really helps you get out of your head. And talking of that, let me tell you, the next time I see your stupid face in the Leningrad Rock Club, I'll cut your ears off and spit in your skull. I'm serious. I've a good sharp knife and nothing would give me more pleasure than to stick it in your eye.

Dear Mikhail Milyukin,

"Your essay in *Ogonyok* on alcoholism in St. Petersburg was a typical example of the kind of journalism that makes this great country of ours an international laughing-stock. Bug spray in a bottle of beer? Shoe polish on a slice of bread! Boiling a wooden table leg with sugar! If nothing else your damnable piece must have served to give drunkards more ideas on how to get drunk. And you have the temerity to blame all of this illicit drinking on Comrade Andropov's anti-alcohol campaign. Why must we wash our dirty linen in public like this? I used to think you were a responsible man, but now I look forward to the day when the forces of law and order return to this country and sweep you and all your dirty kind back into the labour camps where you belong. And when that time comes the bullet you receive in the back of your stupid skull will be less than you deserve. I pray that your grave is marked only with the stool of the man who shoots you.

Comrade Milyukin,

In your recent article in *Krokodil* magazine, you compared St. Petersburg's murder rate to that of New York. But this is rubbish. It is nothing like as great. Anyway, who really cares? Mostly it's the people from the swamps, the darkies from the southern republics, who are killing each other, for drugs, or for hard currency. No one misses scum like that. Except you, perhaps, you mealy-mouthed liberal. Let me tell you I didn't fight in Afghanistan and come home to get soft with criminals. There should be only one sentence for these people: death. I myself have shot lots of these animals to spare the courts the trouble. But it now occurs to me that the country would be equally well served if we sent a few of you so-called special correspondents the same way. So you know what? I'm going to track you down you bastard. And when I do I'm going to turn you into one of your own statistics. Depend on it.

A patriot.

★ ★ ★

Comrade Milyukin,

Do you know the Dieta supermarket, near Mayakovsky Square in Moscow? This morning I went to the meat counter and they were selling mortadella sausage at 168 roubles a kilo. My husband is a schoolteacher. He earns 500 roubles a month. So I ask you: how can we afford prices like this? I ended up buying ten eggs, and they cost me almost 18 roubles. Only a few months ago they would have cost me less than 2 roubles. My point is this: you have the nerve to tell me that things are better now. Well, let me tell you, your new democracy has destroyed the old economic system but you haven't introduced anything to replace it. How I wish Stalin was still alive and you and all your fellow democrats were forced to spend your time working on a collective farm. Better still, I think a few years in Solovki would do you a world of good.

* * *

Mikhail Milyukin,

Your piece about St. Petersburg's "Cosa Nostra" was one of the most stupid, misleading piles of shit I have ever heard anyone gob out on national television. There is no such thing as "the Russian Mafia." The whole idea of a Mafia has been made up by people like you who try and make money out of selling scare stories. There are just businessmen providing people with what they want and, just as often, with what they need—the things you can't buy in the state shops. Our business methods have to be ruthless sometimes if only because in this stupid, backward country of ours there exists no understanding of supply and demand and free enterprise. If someone lets you down in business there is no real legal mechanism to enforce a contract or to have him pay compensation. So we break his legs, or threaten his children. Next time he'll do what he's supposed to. A man doesn't pay a share of his profits to his partners, we'll burn his house to the ground. This is just business. You are an intelligent man. You should understand this. And yet you continue to sell us the dead horse about the Mafia. A number of my business colleagues are very angry about this. They feel that the opportunity cost us by your continuing to peddle this kind of garbage is too high. So a word of warning. Stop it now. Because the next time you choose to describe joint ventures, traders, private businessmen, cooperatives as Mafia-run, you might not live to regret it. You will perhaps be interested to note that due to the large number of men leaving the military the price of a gun is actually coming down at a time when every other kind of price is going up. Think about it.

★ ★ ★

"Ten o'clock," said Grushko when the last letter had been read. Yawning, he stood up and went over to the window. The sky was still as bright as day and would remain so for several hours yet. During the month of June it is actually dark for less than an hour.

"I usually look forward to this time of year," he said. "The *churki* don't much like the lighter evenings. More chance of being nicked, I suppose." He shook his head wearily. "I don't know. Maybe I'm just getting old. But when someone like Mikhail Milyukin gets his box, then I begin to think that whoever did it, well, they must think their chances of getting away with it are good. I mean, they must have known that we'd pull all the stops out. And still they went ahead and did it. It makes me think that they just don't care. That they don't expect to get caught. That they're laughing at us. It's ... it's depressing." He turned and looked at us with a frustrated sort of look.

I shrugged. "Being a policeman isn't so bad. Things might be worse. You could have been a cosmonaut."

Nikolai grunted his assent.

These former heroes were now a cruel national joke: most of them had Alzheimer's disease from useless endurance experiments in poorly shielded Soviet space stations. I thought of another equally tasteless joke that was popular in Moscow at the time.

"Why do policemen have dogs? Because they need someone to do the paperwork."

This time Nikolai guffawed loudly. "That's a good one," he said, slapping his huge thigh.

Grushko smiled, shook his head and lit a cigarette. "You should have been a comedian," he said.

"True," I said, "but my mother says I did the next best thing."

"Your mother too, eh?" chuckled Nikolai.

Grushko was looking at his watch.

"I think we'll call this a day." He collected his jacket off the back of his chair. "Where does your brother-in-law live?"

"Ochtinsky Prospekt."

"You're in luck, comedian. That's where I live. Come on, I'll give you a lift."

We said good night to Nikolai, who said he had some paperwork he wanted to finish.

"Unfortunately I don't have a dog," he grinned. "See you tomorrow."

On the way downstairs to the car Grushko spoke some more about the letters we had read.

"For the Russian writer the real hallmark of his success has always been the number of enemies he makes. Don't you agree?"

"By that standard Mikhail Milyukin must have been a very successful writer indeed," I said.

Grushko nodded grimly.

"By that standard he ought to have won the Nobel Prize for Literature."

We came out of the Big House and stood in front of the huge wooden doors for a moment, enjoying the summer air. A man walking past eyed us nervously and then quickened his step. It was not the kind of place you lingered near. Grushko's eyes followed the man suspiciously.

"We might make a bigger impact if people weren't still so damned nervous of us," he grumbled.

"That," I said, "is going to take a little while."

"I suppose so." Grushko lit a cigarette. His gold lighter flashed in his hand and I found myself again wondering about the generosity of Swiss policemen. What could he possibly have done for them that would have been rewarded with such a generous gift? Or were the Swiss police just so well paid? Nobody would have been dumb enough to flaunt a gold lighter if it had been come by dishonestly. Grushko caught my eye and seemed to sense my curiosity. Maybe he could read palms after all.

"One night I was at home and I got a call from this militiaman at the Moskva," he explained. We went down the steps and along the pavement. "The Swiss police had got themselves into a lot of bother. Some girls had joined them for dinner and they'd helped them spend quite a bit of money—well, by our standards. There were empty bottles of champagne all over the table. Anyway, at the end of the evening the girls, who were hard-currency prostitutes you understand, put it to the Swiss that they should all go upstairs. Only the Swiss thought better of it. But the girls felt that they had wasted a whole evening on them without result: I mean, what's a free dinner next to a hundred dollars, right? So they told the Swiss that they were working girls who needed the money and expected to be paid for their company. There's nothing more rapacious than a Russian whore. But the Swiss disagreed and so the girls called their pimp in to try and settle the dispute. One of the Swiss persuaded a militiaman to give me a call and I had to go and sort it out. I had the militiamen throw the girls in the hotel cage and threatened to pinch the pimp." He pocketed the lighter. "So now you know how I came to own this cigarette lighter." His tone was defensive.

I shrugged. "I'm sure it's none of my business."

"Just as you like," said Grushko.

We found Grushko's car and drove north, across the Neva. Where the reddening sun touched the shiny graphite surface of the river it looked as if someone had washed a murderous, bloody axe in the water.

★ ★ ★

Ochtinsky Prospekt, in the east of St. Petersburg, was exactly like the place where I had lived in east Moscow. Exactly like any big housing estate in Russia, now that I come to think of it. Once, when I was returning from a holiday in the Crimea, I saw my home from the air. It was as if a giant had gone to buy some shoes and tried on every pair in the shop. (This could not have been a Russian shop.) In her concern to make a sale (this could certainly never have been a Russian shop) the assistant had thrown the white boxes all over the shop until the floor was littered with them. That was what my home looked like from the air. Something that had been dropped there, randomly, without any thought. Quite unreal.

Inside one of the boxes, each of them twelve storeys high and housing as many as five hundred families, life was only too concrete, however. At Number seven Sredne-Ochtinsky, where Porfiry Zakharych Lebezyatnikov lived with his wife and child, human habitation was all too substantive. It was not that the walls were too thin to keep out the noise made by the family living next door to my brother-in-law; nor was it that the rooms squeezed between the walls were too small. No more was it that the tiny, creaking lift smelt like a urinal; nor the lack of lightbulbs that made the passageways dangerous at night. It was not the very homogeneity of the landscape that could be viewed from the window-box which Porfiry laughingly called a balcony. But rather it was all these things that, when taken together, contrived to make the inhabitant feel like a rat in a very large and dirty nest.

I was used to feeling like a rat in my particular line of work.

As one of "them who can go abroad," Porfiry Zakharych was better off than most. Frequent business trips to Stockholm, Helsinki and, once, to London on behalf of his employer, the Baltic Shipping Company, had enabled him to acquire all the luxury consumer goods and the hard currency you needed to live well.

I call him my brother-in-law, but he and my sister had divorced long ago because of her alcoholism, and this was the first time I had met his new wife, Katerina. She was a striking-looking woman with a dark, slightly oriental face and the most perfectly formed breasts I had ever seen. With breasts such as these it was hard not to gain the impression that they were the main reason why Porfiry had married her. She wore a low-cut top that looked as if it had been sculpted for her, and a necklace that was made of coral.

Porfiry was less than distinguished. Older than Katerina by at least ten years, he was grey-haired and slightly overweight, with a bad, pitted skin that here and there had erupted in various moles and cysts, not the least of which was a stamp-sized purple birthmark on the side of his fleshy neck. He greeted me with a warm hug and a kiss on both cheeks.

"So," he said, "here you are at last. Tell me, what do you think of Katya? Isn't she gorgeous?"

"Stop it, Porfiry," she giggled, colouring with embarrassment.

"She certainly is," I said, without any false politeness.

"And what about our apartment?" he continued.

I looked around. "It's very comfortable," I said.

Porfiry pointed to a handsome wood cabinet that contained an enormous colour television and VCR.

"Finnish," he said proudly. "We've got satellite, too."

He demonstrated the variety of channels that were available with a remote control that was the size of a small computer.

After Porfiry had shown me his computer, the microwave oven, the stereo music centre, his new camera, and demonstrated how to operate the gas water-heater system in the kitchen, he introduced his dog, Mikki, an enormous bull-terrier, while Katerina made me a bowl of semolina. After I had eaten this we all toasted one another's health with some Georgian brandy that helped to take away the taste of the semolina.

When we had exchanged all our news, I told them

about the murder of Mikhail Milyukin and they said that it had been reported on the television evening news.

"The reporter said that the militia think that it's the work of the Mafia," said Katerina.

"It certainly looks that way," I allowed. "They had more than enough reason."

"And what does the great Grushko think?" asked Porfiry.

"You know Grushko?"

"No, not personally. But he's often on television talking about some crime or another."

"There's a lot of crime here these days," said Katerina. "You're afraid to go out. That's why Porfiry got Mikki. To protect us when he's away on business."

"Or hunting," added Porfiry. "We'll go hunting soon, eh?"

"Great," I said. "If I can get any time off. Milyukin's murder has really made things rather busy for us." I finished my glass of brandy and let Porfiry help me to some more. "Besides, I'm supposed to find out how Grushko does things."

Porfiry shrugged. "Even if you catch the ones who did it," he said, "we'll never defeat the Mafia. You know that, don't you?"

"Why do you say that?"

"Because it's the one thing in this country that actually works."

CHAPTER
SEVEN

★ The next day I was due at the State Prosecutor's Office and so Porfiry, whose journey to his offices in the passenger seaport took him in that general direction, gave me a lift in his car. This was a bright red new Zhiguli and Porfiry was as proud of it as he was of all his other toys. All the way across the city he talked about how he had driven it into the country from Helsinki, and I was quite glad to get out by the time we got to Yakubovica Street.

The State Prosecutor's Office was a decrepit building much like the one I inhabited on Kalayeva Street, with the same green walls, the same ancient lift and the same sour-piss smell. Vladimir Voznosensky's box of an office was on the second floor and he shared it with a broken microwave oven, several tonnes of papers and an ancient army carbine with which he claimed he went hunting, although I could not imagine that it could ever have fired. Voznosensky, a slight, fair-haired figure with a flourishing moustache and a cardigan that, despite the warm weather, he wore zipped up to the neck, greeted me cordially.

"I prosecute most of the cases involving organized crime in this city," he told me. "So I guess we'll be seeing a lot of each other. It's a difficult business. And it's not made any easier by the fact that my predecessor is now Petersburg's number-one Mafioso lawyer."

"Luzhin? He used to work here?"

"I see Grushko's already told you about him," said Voznosensky. "Yes, Semyon Sergeyevich Luzhin was assistant state prosecutor in Leningrad for five years. Now he makes his old monthly salary in one hour. And he's not the only one to have left this place to go and work for the other side." He shrugged and lit a pipe. "Everything comes down to money these days, doesn't it?

"Another thing: when you do make an arrest, what you'll always find is that your Mafioso will claim that whatever it is he's supposed to have done was a personal matter. He'll deny membership of any gang. He's killed another gangster? It was an argument they had about a girl, or an old gambling debt, or an insult received. A Mafia killing? No way. He's never heard of the Russian Mafia; he thought that was something the Party invented to try and discredit capitalism and the free market.

"But our biggest problem is still with the intimidation of witnesses."

I nodded. "It's the same in Moscow," I said. "We've been trying to set up a witness-protection programme, but of course there's not enough money to make it work. And nothing's going to improve until we've changed the way we try racketeering cases in the courts. We need a proper jury system, with jurors compensated for taking time off work. Nobody wants to serve on a jury and get paid nothing."

"Nobody does something for nothing these days."

"Unless you're a policeman," I suggested provocatively.

"Don't you believe it," said Voznosensky. "There are plenty with their paws out for what's available. It's the Mafia's biggest expense. That and weapons."

"What's that? Mostly military stuff for hard currency?"

He nodded. "And it's all top quality, too. There's enough military hardware on the streets of this city to fight a war."

"Tell me, do you get much interference from the military prosecutor?"

"More and more." He muttered a scornful sort of laugh. "Prosecution is the one area of military life that is actually expanding."

He made tea and we talked some more: lawyer's talk, about protocols, evidence, who the best judges were and the latest crime figures.

"So, tell me about Grushko," I said after a while. "What kind of a man is he?"

"Worked his way up through the ranks. The militia's been his life. And never a breath of scandal. Grushko believes in what he's doing. Things are black and white with him." Voznosensky shrugged and tapped his forehead. "To that extent he's like a typical Stalinist. You know—a bit rigid and inflexible sometimes.

"Of course, politically, he couldn't be more different. Stuck his neck out when it was still dangerous to do it, especially for a militiaman. It's a story worth hearing. A couple of years ago, Grushko was selected as the Central Board of Leningrad's delegate to the 22nd Party Congress. He announced his resignation from the Party while making a speech from the lectern. It caused quite a stink at the time, I can tell you. After that about half of the detectives and investigators in the Central Board left the Party, including General Kornilov. These days it's split pretty evenly down the middle between those who support Yeltsin and those who support the old Party. That's your Grushko."

"What about at home?"

"He lives quite modestly really. He's married, with a daughter who's the apple of his eye. Any spare money he's ever had he spent putting his daughter through med school. She's now a doctor at one of the big hospitals here in Peter."

"A sociable man, would you say? I only ask because I don't want to be a nuisance to him if I can help it. But if he's the affable type then it won't matter."

"I wouldn't call Grushko sociable, no. But he's straight with you. He likes a drink and although I've seen him drink a lot I've never yet seen him drunk. Oh, yes, and Pasternak: he loves Pasternak."

★ ★ ★

At the Big House Grushko was not to be found. Nor were Nikolai and Sasha. In the office they shared with two other detectives I found a younger officer, working his way through Mikhail Milyukin's Filofax, telephoning every name and number that was written there. Replacing the phone he stood up and introduced himself.

"Lieutenant Andrei Petrov, sir," he said, shaking my hand. Better dressed than most of the men working for Grushko, Petrov was another of these blond-haired northern Russians. "And this—" he nodded across the desk at a man who was playing idly with an automatic. The man stood up and extended me his hand—"this is Lieutenant Alek Svridigailov—one of your investigators."

"Pleased to meet you, Lieutenant."

Svridigailov was smaller than Petrov and as wiry as a pipe-cleaner. He had the lugubrious face of an undernourished bloodhound.

"Glock semi-automatic," he said, explaining the gun. "Made in Austria. Fires thirteen rounds of .45 ACP-calibre ammunition. Better than anything we've got. You see, there are only thirty-five parts. A real quality weapon. I'd love a gun like this. They took it off some Yakut hood. Can you believe that? You wouldn't think one of those bastards would be intelligent enough to get himself a gun like this, would you."

Andrei Petrov chuckled. "You know what they say about those Yakuts? The only reason they don't eat cucumbers is because they can't get their heads in the jars."

Svridigailov looked at Andrei and then back at me, shaking his head as if to apologise for his colleague.

"Grushko's gone to the TV station," Andrei explained. "He's recording Georgi Zverkov's show. And as for Nikolai and Sasha—" He frowned as he tried to remember where they had gone.

I sat down at Nikolai's desk and glanced over what was on it.

"Doesn't he keep a diary?" I asked. It occurred to me that I might make a note of some of Nikolai's contacts.

Andrei nodded at the safe beside Nikolai's desk.

"I expect he's got it locked up," he said.

"I remember," said Svridigailov. "They went to the Pribaltskaya Hotel. To see some Georgians."

Opened for the 1980 Olympic Games, the Pribaltskaya Hotel stands on the western edge of Vasilyevsky Island, looking out across the Bay of Finland. Triptych-shaped, with seventeen floors and 1,200 rooms, it is one of the biggest hotels in the city and although the citizens of St. Petersburg were forbidden from using it, the hotel's swimming pool, sauna, bowling alley, gymnasium and massage parlour—not to mention the five bars, the five restaurants and the fifteen coffee shops—made it very popular with some of the more nefarious elements of local society. The methods of the Mafia required strong arms to implement them and, like most racketeers, the Georgians liked to work out and use the weights at least once a day. From years of strict regime in the zone, many of them had physiques that would have been the envy of any Olympic athlete, and in their expensive designer track-suits and gold necklaces they would have been easily distinguished from any other people who dared to use the gym at the same time. The gang leader was a swarthy-faced tough called Dzhumber Gankrelidze and he and his lieutenant, Oocho, seemed to be wearing more gold than the rest of the gang put together. These two were among those exercising in the Pribaltskaya gym with a couple of heavies watching the door when Nikolai and Sasha presented their IDs.

"It's all right," said Dzhumber, wiping his hairy neck with a towel. "I think these dogs are here to bark, not bite."

Nikolai pushed the man obstructing his path to one side.

"Who's he? Your secretary?"

Dzhumber Gankrelidze grinned, showing off a status-enhancing gold tooth.

"Yeah," he said, "I get him to take some dictation now and again."

Oocho laughed and continued to work on his grapefruit-sized biceps.

"I bet you do," said Nikolai. "What's his shorthand? Twenty rounds a minute?"

"You're good," said Gankrelidze smiling. "You should be in the cabaret upstairs."

"I'm fussy about who I entertain," said Nikolai.

Gankrelidze kept on smiling. He was used to police harassment. Sasha dipped his head to read the label on one of the Georgians' track-suits.

"Sergio Tacchini," he said. "Very nice. Quite the life-style you boys have here."

"You know what they say," said Oocho. "He who sits near the pot eats the most kasha."

"I guess you're sitting close enough at that," Nikolai observed. "All those cash-cows in the lobby. Business looks pretty good."

"Pick a girl and tell her I sent you," Gankrelidze said negligently. "It'll be my little treat. Your friend too. I like to see the militia enjoying themselves."

"That's the thing I like about you Georgians," said Nikolai. "You're very generous with your mothers and your sisters."

Gankrelidze stopped smiling and picked up a dumbbell. He began to pull it towards his big shoulder.

"What do you want?" he said evenly.

"I've got Georgia on my mind," said Nikolai. "Specifically the late Vaja Ordzhonikidze. Let's start with where you all were the night before last. And don't blow me any smoke rings either. Not five copecks'-worth. You don't have to work for Russian intelligence to decode the way Vaja took his wooden pea-jacket. Someone thought he was a pincher."

Gankrelidze dropped the weight onto the mat and stood up. He was strong, but shorter than Nikolai by about a head.

"You know, normally I don't talk to strangers. But you—you've got a kind face. Me and the boys here spent the whole evening in the restaurant upstairs. Isn't that so, boys?"

There was a murmur of general agreement.

"You don't believe me, you ask your dogs on the front door. They saw us when we arrived at about eight, and when we left again around three."

"No doubt they've had their paws well stroked," sniffed Nikolai.

Oocho laughed and shook his head. "Yeah, well, you hear all sorts of terrible rumours about this city's militia."

The rest of the gang thought that this was very funny.

"So how about this rumour that Vaja was a pincher?" said Nikolai. "That it was his own side that killed him: because he was an informant for Mikhail Milyukin."

"There are people who drink their own urine," said Gankrelidze, "and people who put hot jars on their backs, because they think that it's good for them. But that doesn't make it true. You're looking at the wrong cat, my friend."

Gankrelidze picked up his towel and wiped his face.

"I tell you what I'll do," he said. "I'll give you an invitation to Vaja's funeral. We're giving him a real Georgian send-off. Now does that sound like we thought he was a pincher?"

Nikolai lit a cigarette as he considered Gankrelidze's argument for a moment.

"Did Vaja like watches?"

"He appreciated the value of punctuality, if that's what you mean. What are you aiming at?"

"Only this: someone baited a trap for him with an expensive watch." Nikolai picked up a medicine ball and began to roll it in his dinner-plate-sized hands.

Gankrelidze tut-tutted.

"Good taste. It can be a curse."

"I don't suppose you've any idea who that might have been?"

"You're the local melody, you tell me. I'm just a citizen."

"Sure, you're a citizen," said Nikolai. "And I'm the Grand Duchess Anastasia."

★ ★ ★

"And then we left," he said and unlocked the safe by his desk. He placed his holstered gun inside, took out his diary and locked the safe again.

"What do you think?" I asked. "Would they really execute one of their own and then give him a Mafia funeral with all the trimmings?"

"If it was good for business they'd give the Patriarch a Mafioso's send-off," declared Sasha. "These bastards like to think that they're men of honour, but that's only because they've seen Al Pacino in *The Godfather*. In reality they've got no more respect or honour than a hungry pig."

"It's true," said Nikolai. "They watch that video over and over again. It's like a training film for them. I wish I had ten roubles for every *churki* who thinks he's Michael Corleone."

The big man's phone rang. He took the call and then asked me if I remembered the man who owned the restaurant that had been firebombed.

"Chazov, wasn't it?" I said. "You were hoping to jog his memory?"

"Care to sit in?"

★ ★ ★

We spent a fruitless afternoon with Chazov, who was still too scared of the Mafia to add anything to his original statement. When Nikolai explained that there would be an official investigation into the origin of his meat supplier, Chazov assured him that he had bought it in good faith from a legitimate supplier, although he was unable, or unwilling, to name him. To Nikolai's final tactic, that he intended to find out whether or not the meat had been stolen from the state meat markets, contrary to Article 92 of the RSFSR Criminal Code, an offense punishable by up to four years' deprivation of freedom or corrective labour, Chazov answered with a shrug only. And after he had gone Nikolai banged the table in the interview room with the flat of his hand.

"He knows I've got nothing," he growled. "If I had the first shred of evidence that the meat was stolen I'd have had it impounded and him charged. But how can I ask for a protocol purely on the basis that the very quantity of it makes the supply suspicious? He knows that."

He hit the table again and I didn't fancy the idea of him ever hitting me.

"But I'm not finished with him. I'll keep having him back here until he's so sick of the sight of me, he'll be begging to tell me who's putting the squeeze on him."

I had no doubt that he meant every word of it.

CHAPTER

EIGHT

★ Peter the Great built St. Petersburg as Russia's window on the West. That was before television. Television is today's window on the West. Not that there's much worth watching, unless you like Brazilian soap operas. Which is why so many people beg, steal and borrow to own a video-cassette recorder.

St. Petersburg Television, broadcasting to over 70 million people, from the Baltic to as far away as Siberia, remained the exception to the state's continuing broadcasting monopoly. A mouthpiece for opinions quite different from those expressed on national television, it had long been a hotbed of the new democracy. The studios of St. Petersburg Television were located on Petrogradsky Island, near the top of Kirov Prospekt and easy enough for Grushko to find since they were distinguished by an enormous transmitter-mast that soared over the Neva like a smaller version of the Eiffel Tower.

A middle-aged balding man, wearing his tie askew and his sleeves rolled up, greeted Grushko in his office.

"Yuko Petrakov," he said, introducing himself. "I was Mikhail's producer on *Sixty Minutes*."

"We're speaking to everyone who worked with him," explained Grushko, sitting down, "in the hope that we might find out if he was working on anything that might have got him killed."

Petrakov lit a cigarette and nodded attentively.

"I've already telephoned Mikhail Mikhailovich's editors at *Krokodil* and *Ogonyok* in Moscow. But since I was coming here anyway I thought I'd speak to you in person, Mr. Petrakov. Did you know him very well?"

"Yes, I did. He was one of our finest journalists, and I don't just mean here on Petersburg TV. He was one of the country's finest journalists. The Golden Calf Literary Award, the Ilf and Petrov Prize for Satirical Journalism, Journalist of the Year two years running . . . There has never been anyone quite like Mikhail. Not in Russia, anyway. It was no surprise to me to learn that he had been lured away by national television."

"He was leaving the station?"

"Yes. He told me himself exactly a week before he was murdered. Well, of course he was only ever a freelance. As you know he had other commitments besides us. But they wanted him and were prepared to pay handsomely to get him. More than we could afford, anyway. We are not as well off as they are, colonel. In fact we're losing money. Our major source of funds remains the state budget. I dare say we'll end up as part of the great Russian broadcasting company. They already own a fifth of our equipment and technology." He shook his head. "But here, you don't want to hear about our problems, do you?"

"Was there any resentment at Mikhail leaving?'

"Some. But not from anyone who knew him. Mikhail wasn't a wealthy man at all. Some people imagined that because he was famous he was rich. It simply wasn't true. Mikhail wasn't very good with money. He was never paid well for what he did. So I didn't blame him at all for wanting to leave. And of course he wasn't the first person to be enticed away. Bella Kurkova went last year. I don't sup-

pose they'll waste any time looking for someone to replace him."

"Do you know what they wanted him to do?'

"The same thing as for us: make five or six documentaries a year." He shrugged. "To tell the truth, as he saw
it. I guess that's why he was killed. I'm not sure they
would really have known how to handle a man like
Mikhail. There was never much editorial control from me.
Mikhail liked to do his own thing, and sometimes that
meant upsetting people."

"Yes," said Grushko. "I've already seen a sample of the
kind of fan mail he received. Was the day he told you he
was leaving the last time you spoke to him?"

"I think it was, yes. Under the terms of our original
agreement he had one film left to do for us and so we also
talked over an idea he had for another film about hard-
currency prostitutes."

The phone rang. Petrakov stubbed out his cigarette and
answered the call. Then he replaced the receiver without
speaking.

"That was Zverkov. You're to go down to make-up in
ten minutes. I'll show you the way when it's time."

"This film about hard-currency prostitutes," said Grushko. "Did he mention a Mafia connection? The Georgians?"

"If he did I doubt it would have registered," said
Petrakov, lighting another cigarette. "Mikhail got to be a
bit of a bore about the Mafia sometimes. Well, to be quite
frank with you, he was obsessed with it. He saw the Mafia
everywhere, in everything."

Grushko was half inclined to say that he agreed with
that assessment. Instead he reminded Petrakov that the
Mafia had threatened Milyukin's life on a number of occasions.

"I'm afraid that's just an occupational hazard for any
journalist, Colonel," shrugged Petrakov. "Especially in

Russia. About the only thing that isn't rationed these days is stupidity."

"Would you have known if he was ever scared by one threat in particular?"

"No. And I think he took them all quite seriously. At least to the extent of taking taxis instead of public transport." Petrakov laughed. "Always allowing for the vagaries of Petersburg taxi-drivers. That's why he never had any money."

He frowned as his lips tugged at his cigarette. "But you know, now I come to think of it, I do remember him being quite agitated by something. I don't know that you would call it a threat exactly ..."

"Oh? What was that?"

"He found out that his phone was being bugged."

"Bugged? By who?"

"The KGB, Colonel. Or the Russian Security Service, or whatever it is that the Department is calling itself these days. Who else?" He grinned at Grushko as if he didn't quite believe that the detective could not have known about it.

"You look surprised," he said. "I would have thought ..."

Grushko shook his head irritably. He hated when people assumed that the Central Board was still party to the Department's dirty tricks.

"Did he know he was being bugged?"

"Well, I think he was able to guess. I mean, they're hardly very subtle about it. Clicks on the line and all that kind of thing."

"But why?"

"The Department is reformed only of its Communists, not its anti-Semites. There are factions in the KGB who would like to see every Jew in Russia on a plane to Israel."

"And that's why Mikhail Mikhailovich thought that they were operating a surveillance?"

"Yes."

"I didn't even know that he was Jewish."

"Oh, Milyukin wasn't his real name. His real name was Berdichevski. When he came to live in Leningrad, in 1979, he changed it to avoid discrimination. It was hard for a Jew to write anything then. The Russian press— especially the *Russian Literary Gazette*—is still quite anti-Semitic. Even now, more than ten years later. They're even saying that Lenin was a Jew. Or don't you notice these things?"

"I notice them."

"And?"

Grushko shrugged. "This is Russia. This is the home of conspiracy theories." He didn't much like being pressed for his opinion. He felt he knew what was right and what was wrong but that it was a matter between himself and his own conscience. He concealed his irritated frown with a strong-tasting puff on the last millimetre of his cigarette.

"How well do you know Mrs. Milyukin?" he asked.

"Hardly at all. Why?"

"Oh, I was just wondering why she didn't think to tell me any of this herself." He shook his head. The last puff had been stronger than he had expected. "It's sad, really. When I read his letters last night I thought I'd encountered just about every possible shade of hatred for the man. And now I find one, in my own backyard, that I didn't even know about: the Department."

Petrakov raised his toothbrush-shaped eyebrows.

"Yes, well, while you're busy compiling a grudge list against Mikhail, don't forget the army. His early stand against the war in Afghanistan won him a lot of enemies. A lot of friends too, it's fair to say. But nobody ever hunts you down just to shake you by the hand and clap you on the back. Not in Russia."

He glanced at his watch and stood up. "We'd better go," he said.

Grushko followed Petrakov out of the door.

When the make-up people had done their best to soften Grushko's fist of a face, he waited in the hospitality suite until Zverkov came to talk to him.

He was a handsome man in an unshaven, macho sort of way and, wearing a smart leather jacket and a pair of jeans, he looked like nothing so much as one of the "businessmen" who might have been found over at Deviatkino Market. But worse than this Zverkov was also arrogant in the way that only so-called "creative people" can be. If he had been Nijinsky he could not have thought more of himself. He did not offer to shake Grushko's hand and the studio's hospitality only ran as far as a glass of tea. Zverkov was of the opinion that the militia needed his programme more than he needed the militia.

It had not always been that way. It had been Grushko who first asked Zverkov to film at the scene of a crime in the hope of soliciting information from the public. He had hardly realised that this would be the basis on which Zverkov would create a whole style of television journalism. Most commonly this involved getting as close to the perpetrators and their victims as quickly as possible. Nothing was hidden from the lens of Zverkov's outside-broadcast team, with Zverkov's microphone there to record the sound of their complaints, their confessions, their cries of pain and, quite often, their last breaths as well. Realism, they called it. Pornography, some said. Either way Grushko cared even less for Zverkov's work than he did for his manners.

"We'll show some clips of Milyukin's documentaries," he explained smoothly. "And then I'll ask you to say something about the circumstances of his death, appeal for information. Do you know the kind of thing I mean?"

"I should do," said Grushko. He was starting to have a bad feeling about this interview. "It was me who got you started doing this kind of thing."

Zverkov nodded sullenly. A few minutes later Grushko took his place on the set next to Zverkov and watched the short videotape which had been made about Milyukin: there were shots of him interviewing black-marketeers, prostitutes and the generally disaffected; shots of the Chernobyl nuclear-reactor accident; shots of Milyukin walking through a hospital ward containing firemen with fatal radiation burns with tears streaming down his face; shots of Milyukin speaking to citizens queuing for meat outside a state meat market; and, lastly, Milyukin speaking directly to the camera in the assembly hall at the Smolny Building where the victory of the Socialist Revolution was announced on the night of 25-26 October 1917.

In life Mikhail Milyukin had been a small, intense-looking man with curly black hair, a rodent-like face and, it seemed to Grushko, a rather purplish, boozer's nose. To look at, a quite unprepossessing sort of character, as might have worked pushing paper around some forgotten government department. But it was for his dry humour and his consistent honesty, not his appearance, that he had been much beloved. As Grushko watched the tape, Milyukin's usual candour was tinged with such obvious pessimism that he was almost inclined to consider the possibility that Milyukin had known he was about to be killed.

"The urgent need for foreign capital seems obvious," said Milyukin, "but what is there that's actually worth investing in? Our factories are hopelessly antiquated. The rudiments of political stability are missing. Individually we lack something as ordinary as a work ethic: everyone knows the saying "They pretend to pay us, and we pretend to work." But even the most basic human instinct of all—the profit motive—seems to be missing from all but a small and not always law-abiding section of society. After seventy years of this—" here Milyukin waved his hand at the enormous portrait of Lenin that dominated the empty assembly hall—"many people are coming to realise that the task of redeveloping Russia may not just be difficult. It might actually be impossible."

The film sequence concluded with the black Volga in the forest and several of the gory close-ups of the two dead bodies that were the hallmark of Zverkov's veracious style.

Grushko's interrogator fixed a sober look to his designer-stubbled face and looked away from the monitor to the camera.

"The murder of Mikhail Mikhailovich Milyukin is being investigated by Colonel Yevgeni Grushko of the Criminal Services Department of the Central Board of Internal Affairs." Zverkov turned to face Grushko.

"The other man found dead with Mikhail Milyukin, Vaja Ordzhonikidze: he was a Georgian Mafioso, wasn't he?"

"That's correct," said Grushko, shifting uncomfortably in his swivel chair.

"And I believe it has been suggested that the two men were shot because Ordzhonikidze was giving information to Mikhail?"

"Well, that's one possibility," Grushko allowed, "but it's still too early to treat it as anything more than that. Obviously we would like anyone who saw or had contact with either of these two men recently to come forward as quickly as possible. For that matter we would like to speak to anyone who might be able to shed some light on the nature of the connection between them."

Zverkov nodded. His expensive leather jacket creaked as he glanced down at the notes on his lap.

"I'm sure people will do everything they can to help bring these murderers to justice," he said quietly.

"But now let me ask you this." His tone became harder, more aggressive even. "What are St. Petersburg's militia doing to help the people? When are you going to put a stop to the Mafia in this city?"

Despite his intuitive feeling about appearing on Zverkov's show, this was more than Grushko had bargained for. But he did his best to field the question.

"If we are going to defeat the Mafia, it will have to be a joint effort," he said coolly. "The Russian people and the militia acting together. We can only secure convictions of Mafia figures if people are prepared to come forward and give evidence to—"

"What, are you saying that the militia can't do the job?" Zverkov smile contemptuously.

"No, that's not what I'm saying at all."

"But isn't it a fact that people within your own department believe that the Mafia is now so strong that any attempts to combat it are doomed to fail?"

"It's true," admitted Grushko, "there are such people. But I'm not one of them. No, I feel more optimistic about the—"

"Well, we'll all sleep more safely in our beds tonight knowing that you feel more optimistic, Colonel Grushko. But what's that optimism based on? Georgian brandy?"

"Now, wait a minute—" growled the detective.

"No, you wait a minute." Zverkov was almost shouting now. "You cops can't even stop the Mafia from stealing free food from the EEC."

"The particular crime I think you're referring to was committed in Kiev," said Grushko. "I don't see that you can hold this city's militia responsible for solving that. You want to find out what happens to the food aid that arrives in St. Petersburg from the West, then I suggest you ask the city councillors. And you—" Grushko reached forward to feel the leather of Zverkov's leather jacket—"I'm sure we'd all like to be able to afford a nice leather jacket like this. How much was it? Fifteen? Twenty thousand roubles? That's two or three years' salary to one of my men. And you've got the nerve to lecture me about—"

"That's not the point—"

"It is exactly the point," said Grushko, his face growing redder by the second. "It's *exactly* the point. If you and others like you weren't so hell-bent on getting your hands on Western clothes and goods, the Mafia wouldn't stand a chance. You can't condemn the militia for fighting a losing battle with the Mafia when you yourself shop with these criminals."

"So you admit you're losing the battle?"

"I admit nothing of the sort."

The argument continued in this vein for several more minutes until, unable to tolerate Zverkov's insults any longer, Grushko snatched the microphone from his tie and walked off the set and out of the television studios.

Later on, when Grushko watched the broadcast at home with his wife and mother-in-law, his anger quickly gave way to depression as he considered what General Kornilov would make of his performance.

"Well," he sighed, "I walked straight into that one, didn't I?"

Grushko's wife Lena was more inclined to look on the bright side of things.

"But you were right," she said. "What you said about the need for people and militia to act together if the Mafia is to be defeated."

"You lose your temper, you lose the argument," opined Lena's mother.

"Don't worry, dear," said Lena. "Nobody likes that man these days. Not even mother. Do you, mother?"

"He looks like a *churki*," said the old woman. "Either that or a Yid . . . One of those homeless cosmopolitans."

"Mother," said Lena smiling gently, "you mustn't say such things."

Grushko poured himself a glass of home-made whisky and sipped it gently. This was the smoothest stuff he had distilled so far, made from vegetables grown on the allotment he shared with a detective in the vice squad, and it had a deceptively sweet taste. He only wished he could have grown some maize to make a corn-based liquor, but the beetroot whisky and the cucumber wine now fermenting in bottles on top of the lavatory cistern were better than queuing for hours to buy vodka in the state shops—when they had any. What vodka he did manage to buy he usually kept for trade. So Grushko sipped his whisky, confident that it wasn't the kind of stuff that included alcohol taken from glue or toothpaste, and counted himself lucky in that at least.

They heard the front door. It was Tanya, Grushko's daughter. She came quickly into the tiny sitting-room.

"Have we missed it?" she said, looking at the television.

"I wish I had," said Grushko.

"How was it?"

"Your father lost his temper," said Lena.

Tanya looked hardly surprised to hear this, any more than she was surprised to see the look of distaste on her father's face when Boris, her boyfriend, followed her into the room.

"Boris," said Lena warmly, "how nice to see you."

Grushko merely grunted. He made no secret of his dislike of Boris. It was not that he objected to the young man's manners or his appearance. Boris was as polite as he was well-dressed. He had a good job, too. As a broker on the St. Petersburg Commodities and Raw Materials Exchange, buying and selling everything from ox-tongues to railway sleepers, Boris was making a lot of money. What bothered Grushko was the discovery that a seat on the Exchange that had once cost a staggering 50,000 roubles now cost an astronomical 6 million.

"Just look what Boris gave me," said Tanya slipping the stopper out of a bottle of Christian Dior perfume and holding it under her mother's nose.

"Mmmm, that's lovely," said Lena.

Grushko took his time sniffing the scent. A lot of what was sold as French or American perfume was no more the real thing than a bottle of his cucumber wine. But not this. He nodded appreciatively.

"The real thing," he said. "Hard currency, was it, Boris? Must have cost a lot of money, anyway."

Boris shrugged nervously. Tanya's father made him nervous. "No," he said, "not that much really."

"You surprise me, Boris," said Grushko. "Tell me: how are things on the Exchange? Whose birthright were you selling today?"

"Dad, please," said Tanya.

"Well, I can't complain . . ."

"No, I wouldn't have thought you could, Boris. Oh yes, you'll be all right—"

"Lay off, will you, Dad?"

"—whatever happens to the rest of us."

"Yevgeni Ivanovich," Lena said sternly, "that's enough."

The phone started to ring. Grushko had a shrewd idea who it was. For a moment he was tempted not to answer it, but then he realised that everyone wanted him to, if only to get him out of the room for a few minutes. He walked into the hallway.

"Saved by the bell," grinned Boris, and then glanced at his gold watch. "Well, I guess I'd better be going."

"I'm sorry about Yevgeni," Lena said. "Georgi Zverkov gave him a hard time."

"So he takes it out on the rest of us," said Tanya.

The telephone was by the front door and Tanya made a point of kissing Boris with an extra amount of passion before saying goodnight, just for her father's benefit. Then she went into the bedroom she shared with her grandmother and closed the door without another word. Grushko replaced the receiver and returned to the sitting-room, where he drained his glass.

"Yevgeni Ivanovich, what comes over you sometimes?"

"I'm sorry, love," he said. "I can't bring myself to like the man. I can't get it out of my head that a seat on the exchange costs 6 million roubles—6 million. Now where does he get that kind of money? Where does anyone get it?"

Lena glanced up at the little reproduction icon on the wall, as if the Madonna and Child might have provided her with an answer that could satisfy him. She was anxious that Grushko should like a man with Boris's good prospects.

"Perhaps he borrowed it," she suggested. "From Gosbank."

"Maybe I should go in and see them myself," he laughed, and poured himself another whisky.

"Who was on the phone?"

"General Kornilov. He just told me to report to his office first thing in the morning. Then he hung up." Grushko swallowed half of the whisky in his glass. "Which is probably what he means to do with me."

★ ★ ★

Kornilov was not a man to look or sound angry, even when he was furious. Grushko would have preferred it if he had been. At least you knew where you were with a man like that. But Kornilov was as inscrutable as a field of bison grass.

As Grushko came through the door the general nodded at the chairs in front of him and carried on with the protocol he was writing. Grushko sat down, reached for his cigarettes and then thought better of it. Perhaps it was best not to seem in any way relaxed about what had happened. Finally Kornilov put down his fountain-pen and clasped his hands on the blotter in front of him. Grushko's eyes noted how the fingernails on Kornilov's right hand were so badly stained with nicotine they looked as if they were made of wood; they seemed to underline Grushko's impression of Kornilov as something hard and inhuman.

"What the hell did you have to go and make that stupid remark about the city councillors for?"

Grushko shook his head and shifted uncomfortably under his senior officer's scrutiny. It was said that Kornilov had once stared down Bobhov, formerly the first deputy chairman of the KGB. Grushko could easily believe it.

"He was trying to provoke me," he said.

"I'd say he damn well succeeded, wouldn't you?"

Kornilov lit one of the Boyars he liked to smoke. Grushko watched the incriminating smoke curl round Kornilov's fingertips. Not wood, he thought, but smoked fish. Kornilov was kippering his own fingers. He wondered what the man's lungs looked like. For that matter, what did his own lungs look like?

"I had Borzov from the mayor's office on that phone for fifteen minutes this morning," grumbled Kornilov. "He made his feelings quite plain about your performance, Grushko."

Grushko winced. It was always bad when Kornilov called him by his surname.

"Did he, sir?"

"He suggests that we need to solve this business with Milyukin as quickly as possible in order to demonstrate that we are winning the war against the Mafia. Otherwise—"

"Borzov," sneered Grushko. "That idiot. It's only a few years since Borzov was telling people, Mikhail Milyukin included, that there was no such thing as the Soviet Mafia."

"Otherwise," Kornilov repeated more loudly. "things might go badly for us when it comes to renewing our budgets. I need hardly remind you of the shortages we already have to cope with. Petrol, paper, handcuffs, photocopiers, to say nothing of proper leisure facilities for off-duty officers."

"No, sir."

"I want results, Grushko. And I want them soon. Is that quite clear?"

"Yes, sir."

Kornilov picked up his fountain-pen. His yellowing fingers began to write.

"That's all," he murmured.

CHAPTER

NINE

★ When the old man, whose name was Semyonov, had answered all our questions, Sasha thanked him for coming in and, wishing to humour him a little, asked him how he had come by the impressive row of medals he was wearing on his jacket.

"During the blockade of the city," said the old man. "I was on the Pulkovo Heights. Four years facing the German 18th Army. Most of them are service medals. But this one I got for commanding the execution of eight German officers. We built a gallows right here in the centre of Leningrad and after a bit of a trial we put them on four trucks, two apiece, parked under the beam and then strung them up. Half of Leningrad came to watch." The old man grinned cariously. "First decent bit of entertainment folks had seen in three years."

Sasha nodded politely but I could see that he was shocked. Neither of us was old enough to think of the nine-hundred-day siege, when over a million citizens of Leningrad had died, as anything more than another morbid statistic in our country's bitter history. Distracted from his continuing telephone inquiry by old Semyonov's story, Andrei nodded grimly.

"Still," he sniffed, "I expect they deserved it."

"That they did," said Semyonov. "They were war-criminals. The only pity is that we didn't hang more of them."

Grushko emerged from his dressing-down in General Kornilov's office and directed a face the colour of blood towards Andrei.

"Haven't you finished making those calls yet?" he snarled. "What's the matter with you: sleeves too long or something?"

I smiled. Sleeves that were much longer than a man's arms had been a mark of the privilege that the tsars enjoyed, showing that they did no work.

Andrei picked up the phone and extinguished his cigarette. "No, sir."

"Well, get on with it then. And where's Nikolai Vladimirovich?"

I stood up and walked towards him. I was just about to remind Grushko that Nikolai and Alek Svridigailov had spent half the night keeping an eye on the Georgian gang at the Pribaltskaya when the two of them appeared in the corridor behind him.

"Where the hell have you been?" said Grushko, but before either one of them could answer he had turned to me. "And who's the Hero of the Soviet Union with Sasha?"

"Mr. Semyonov," I said. "Reckons he saw Milyukin on the night he was killed."

"Why the hell doesn't anyone tell me what's going on around here?" Advancing on the old man he fixed a grumpy sort of smile to his face.

"Hello, sir," he said. "I'm Colonel Grushko."

The old man rose half out of his chair and touched his forehead with his forefinger in what looked like a salute.

"Yes," he said, "I know. You were on television last night. I saw you. That's why I came."

Grushko winced at the memory of it, and I saw Nikolai and Sasha exchange a smile.

"I hear you think you saw Mikhail Milyukin on the night that he was murdered."

"It's what I've been telling the two detectives here," said Semyonov. "I was in the Poltava Restaurant, at the Peter and Paul Fortress, dining with some old army friends. We were in the blockade together, you know, and we always meet around this time of year. Of course the Poltava is expensive and so we have to save up a bit, but it's always worth it."

Grushko nodded patiently.

"Milyukin was at another table and he seemed to be waiting for someone."

"When was this exactly?"

"Well, we got there around eight. And he came in not long after that I think. He waited almost two hours, until about ten."

Semyonov drew the sleeve up his bony old arm to reveal a new army watch of the kind you could buy from any street-corner spiv.

"I'm sure about the time, because my daughter bought me this watch for my birthday and I kept looking at it all evening. Anyway, whoever Mr. Milyukin was waiting for didn't show up. He kept looking at his watch too. That's why I noticed him in the first place. I wondered if he had a new watch as well."

"And you're sure it was him?"

The phone rang and was answered by Andrei.

"Oh yes," said Semyonov. "It was him all right. He's on television as well, you see. And I never forget a face that's been on TV."

"Thank you, Mr. Semyonov," said Grushko. "You've been most helpful."

"I know this restaurant, sir," said Nikolai.

"You would."

His hand covering the mouthpiece of the telephone receiver, Andrei waved it at Grushko.

"I've got a Lieutenant Khodyrev on the line," he explained. "From Militia Station 59. She says that Milyukin reported a break-in there, two days before the murder."

"So where the hell have they been?" said Grushko. "On holiday?"

"Do you want a word with her?"

Grushko reached for the phone and then seemed to think better of it.

"No," he said glancing at his watch. "Tell her to meet us at Milyukin's address in half an hour. We can go there on our way to this restaurant, Nikolai."

As Andrei relayed the message, Grushko looked at me inquiringly.

"Yes, I'll come."

"Sounds like a few of our pigeons coming home," said Nikolai.

"You've got a car, haven't you?" Grushko said to Andrei when he had finished the call.

"Yes, sir." There was no mistaking the alacrity in Andrei's young voice. Later on, Nikolai told me that this was Andrei's first month with Criminal Services.

"Good. Because there's something I want you to do. I want you to take Mr. Semyonov home."

Andrei's face fell, but he knew better than to argue with a man like Grushko.

★　★　★

Lieutenant Khodyrev was an attractive-looking woman in her early thirties, with dark hair gathered in a bun at the back of her head and the healthiest teeth I had ever seen in any Russian's mouth. No one goes to the dentist very much these days: the cost of any kind of health care is hugely expensive and most people rely on folk remedies and old wives' tales when they get sick.

She was wearing plainclothes and although Grushko seemed too preoccupied to pay Khodyrev much attention, it was clear to see that Nikolai was very taken with her, holding open every door for her as if he had learned his manners at the court of the tsar.

"Have you been with the militia very long, Lieutenant?" he asked her as the four of us came upstairs to Nina Milyukin's flat.

"Four years," she said. "Before that I was a gymnast with the Olympic team."

Which explained her generally healthy demeanour.

"Colonel Grushko, sir," she said, "there's something else I've discovered."

"Something else that slipped your mind? Or are you intending to impress us with your investigative abilities in instalments?"

"No sir," she said patiently. "The fact is I've only just been transferred to Station 59 and it's taken a little while to find my feet there. I found out about this other thing just as I called the Big House."

We arrived on the landing outside the flat.

"Well, what is it?"

"About three months ago, before I went to Station 59—"

"All right," said Grushko, "I get the picture. None of this is your fault."

"Thank you, sir. Mikhail Milyukin came into the station and asked for police protection. He said that the Mafia was after him. He would have got it too, only my predecessor, Captain Stavrogin, was ordered to turn him down."

"Ordered? By who?"

"Someone in the Department. I don't know why exactly. But the official reason was that no Russian citizen should be given any special privileges."

"I'd like to speak to this Captain Stavrogin," Grushko said thoughtfully.

"I'm afraid you can't, sir," she said. "He died of lung cancer, a couple of weeks ago. That's why I've been transferred. All I know is that when he told Mr. Milyukin the decision, the captain advised him to hire a private bodyguard?"

"And did he? Hire a private bodyguard?"

Khodyrev pursed her voluptuous lips. "It doesn't look like it, sir," she said.

Grushko nodded curtly and then rang the sonorous doorbell.

Nina Milyukin looked less than pleased to see us.

"I'm sorry to bother you again," said Grushko. "Just a few more questions. It won't take long."

"You'd better come in," she said and stood aside..

We advanced into the hall and then waited politely while she bolted the door behind us.

"Would you like some tea?" she said and led the way into the communal kitchen.

I was disappointed by this invitation. I had been hoping to get a chance to step inside that wardrobe-study again and get another look at the photograph of her that was on Mikhail Milyukin's pinboard.

The kitchen was the standard arrangement. Two fridges, two cookers, two sinks and, hanging on the wall, two bathtubs. Suspended from the ceiling was a large wooden clotheshorse on which the day's wash was drying as well as it was able in that damp old flat. A large and battered brass samovar stood on a well-scrubbed wooden table and in the corner of the room lay any equally large, equally decrepit-looking black cat. Nina Milyukin found some glasses, drew off some tea and handed it round.

"I'm afraid there's no sugar, and no milk," she said.

We all shook our heads dismissively.

"A couple of days before he died," Grushko began, "Mikhail Mikhailovich reported a break-in."

Nina Milyukin's head sat back on her shoulders.

"A break-in?" She smiled. "There's been no break-in here. Surely you've seen our front door?"

Lieutenant Khodyrev shook her head. "According to the report, Mr. Milyukin believed that they gained entry using keys that he had lost."

"Yes, he did lose his keys," she said thoughtfully.

"Apparently his Golden Calf Literary Award and fifty roubles in cash were taken," said Khodyrev.

"It's the first I've heard of it. But now you come to mention it, I had wondered about the Golden Calf. I haven't seen it in a while. Even so, I can't imagine why anyone would have wanted it. After all, it's not real gold." She smiled sadly. "If it were we would have sold it."

"Well, whoever took it obviously thought it *was* real," said Grushko. "Have you noticed anything else that's missing?"

She sipped her tea and shook her head silently.

"Perhaps some papers? Tapes?"

"How could I? You took most of Mikhail's things away with you the other day."

"Yes, I did," said Grushko. "Well, how about before that?"

"No."

"This is good tea," said Grushko.

I heard myself grunt in agreement.

"I was speaking to Yuri Petrakov at St. Petersburg Television, the other day."

"Yes, I saw the programme. Zverkov gave you a rough time, didn't he?"

Nina was smiling. I almost thought that she might have enjoyed that: Grushko being cross-examined.

"Zverkov's a bully," she added. "Mikhail never liked him. He said that underneath the pretence of being pro-reform he was really a wicked man. But you only have to look at his work. The man's a complete opportunist. He doesn't care about people at all. They're just stories to him. All Zverkov cares about is Zverkov."

"What did he think of Mikhail?"

"There was no love lost there," she said. "A couple of years ago there was an evening organised by the Leningrad branch of the Soviet Cultural Fund, to mark the fiftieth birthday of the writer Josef Brodsky. It was held in the Public Library on Ostrovskovo Square. After it was over the two of them bumped into each other and exchanged a few insults. Zverkov had said something disparaging about Yeltsin. That he was a drunkard or some such nonsense. Mikhail called Zverkov a Fascist. There was a scuffle and Mikhail got his eye blacked.

"About six months after that there was a three-day conference at the Academy of Sciences." She snorted with laughter. " 'Man in the World of Dialogue,' or some such nonsense. And they had another argument. I think it was about Lithuanian independence. Or was it Latvian independence? I don't remember." She shrugged. "Either way, who cares?

"Anyway, no one was really hit, but Mikhail kicked Zverkov's car and damaged it. Since then, nothing. They never spoke. But after the August coup was over Mikhail kept agitating for Zverkov's programme to be taken off the air. He said Zverkov had been sponsored by the KGB. The only reason Mikhail accepted a job offer from national television was because he knew they were also considering Zverkov for the same spot."

Grushko said nothing for a moment but I could tell what he was thinking: did Zverkov have sufficient reason to have wanted Milyukin dead?

"I find it extraordinary that he said nothing about all this."

"What do you expect of a man like that? He's a hypocrite," said Nina.

"Yuri Petrakov said that Mikhail had discovered that your phone was being bugged by the KGB."

Nina shrugged.

"Did you know about it?"

"Yes."

"Mr. Petrakov also said that Mikhail believed that he might have been the target of an anti-Semitic faction within the Department."

"You'd better ask them about that, hadn't you?"

Grushko sighed. "Mrs. Milyukin, I'm just trying to find out what your husband believed."

"He believed in all sorts of things, Colonel. Really, you've no idea. In some ways he was a rather credulous sort of person to have become a journalist. I suppose he wanted things to be true so that he could write about them. Faith-healing for instance. Did you know he believed in that?" She lit a cigarette, and shook her head impatiently. "Look, what does it matter what he believed in now? He's dead. Why can't you just leave him alone?"

"Surely what matters most," argued Grushko, "is that the people responsible for his murder are caught and punished."

Nina sighed theatrically and stared out of the filthy window. When she said, "Why can't you just leave him alone?" I assumed she meant "Why can't you leave *me* alone?" But Grushko was not to be put off.

"Did he ever talk about hiring himself a bodyguard?"

"A bodyguard?" Nina smiled. "Look around you, Colonel. We're not wealthy people. We couldn't even afford a washing-machine, let alone a bodyguard. This was Mikhail Milyukin, not Mikhail Gorbachev."

Grushko finished his tea and placed the glass on the table. By now the cat had stirred from its corner. It arched its black back, tiptoed forward and then curled its tail around Nikolai's trouser leg.

"No you don't, Bulgakov," said Nina, and shooed the animal into the corridor. She probably wished she could have been rid of the militia as easily. I smiled to myself. It was just what you would have expected a writer to have called his cat.

"Your husband had asked the local militia for protection, you know," Grushko persisted.

"Then I hardly see why he would have needed to hire a bodyguard," retorted Nina.

"The militia turned him down."

Nina gave Grushko a look of dim disapproval and then turned away.

"Well, I don't suppose it even occurred to him to offer them money. Mikhail could be quite naïve."

"It wasn't a question of money," said Lieutenant Khodyrev.

"No? What was it a question of?"

Khodyrev paused as she struggled to find an explanation that wouldn't have left her station looking like KGB poodles.

"I think," I said, "that it was simply a question of manpower. Things are already stretched almost to the breaking point. There are militia patrols that don't leave their stations for lack of spare parts and—"

"Now I see why you go around in threes and fours," said Nina. "It saves petrol. And it makes explanations so much easier."

"Thank you for your time," Grushko said crisply. "And thank you for the tea."

When we were outside in the street, Grushko thumped on the roof of his car.

"What the hell's the matter with that woman? Anyone would think she didn't care whether we caught her husband's murderer or not."

"She's feeling upset," said Khodyrev. "Who knows? Maybe she holds us partly to blame. For not providing him with protection in the first place."

"On the other hand," said Nikolai, "perhaps she just doesn't like policemen. My wife's the same."

"Living with you, I can't say I blame her," said Grushko. "Maybe you're right Lieutenant Khodyrev, I don't know. Meanwhile, see if you can manage to trace that Golden Calf. Before Moses."

"Sir?"

" 'And he took the golden calf which they had made and burnt it with fire, and ground it to powder, and scattered it upon the water, and made the people of Israel drink it.' "

★ ★ ★

Standing on a small island in the centre of the Neva Delta, the three-hundred-year-old Peter and Paul Fortress was the nucleus around which St. Petersburg had grown. The twelve o'clock cannon fired as Grushko drove across the wooden Ivan Bridge towards the main entrance and, instinctively, we all three of us checked our watches.

It seemed an odd place to locate a restaurant. It was true, the fortress was very popular with the tourists, but so many people had met unpleasant ends within its granite walls that it would have quite taken the edge off my appetite.

The Poltava Restaurant, named after the battle Peter the Great had won against the Swedes, was located in what had once been the officers' club. We pulled up outside and knocked on the heavy wooden door. The fat greasy man who opened it was typically obstructive, no doubt in the hope that we would pay more to get a table for lunch.

"You've got no chance today," he said. "We're all full up."

Grushko flashed his identity card. "Save it for the starving," he said and pushed his way inside.

The mood was more rustic than military. Old prints, including one of Peter the Great's wedding party, decorated the snow-cemmed walls beneath heavily beamed ceilings that were hung with wrought-iron chandeliers. And somewhere, we could detect the mouth-watering smell of pastry cooking.

"I'd like to speak to the manager, please," said Grushko.

"I'm the manager," said the man who had let us in.

Grushko showed him a photograph of Milyukīn.

"Ever see him in here? His name is Mikhail Milyukin."

The manager took the photograph in his grubby hands and looked closely at it for several seconds. He shook his head.

"Looks too thin to be one of our regulars," he said.

"We think he was in here three nights ago."

"If you say so."

"He was supposed to meet someone, only the other party didn't show up."

"A girl was it? We get a lot of courting couples in here."

"That's what we'd like to find out," said Grushko. "Perhaps if you could check the booking?"

The manager led us into a small alcove where, on a tall oak table next to an ancient telephone, lay a large leather-bound book. He opened it, licked his finger, turned back several pages and then ran the same finger down the page, smudging some of the writing as it went.

"Here we are," he said. "Yes, now I remember. Party of two for eight o'clock, it was. But the booking was made in the name of Beria."

"Beria?" exclaimed Grushko. "You're joking."

The manager turned the book towards Grushko.

"Take a look for yourself," he said.

"Yes, you're right," said Grushko. "It's just—it was just that Beria was the chief of Stalin's secret police."

"You don't say," shrugged the man. "I'm too young to remember that myself. But we get all sorts in here."

As he spoke a swarthy, southern type with a droopy mustache and a sharp suit stepped out of the dining-room, heading for the lavatory. Each squeak of his patent-leather shoes seemed to suggest that he was Mafia. Grushko's eyes followed the man—he would have called him a *churki*—with distaste.

"I'll bet you do," he murmured and then returned his attention to the reservations book.

"What I mean is that it's obviously a false name," he said.

"Not obvious to me," said the manager.

"How was the booking made?"

"Telephone. No one ever books in person. Not unless they're a regular. Being on an island, well, it's not exactly on anyone's way."

Grushko pointed to the blue biro Cyrillic letters that constituted Mr. Beria's booking.

"Is this your writing?"

"Yes."

"Can you remember anything about the person who phoned?"

"It was a man, I'm sure of that anyway." He thought for a moment and then shrugged. "Apart from that, nothing at all."

"Did he have an accent? Georgian? Chechen, maybe?"

"Look, I'm sorry, I really don't remember. Like I say, we get all sorts here."

"When Mr. Milyukin, the man in the photograph, left, did he offer any explanations as to why the other man hadn't shown up?"

"He paid his bill and then collected his coat. I helped him on with it. I said I hoped that we might see him again, and he said he hoped so too. I even opened the door for him. I think he was on foot—I mean, I don't remember hearing a car start."

"Well, thanks anyway," said Grushko.

"Well, now you're here, gents, why not stay and have a bite of lunch?" said the manager. "On the house. We've got homemade Peter's soup . . ."

"Peter's soup," Nikolai repeated hungrily. "That's what I can smell."

The Mafia type returned from the lavatory.

"Thank you, no," said Grushko, eyeing the man. "We usually like to get away from our clients during the lunch hour."

Nikolai's face fell and reluctantly he followed Grushko and myself out of the Poltava's door.

When we were outside Grushko looked squarely at the big man as if waiting for him to say something about walking away from a free meal.

"What?" he said finally. "No complaints about your stomach?"

Nikolai lit a cigarette and looked up at the golden spire on the nearby cathedral.

"No," he said, "you were right. The food smelled better than the people eating there." He slowly tightened his belt a notch. "But I don't mind telling you, this honesty is damned hungry work."

CHAPTER

TEN

★ An investigator's job can only begin when a detective has made a statement to the effect that a crime has been committed and that a man should be arrested. All protocols follow this one-sentence declaration.

After our trip to the restaurant in the Peter and Paul Fortress I had a busy afternoon issuing several arrest protocols to two detectives from Grushko's department. A gang of Kazhaks had been preying on Jews who were about to emigrate to Israel, robbing them on the eve of their departure when all their belongings were neatly and—for the robbers—conveniently gathered together in bags and boxes. A man called the Goose had murdered an old Jewish woman in cold blood in her apartment on Bakunina Prospekt when she offered the gang resistance.

Having signed these arrest protocols, the next task was to justify them, and this required me to sign personal-search protocols and interrogation protocols. But to search the Goose's apartment for goods stolen from the old woman meant that I was going to need the relevant protocol stamped by the State Prosecutor's Office. So I called Vladimir Voznosensky and then went straight over there with the two detectives in their car. To some this might have all sounded rather bureaucratic, but that would have been to forget that the investigator was the best guarantee of a suspect citizen's rights.

I had not long arrived back at the Big House when I received a call from an old friend at the GUITI, the Chief Directorate of Corrective Labour Institutions. I had telephoned him earlier that same day to check on Sultan Khadziyev, the Chechen pimp whom Mikhail Milyukin had helped to put in the zone. My friend, whose name was Viktor, had been able to discover that Khadziyev had been serving his sentence in Beregoi 16/2, a camp that was close to the Kazakh border in western Siberia. Now he told me that Sultan had been released four weeks ago. For good behaviour.

"But he couldn't have served more than half of his sentence," I said.

"I don't understand it myself," said Viktor. "I called the regime chief at the camp and he assured me that a proper release order, authorised by this Directorate, had been received. Believe me, I intend to investigate this matter thoroughly."

"Does the camp commander know where Khadziyev went?"

"Apparently he spent a few days in the camp infirmary taking advantage of the medical facilities. The way things are on the outside these days, if you get sick you're better off as a *zek*. After that they gave him a salary cheque for seventy-five roubles and a railway warrant from Omsk back to St. Petersburg."

"Let me know what you find out, Viktor."

I was about to call Grushko and tell him what I had learned when the phone rang again. This time it was Nikolai.

"I'm downstairs," he explained. "There's been a hit. The boss wants to know if you can come with us."

"I'll be right down."

I found Nikolai, Sasha and Grushko waiting in Grushko's car on Kalajeva Street.

"It looks like the gang war might just have started," said Grushko, turning south on to Liteiny Prospekt. "A couple of Mafiosi just got their wooden pea-jackets."

I told them about Sultan Khadziyev.

"Good behaviour, eh?" he said. "Well, that'll give us something to talk about when we've got him in our bag of maybes."

"Want us to find him, Colonel?" said Nikolai.

"Unless the dull definition of detective has escaped you. Let's just hope he's not today's dead meat."

Bordered by apartment blocks and the Hotel Pulkovskaya, Victory Square is in reality an enormous roundabout at the southern end of Moscow Prospekt. Marking the former front-line of the Nazi advance on the city is a wide keyhole-shaped area of paving stones and sculptured groups that constitutes a monument to the heroic defenders of Leningrad. At its centre, standing within an incomplete circle of granite, is a fifty-metre-high obelisk, near to which base is another typically Soviet group: a Red Army soldier supporting a woman faint from starvation; a wife comforting her wounded husband; and a mother holding the lifeless body of her child. It was only a couple of weeks since Remembrance Day and several bunches of flowers still lay at the feet of these heroic figures. At the base of the granite plinth they occupied lay the bodies of two men, cut to pieces with a machine-gun that was at least the destructive equal of the one carried by the bronze soldier. Each man had been hit fifteen or twenty times, but before running away the killer had, according to a witness, stopped to light a cigarette and sweep some of the flowers off the plinth and onto the bodies. There was blood everywhere, as if someone had dropped a five-litre jug of wine from the top of the obelisk. One of the dead men still clutched a handful of the dollars he had been about to hand the other, while stray bills blew around the stone circle like dead leaves.

Dead meat was right, I thought. It was hard to think of these two men as at all human now. They looked ready for a butcher's hook.

The man clutching the dollars was dark-skinned, with moustaches that were the same length, colour and shape as his eyebrows. In the breast pocket of his suit was a pair of aviator-style sunglasses and he wore his tie in a double-knot that managed to make it look too small, as if it were a schoolboy's tie. Grushko reached inside the man's blood-stained jacket and withdrew a wallet and an identity card.

"Ramzan Dudayev," he said. "Sounds like a Chechen name. But it's hard to tell with these *churki* bastards."

The wallet produced several stolen credit cards and yet more dollars, while Nikolai found a revolver tucked underneath the dead man's snakeskin belt.

"You can't be too careful these days," he muttered.

The second man was younger, with spiky hair and several days' growth of beard. His lightweight suit was of a better cut than his friend's but no more bullet-proof and he wore a button-up vest instead of a shirt and tie. His wallet had been neatly holed by a bullet. Grushko tried to read the name on the bloodstained identity card.

"Abu Sin . . . something or other," he said. "Sinbad the bloody sailor."

Sasha turned up a set of amber prayer-beads, a large and greasy wad of roubles, a flick knife and a small cigarette case with the picture of a naked model embossed on the lid. He opened the case and sniffed at the roll-ups it contained.

"Kojaks," he said.

"These Muslims like to smoke their bit of clover," Grushko observed. He stood up and turned towards me.

"So, how do you like our Petersburg Mafia? The price of a hit like this is 50,000 roubles. Or around $230, if you want to pay hard currency. For an outside job. Of course the Georgians might just have preferred to have done it themselves. They take their revenge very personally."

"Do you think that these are the two who murdered Milyukin and Ordzhonikidze?" I asked him.

He took out his handkerchief and wiped some of the blood off his fingertips.

"Assuming that the Georgians do think that it was the Chechens who were behind it, no, I reckon they just put these two on account. At least until they have a better idea of who killed Vaja. You see, with the Mafia it's almost as important that you hit someone as it is that you hit the right person. Otherwise it looks bad for business. Like you're letting things slide."

I shook my head at the sheer waste of it all.

"You'd better get used to this sight," he said. "You can bet you'll see a lot more." He spat copiously, lit a cigarette and started towards the steps leading up from the stone circle. "And it makes finding Sultan Khadziyev even more urgent. Before the Georgians can book him on the same flight as these two."

"Sultan's a pimp, sir," said Nikolai, following. "Chances are he'll find a couple of cash-cows and get himself started again. Why don't Sasha and I check a few of the hotels? Speak to some girls and the local melody. Maybe they can point us in the right direction."

"I've got a better idea," said Grushko. "Check *all* the hotels."

As we came up the steps, the Central Board's Scientific Research Department van was drawing up alongside the circle's entrance.

"Sorry we're late, sir," said one of the experts, "but our van broke down."

Grushko shrugged and continued on his way. When he reached the car he looked around at the monument to victory.

"Did we really win?" he said, shaking his head sadly. "Or did the krauts just lose?"

★ ★ ★

Grushko was right about the ubiquity of Mafia killings, although the next one happened sooner than even he might have expected. Less than two hours after returning to the Big House, Grushko and I were summoned to the scene of yet another murder. Meanwhile Nikolai and Sasha had gone off to look for Sultan Khadziyev.

It was seven o'clock in the evening when we drove up to the gate of the Alexander Nevsky Monastery. Outside the Moskva Hotel on the other side of the road, a small jazz band was playing "When the Saints Go Marching In."

"Sounds appropriate," said Grushko.

We waved our identity cards in the tired faces of the young militiamen who were holding back a crowd of curious bystanders and made our way along a cobbled path that was flanked by the walls of two cemeteries—the Lazarus and the Tivkin, where the bodies of Dostoevsky, Rimsky-Korsakov and Tchaikovsky were buried.

"Well," said Grushko as we approached the terracotta-coloured monastery that lay on the other side of a small moat, "you can't say that we haven't been showing you our beautiful city."

The small bridge across the moat was busy with experts and local detectives, one of whom, seeing Grushko, detached himself from the rest and came over to talk to us.

"What have you got?" said Grushko.

"Another *churki* killing," the detective said negligently and spat across the parapet into the water. "This one won't be walking up Rustaveli Avenue again."

"A Georgian?"

The detective nodded and led us on to the bridge where, slumped against a wall, with a hole the size of a saucer in his chest, lay the body of a handsome young man.

"Name of Merab Laventrivich Zodelava," he said. "A drug-dealer, apparently. His pockets were full of wheels." He showed us a plastic bag containing lots of pills. "Amphetamines, I should say. The whores buy them to keep awake on the job. Anyway, it seems like he was standing here about to make a sale when this other *churki* showed up and blasted a window in him with a sawn-off. Both barrels, it looks like. Makes the autopsy easy, I suppose."

"Any witnesses?"

"Just the one. But don't get too excited." The detective jerked his head at an old man who was sitting patiently on an empty beer crate under the watchful eye of a militiaman. The man had one leg.

"See that one leg?" he said. "Well, he's got just the one eye to match."

"Great," said Grushko.

"He was here to beg a few copecks off the people going into the cathedral. I reckon the only reason the gunman didn't pot the old man as well was because of those dark glasses he's wearing. Probably thought there was no point in shooting a blind man."

"Did he give you a description?" asked Grushko.

The detective flipped open his notebook.

"It's not much. He didn't stare too much in case he got a dose of lead. 'Well dressed, aged about thirty, dark hair, dark moustache, dark complexion.' " He shrugged. "Like I said, a *churki*."

"What about the pipes?" asked Grushko. "Did he take it with him?"

The detective shrugged.

"Drag the moat anyway," Grushko ordered, "just in case he dumped it. And better check both cemeteries in case he tossed it over the wall on his way out."

"What's the form on this one, sir?" asked the detective.

"Have we got another turf war on our hands? One of the scientific boys was saying something about a couple of Chechens getting their tickets to Allah this afternoon."

"I don't know about a turf war," said Grushko, "but there's plenty more blood where this lot came from."

CHAPTER

ELEVEN

★ Vaja Ordzhonikidze's funeral cortège represented a small fortune in motor vehicles: Mercedes, Saabs, Volvos, BMWs—there wasn't one that would have been within the purchasing range of a whole syndicate of militiamen, always assuming that they were straight. Not in this lifetime.

I thought of my own battered Volga back in Moscow, awaiting a new head gasket from the factory in Nizhni Novgorod, and cursed the luck that had made me an honest man. Well, almost an honest man. Honesty is not always so clear-cut. The nature of what I do requires that sometimes I have, as Dostoevsky might say, a Double, to do things of which one disapproves, such as misplace some evidence, or look the other way. Or to search a man's desk when he is out of his office and look for a sign of that man's corruption: a bank book, a name in a diary, a letter, a receipt from an expensive restaurant. A man who might have worked alongside you and thinks of you as his friend. A lie can sometimes illuminate the truth, but this can be hard. Still, nobody ever said the world was perfect.

The cars came down Oktabrisky Prospekt and pulled up at the gate of the Smolensky Cemetery. Several well-built men in dark suits and white shirts jumped out and stared with paranoid expectancy in several directions. Satisfied that there were no likely threats in the area they squired their team leaders and bosses, the Georgian Mafia élite, out of the cars.

From the other side of the canal, on Decembrist's Island, we watched the Georgian funeral through binoculars—Nikolai, Sasha, Dmitri our photographer and myself. Grushko was the last to arrive, with General Kornilov.

Grushko shot a look of puzzlement at Dmitri and then leaned towards Sasha.

"Who's he?" he said. "Where's Arkady, our usual man?"

"Sick," said Sasha. "This is Dmitri."

Grushko nodded uncertainly and watched Dmitri turning the focus on a huge telephoto lens.

"You needn't worry about him, sir," said Sasha. "He used to do surveillance work for the KGB, until he got made redundant."

"Oh? And what does he do now?"

"Weddings, mostly."

Grushko sighed and raised his binoculars.

"Weddings," he muttered darkly.

A group of Georgians were taking Vaja out of the hearse. He lay on an open bier like Lenin, covered with flowers. They lifted him onto their broad shoulders and, preceded by a priest of the Georgian Orthodox Church reading from a prayer-book, his acolyte swinging a censer and a third man bearing an icon, the funeral party started to proceed into the cemetery.

"That's Dzhumber Gankrelidze," said Nikolai. "The one straightening his tie. He's the boss."

The power-wind of Dmitri's camera whirred busily.

"It's quite a show," observed the general. "It doesn't much look as if they could have thought Vaja was an informer."

"This is nothing compared to the Little Gypsy's funeral

in Sverdlovsk last year," said Grushko. "Brought the whole town to a standstill."

"Yes," said Kornilov. "Gregory Tsyganov. Who was it killed him?"

"Azerbaijanis."

"Still, it's quite a show by our standards."

"And then, the year before that, there was Bosenko's brother."

"The Black Swan? I'd forgotten that one."

"Blown up in his car, he was," said Grushko. "There was hardly enough of him left to fill a shoe box, let alone a coffin, but the Cossacks still gave him the brass handles." He smiled.

"All right, Yevgeni," said Kornilov. "You've made your point." He didn't enjoy taking lessons from Grushko. "Do we know where they're holding the party afterwards?"

"Our informers told us they're going to a restaurant called Tbilisi. It's a little Georgian place on the other side of the Neva, in Petrogradsky Region. I've had the place bugged, just in case they say anything coherent."

The procession passed inside the cemetery and everyone lowered their binoculars. Dmitri started to wind back his film.

"And what about this pimp?" said Kornilov, lighting a cigarette. "The one who might have had a grudge against Mikhail Milyukin. Any sign of him yet?"

"We're keeping an eye on all the tourist hotels," said Grushko. "If he is running a new herd of cows then that's where we'll find him"

"Yes, well, make it soon, Yevgeni. Since you mentioned Sverdlovsk, then remember what happened there. It was a war."

"Yes, sir."

"What puzzles me is how he got out of the zone so early?"

"According to my contact in the GUITI," I said, "it was someone in the Department who fixed it."

"Does he have any idea who?"

I shrugged and shook my head.

"What are they up to?" he muttered. "Let's just hope you're right about this Chechen, Yevgeni. You know, without him, you've really got nothing. Nothing."

I could see Grushko didn't much like to be ridden by Kornilov in front of us, but he just bit his lip and nodded sullenly. That was why Nikolai, Sasha, Andrei or any of his men would take it from Grushko: because they knew he had to take it from Kornilov.

"By the way," said Kornilov, after the funeral procession had disappeared from view. "That icon they were carrying. Who was it?"

Grushko smiled thinly.

"It was St. George, sir. Who else for Georgians?"

There has been a police prison on the site of the Big House since the time of Catherine the Great. After the assassination of Alexander II the site at Number six Liteiny Prospekt became the headquarters of the newly created political police, the Okhrana. Following the abandonment of Leningrad as the country's capital, the Leningrad NKVD plotted the murder of Stalin's rival Kirov from the old building at Number six. They then used his death as a pretext for purging the local party and, for that matter, the local NKVD as well. Stalin's most notorious henchman, a Georgian named Laventri Beria, had spent some considerable time working in the newly built Big House. His desk and typewriter were still in use. It was small wonder people joked that from the top of the building you could see Solovki, the most notorious of all Stalin's White Sea Canal labour camps, where hundreds of thousands of people had perished; and it was only fitting that the Department, even in its post-Party truncated form as the Russian Security Service, should occupy the top two floors.

Grushko walked along the corridor and reflected that even now, after the demise of the Party, things were still more comfortable for the KGB than for their poor cousins downstairs. There were fresh towels, soap and lavatory paper in the washrooms. The floors were covered with thick blue carpets instead of dirty brown linoleum, while in every office were computers, fax machines and photocopiers.

He entered one office where a woman in her forties with neatly cut auburn hair and wearing a smart blue two-piece suit was taking books down from her shelves and packing them into cardboard boxes. Vera Andreyeva seemed more like someone who read the news on television than a major in the KGB.

"What's this?" said Grushko. "Are you moving into better offices?"

Andreyeva smiled at Grushko's little irony.

"As a matter of fact I am," she said. "I'm leaving the Department, Yevgeni. What's left of it, anyway."

"Leaving? Surely they're not getting rid of you as well, Vera Fyodorovna? I thought that the Department was going to use its best resources to fight organized crime and economic corruption."

"Oh, they are," she said. "But then so is the army. And the navy. And for all I know the air force as well. All of us looking for a new role in life. And stepping on your toes." She shook her head. "Wasn't it Chekhov who said that when a lot of remedies are suggested for a disease, then it can't be cured?"

"I never liked Chekhov much," said Grushko. He picked up a book from her desk. *"Reforming the Soviet Economy: Equality versus Efficiency."* He inspected another. *"The Nature and Logic of Capitalism."* You are on the move, Vera. What will you do?"

"I've been offered a job with a Russo-American joint-venture company," she said happily. "They're planning to open a chain of real hamburger restaurants throughout Russia. I'm in charge of recruitment."

"An ex-KGB major in charge of recruitment? It figures."

Vera turned towards Grushko and gave him a look, as if she were measuring him up.

"I wonder," she said thoughtfully.

"What?" he said.

"You, Yevgeni? How would you fancy handling security for us? We could use a man like you. The price of meat being what it is, security will be one of our most important considerations."

"Oh, I don't doubt it," smiled Grushko. "But you're serious, aren't you?"

"Why not? Just think of the pay. You know what the Department was going to retire me on? Seven hundred and fifty roubles a month. You know how much I earn with the joint-venture?"

"Please don't tell me," said Grushko.

"Thirty thousand roubles a month. That's forty times as much."

Grushko smiled weakly. "The same as a miner," he joked, knowing that the joke was on him: since the miners had settled their strike, 30,000 roubles was indeed what one of them earned in a month.

"Someone with your background could very probably pick up the same."

"What use would I have for that kind of money?"

"Knowing you, Yevgeni Ivanovich, none at all. But your wife—now she's a different story. I don't doubt she'd find plenty to spend it on. Even in the state shops."

" 'The riddle of the money fetish is therefore the riddle of the commodity fetish now become visible and dazzling to our eyes.' "

Vera looked taken aback.

"I never thought I'd live to hear it," she said. "Of all the people to quote Marx . . ."

"I couldn't remember any Chekhov," said Grushkov. "Look, Vera, thanks for the offer but I'm not here to talk about myself."

"You want to know about your Georgians, don't you? Well, I've had a word with our friends in the seventh CD and the surveillance is in place. So you can relax."

"And the information about Mikhail Milyukin?"

Vera Andreyeva lifted another cardboard box onto the desk.

"Tapes, transcripts, files, everything, like you asked."

Grushko peered curiously into the box.

"But why was his phone tapped at all?" he said. "I mean, why now?"

She shrugged. "Oh, I dare say it always had been and nobody thought to have it removed. Things are a bit like that these days: we're a place on automatic pilot, only the captain's already bailed out." She lifted an armful of books and dropped them into another box. "Well, now it's my turn."

"And does that mean you can talk freely?" Grushko's tone was cautious.

Andreyeva lit a cigarette and sat on the edge of her desk.

"Try me."

"Your colleagues . . ."

"Correction: my former colleagues . . ."

"Would you say that many of them are anti-Semitic?"

"The Department has its fair share of prejudice, Yevgeni. Just like everywhere else."

"All right then, let me ask you this: is there anyone here who might have had it in for Mikhail Milyukin?"

"Enough to kill him? No, I don't think so."

"Enough to scare and harass him maybe?"

She thought carefully for a minute.

"I couldn't ever repeat this," said Vera. "At least, not before an investigator."

Grushko shook his head. "Between you and me then," he said.

"All right," she said. "I believe there was someone in the second CD who tried to persuade Milyukin to spy on a couple of English journalists. I think he probably tried to squeeze him a little." She shrugged. "Well, that's the way they work, of course. But not what you're suggesting. Anyway, they've left now. The officer and the two journalists."

Vera Andreyeva picked up a smart new pigskin briefcase and took out a copy of *Ogonyok*. On the front cover was a picture of Milyukin.

"You know, a lot of people in this Department admired Milyukin," she said. "Myself included."

"But you're leaving," said Grushko. "It wouldn't be the first time that this Department has got rid of its liberals."

"Half the KGB is going to be looking for a new job," she said insistently. "It's not politics that runs the system now. It's the International Monetary Fund."

"You'd know more about that than I do." He picked up the box containing the information on Mikhail Milyukin and walked to the door.

"Thanks for this," he said. "And good luck with the hamburgers."

"Promise me you'll think it over," she said.

Grushko nodded.

"I promise," he said. "But if unemployment is set for a big rise then that's good news for the Mafia. The way things are shaping up Petersburg will be just like Chicago in the twenties." He grinned. "And it's not much of a story if there's no Elliot Ness."

★ ★ ★

It was while I was leaving the synagogue on Lermontovsky Prospekt after the service for her husband that I first saw the beauty of Nina Milyukin. Taller by a head than the friends and relations surrounding her, she stood waiting for the cars to take us down to Volkov Cemetery, without tears but with such a look of sadness as I had never seen. Before, I had thought her face merely clever. Now she struck me as something more distinguished, aristocratic even, like some long-lost Romanov princess from that old tragedy. These are odd words for a lawyer but they must be said, for this is not only Grushko's story, it is also mine.

I do not know whether Grushko made it to the synagogue or not, as I did not actually see him until the funeral party arrived at the cemetery, which was not surprising given the large number of people, many of them Milyukin's readers, who had turned up to pay their respects to him. Even the Mayor of St. Petersburg was there, his office having given permission for Milyukin's burial in one of the city's oldest and most exclusive cemeteries, where some of the country' best writers—Belinsky, Blok, Turgenev and Kupin—were buried.

The funeral could not have been more different from the Georgian's. The State's contribution of 100 roubles was as nothing compared to the cost of the cheapest coffin: at 2,000 roubles apiece these were hard to find and, but for a whip-round in the Big House organised by Grushko, Nina Milyukin might easily have been forced to hire a coffin for the trip to Volkov Cemetery and then to transfer her husband's body to a plastic bag for the actual burial. None of the cars, with the possible exception of the mayor's Zil, would have excited much interest. Nor were there any enormous wreaths, only single carnations. But there was no mistaking the sense of real grief that affected everyone who was there that warm June afternoon.

Afterwards, as the crowds drifted slowly away, Nina remained standing by her husband's grave and watched as the gravediggers began to fill it in.

Grushko spoke to Nikolai, Sasha and myself.

"Wait in the car," he told us. "I'm going to try and have a word with her. If she is holding back on us then now's the time to squeeze her."

To me this seemed insensitive of him but I said nothing until the three of us were back in the car.

"How can he do that?" I asked. "Surely she has the right to a little privacy at her husband's funeral?"

Nikolai pointed to the television crew that had covered the event and were now loading their equipment back into a van.

"What privacy?" he said.

"No, he's right," said Sasha. "Grushko can be a hard bastard sometimes."

Nikolai pursed his lips and lit a cigarette.

"I'll tell you something," he said. "I never met a fairer cop. Not anywhere. If he said he thought the Patriarch himself was a crook, then I'd believe him. If Grushko thinks that she needs a squeeze, then that's good enough for me.

"Besides," he added, "if she's not telling us the whole story then now's the best time to find out. When she's feeling vulnerable. There's no telling how long a woman like that might give you the run-around."

★   ★   ★

Grushko found Nina walking alone on the Poet's Pathway.

"May I talk to you?"

"It's a free country now," she sighed. "So they tell me." He took a deep breath and spat it out.

"I don't think that you've been entirely honest with us," he said. "Have you?"

She was silent for a moment.

Grushko repeated the question.

"You know, Colonel, when I was younger, I used to imagine that my father was buried here. You see, he was a writer too. Not that I really knew him. I was just a baby when he was arrested. We never found out what became of him. Where or when he died. I like to think that if he had lived, he would have been good enough to come here with the rest of them." She smiled sadly. "Ironic, isn't it? I never thought I'd ever marry a man whom they buried here. I don't suppose it would have crossed Mikhail's mind either."

"I didn't know about your father," said Grushko. "I'm sorry. But look, things are different now."

"Are they?" She shrugged. "I don't know. Maybe."

"So how about it? Some straight answers."

She looked up at the blue sky and Grushko saw that there were tears in her eyes.

"You were right," she said. "When you asked about that bodyguard? Mikhail did try and hire one. But it wasn't because he was scared of anyone in particular."

"I'm not sure I understand."

"It was more of a collective thing really. You see, Mikhail was never happy unless he was working on a story that involved a degree of risk. He was always in danger from somebody or other. He thrived on that. Despite all the threats, all that hate, he wouldn't have changed places with anyone. As I told you before, it was beginning to get to him. But the idea of having a bodyguard seemed to be a way of helping him to cope with the pressure of what he was doing. That and his drinking. So he tried to hire one of your own police thugs: the ones they use to put down riots."

"The OMON squad?"

"Yes. Only the man wanted too much money. That's why I told you we couldn't afford it. I'm afraid I was rather angry with the militia, Colonel. I was bitter at the idea that, but for a few more roubles, Mikhail might still be alive."

"This man from the OMON squad: do you remember his name?"

"Georgi . . . Rodionov."

Grushko made a note of the name. Nina sighed deeply and laid her hand on her chest.

"And now if you don't mind, I'd really like to be left alone for a while."

★ ★ ★

While we were waiting, Iron Lenya rang from the morgue on Grushko's car phone. There was a body she wanted us to come and have a look at. When Nikolai had finished speaking to her, Sasha groaned loudly.

"I hate the morgue," he said.

Nikolai fed another cigarette into his mouth, lit it with the last one and chuckled.

"Look on the bright side," he said. "At least it'll take away your appetite."

CHAPTER

TWELVE

★ Of the two to three hundred people who died everyday in St. Petersburg, most were taken north-east across the Riva Neva, past the Piskarov Memorial where 500,000 victims of the blockade were buried, to the suitably contiguous Bureau of Juridical Medical Examinations.

It was late in the afternoon when we followed this sad trail of Piskarovsky Prospekt and on to a rough track leading down the side of the pre-Revolutionary Mechnikov Hospital. Seen from a distance, the fortress-shaped building that was the Bureau could not have looked less morbid. Sunlight warmed its pink brick and illuminated the yellow-tinted windows so that it resembled some fantastic sugar-candy palace in a children's fairy-tale. Certainly there was nowhere else like it in Russia. Grushko told me that the Director, Professor Vitali Derzhavin (who was descended from the great Russian poet), claimed that only Helsinki and New York had a similarly comprehensive forensic facility. Catching my eye in his driving mirror, he added:

"You'll make a friend for life if you take my advice and say something nice about the place. Derzhavin's very proud of it. So proud he even had a time capsule installed in one of the walls telling the story of him and all his staff."

We parked the car and were ushered into Professor Derzhavin's office. While we waited for him to finish his telephone call I studied his collection of silver roubles that was displayed in several glass cases on the walls.

"Thallium," he said. "Yes, that's what I said. Thallium 203." He waved at us to be seated. "Oh, highly poisonous. They used to use the sulphate as a rodenticide. Well, she's a Professor of Chemistry, isn't she, Lieutenant? It wouldn't be too difficult for her to get hold of some. All right then. No problem. Yes, you'll have the written report in the morning. Goodbye."

He replaced the receiver, stood up, and shook hands all round. Grey-haired with a light suntan, he wore a white coat and an easygoing sort of expression.

"How about that?" he said, to nobody in particular. "Some bitch has been poisoning the people she shared her flat with. With thallium. Just to get hold of an extra couple of rooms."

"Is that a good way of doing it?" asked Grushko. "Only my neighbour has this piano. The kid practises all the time, and it's not even in tune."

I thought of my own wife and her music-teacher lover. Thallium. I never thought of that.

The Professor grinned, collected his cigarettes off the desk-top and buttoned his coat.

"Get my secretary to order some for you," he said.

We followed him out through his secretary's office. She looked up from behind a smart new IBM typewriter and smiled sweetly.

"Colonel Shelaeva's waiting for you in Detective-Room Number five," she announced and carried on with her typing.

The professor led the way out of the office and turned down a long, sloping corridor.

"I sectioned this fellow myself," he explained. "We left him on the slab for you, just in case you were thinking of having lunch."

"Very thoughtful of you," said Grushko.

"The militia found him early this morning. Not far from where Mikhail Milyukin was murdered. Unfortunately, due to someone's incompetence, the body was removed and brought here before it was realised that these homicides might be connected. Lenya's pretty mad about it."

"I'm sure," said Grushko.

"He's been outside for about a week I'd say, and you know how warm it's been. Also I think some small animal has been feeding on him. One side of his face is more or less eaten away, so I'm warning you, gentlemen, he's no icon."

We went through a set of swing doors and were met with a strong smell of formaldehyde and a traffic jam of trolleys, each of them bearing a naked body for autopsy. Even in death, most of them through old age or accident, Russians were still obliged to wait in line.

The professor stopped by a door and opened it. Colonel Shelaeva stood up, collected her papers and joined us in that dreadful corridor.

"What took you so long?" she said to Grushko.

"We were at Mikhail Milyukin's funeral," he said.

"All of you?" she said frowning. "For that trouble-maker?"

Grushko nodded.

Shelaeva shook her head, offended by this waste of manpower. Professor Derzhavin spoke quickly as if to defuse a potential disagreement.

"We're in the blue section-room," he said. "If you'll come this way?"

We proceeded down the corridor, through a gauntlet of dead bodies.

"And what mood is blue?" said Grushko.

"Efficient and businesslike."

Grushko explained to me that Professor Derzhavin had ordered the morgue's builders to tile each section-room in a different colour, so that the staff working there might be spared any further lowering of their spirits that could have been occasioned by something more homogeneous.

There were two section tables. On one of them a beautiful young woman was being cut open, her body a yellow coat half-stripped off the meaty skeleton that had worn it. Berzhavin's staff worked loudly, like workers in a meat-processing factory, habituated to what they were doing, wielding knives and handling viscera with rubberised bloody fingers staining the butts of their blasé cigarettes.

At the other table, the table that we gathered round like a group of black priests performing a service of communion, lay a naked man of about forty-five years old, his upper torso still positioned on the dissection block, his arms outstretched as if he had fallen from the ceiling. That which was never meant to be seen—intestines, lights and brain—had been bundled back inside his stomach, and the body crudely stitched up like a piece of Red Indian buckskin.

Derzhavin had not exaggerated the man's facial injuries. One of his ears was missing while the cheek and the underside of his chin were cratered with coin-sized wounds.

"He's not yet been identified," said Colonel Shelaeva. "There was nothing but air in his pockets." She opened a file and handed Grushko a photograph. "But I think we can agree that it's not Sultan Khadziyev."

Grushko nodded silently.

"Still, I asked you to come here because it seems that your hygiene-conscious smoker was on the scene." She shot Nikolai a meaningful look and then showed us a plastic bag containing another soft-pack of Winston that had been opened upside down.

"They found this near the body," she said.

I lit a cigarette that helped to keep my nose, my mind and most importantly my stomach off the smell.

"Cause of death?"

"He was shot once through the head," said Professor Derzhavin. "At first I thought it was another animal bite. But if you look at the centre of his forehead you can see the bullet hole. Whoever shot him pressed the gun right up against the skull. The muzzle has pinned the force of discharge onto the scalp, splitting the entry wound. An executioner's shot."

"It's too early to say that it's the same gun," said Shelaeva, "But I shouldn't be at all surprised if it was."

"Any idea when he died?"

"About a week ago," said the Professor. "Perhaps a little longer. It's difficult to be more precise than that. Not with all the sunbathing he's been doing."

"A week or a little longer," Grushko said ruminatively. "Then he could have been dead before Milyukin?"

"Yes, I'd say so."

"What about those triangular marks on the chest and the stomach?"

"Burn marks, inflicted before death," said Derzhavin.

"Inflicted with an electric iron," Shelaeva added.

"The Mafia meat-tenderiser," murmured Nikolai.

"Just so," said Grushko. "I wonder what they wanted to know?" He lifted the dead man's hand. "What's this, under his fingernails?"

"Diesel oil," said Shelaeva. "There's more on his clothes and his boots."

She drew a cardboard box across the floor and pointed inside. Grushko bent forward and picked out one of the dead man's boots. He looked into the boot and frowned as he tried to make out the name of the manufacturer.

"Lenwest," he said finally.

"Perhaps he was a mechanic, sir," suggested Nikolai.

Grushko nodded silently, turning the boot over in his hands as if it were some fossil recovered from a palaentologist's dig.

"Or a driver, maybe," he said. "Take a look at the wear on his boot. It's heavily worn on the right heel. That could be from repeatedly pressing an accelerator."

"A bus-driver?"

"Could be. Or a truck-driver."

"I'll have a better idea for you when we've had a chance to analyse that oil," said Shelaeva.

"Oh, one more thing," said Professor Derzhavin. He turned to one of his staff and called her over.

"Anna, that liver, could you do the honours?"

The girl Anna was a small, red-haired creature who looked hardly old enough to vote, let alone dissect a human cadaver. She produced a bucket from underneath the table and removed a glutinous black-red hunk that she then lay on the slab by the dead man's feet.

"It's pretty enlarged," said the professor, "so I thought he might be a heavy drinker. But I thought we'd wait for you before we made sure."

The girl produced a curette and prepared to slice the liver in two. "When she cuts the liver open, I want you to get a sniff of it." We leaned towards the liver. "All right, Anna."

As the curette moved perfectly through the dead man's organ, the air was filled with such a stench of stale alcohol that I thought I would choke. We reeled back from the table, coughing and laughing disgustedly.

"Well I don't think there can be any doubt about that," chuckled the professor. "But what *is* curious is that he seems to have been a vegetarian."

"Yes, that is unusual," agreed Grushko.

"Oh I don't know," said Nikolai. "Have you seen the price of meat lately?"

Sasha groaned as one of the staff working on the girl's body opposite began to remove the top of her skull with an electric saw.

"I don't think I'll ever eat meat again," he muttered weakly.

★ ★ ★

Nikolai had asked Chazov to come and see him at the Big House again, only on this occasion he had chosen a time more inconvenient to the restaurateur, in the early evening, when he would normally have been preparing to open for dinner.

I left the two of them arguing, to deal with the investigation of the Kazakh gang that had now been arrested for the robberies of the Jewish emigrants and, in particular, the Goose.

The Goose was a big man with a shaven head and a long, scrawny neck and it was easy to see how he had come by his nickname. Although he could speak Russian fluently I asked him if he wished to have the services of an interpreter. The man shrugged and shook his head. Then I read him the rules of his interrogation as laid down in Article 51.

"You have the right to remain silent," I told him. "You have the right to an advocate. You have the right to appeal to the State Prosecutor and say why you have been wrongly arrested. You may add something to this protocol if you wish to do so."

The Goose knew that the two arresting detectives had obtained plenty of evidence to convict him and he was an old enough hand at the game to exercise his right to silence. He signed the protocol and then they took him back to his cell. At some later date I would have to reacquaint him with the charges pending against him in the presence of his lawyer.

After this my wife telephoned to say that the gasket for my car had arrived and when would I be coming back to Moscow to repair it and drive it away? I told her, in a few days. I wanted to tell her I missed her, but something stopped the words in my mouth. Maybe because it wasn't true. I missed my own bed, my television set, my fishing rods, my books and having my meals cooked for me, I even missed my daughter. But her? No way.

"So how are things at home?" I asked. "How's my daughter?"

"She's fine. Sends her love."

"How's Moscow?"

"The prices are just ridiculous. Everything is so expensive."

"Yes, it is," I said.

"How's Leningrad?" she asked.

"St. Petersburg. You get sent to the zone for calling the place the wrong name. Things are all right. I'm on a case already."

She grunted. She never was much interested in my work as an investigator. She always wanted me to go into business for myself, as a lawyer. To make real money.

"How's Porfiry?" she asked.

"He's much the same. Thinner."

"Everyone's thinner."

"Are you feeding Misha?"

Misha was my dog.

"He gets as much porridge as he can eat."

"Well, I guess his breath won't smell so bad."

"When you do come back for your car—"

"Yes?"

"Could you bring some cheese perhaps?"

"Cheese?"

"I've heard that there's plenty of cheese in Leningrad.

I mean St. Petersburg. There's none in the whole of Moscow. Naturally I'll pay you for it."

"I'll see what I can do. Anything else?"

"Not that I can think of."

"All right. I'll ring you before I come." I laughed unpleasantly. "Nice doing business with you."

★　★　★

A little later on I went round the corner to find Grushko.

He was in his office. There was a tape-recorder on his desk on which he had been listening to the tapes the KGB had made of Mikhail Milyukin's telephone conversations. He seemed troubled by something and I was just about to ask him what it was when Sasha came into the office, his face eager with what he had to tell.

"I've had a call from the drugs squad," he explained. "There's a friend of mine who works there who told me that on the night of Milyukin's murder they had some information that a suspect they were after was driving around in a green Mercedes. Well, they checked with the GAI and found that there are only three such cars in the whole of Peter. Anyway, in the process of eliminating these two other Mercs, they saw one of them driving down Nevsky at about eleven o'clock that night. It's registered to Dzhumber Gankrelidze."

"That would put the Georgians a long way from where they claimed they were," said Grushko. "In the restaurant at the Pribaltskaya Hotel." He lit a cigarette and leaned forward in his chair.

After a moment or two I nodded at the tape machine.

"Anything there for us?"

"Listen to this a minute, will you? This was recorded a week before the murder."

He switched the tape on.

" 'Mikhail Milyukin,' " said the first voice, which was

easily recognisable from Milyukin's many television reports.

" 'This is Tolya.'

" 'Ah yes, Tolya. I was hoping you'd call.'

" 'You got my letter?'

" 'Yes, I did. And I'm very interested in what you wrote. But is it really true?'

" 'Every word. And I can prove it.'

" 'Then I think it could make quite a story.'

" 'You know it would.'

" 'Look, it's best we don't talk about this on the phone. Where can we meet?'

" 'How about the Peter and Paul Fortress? Inside the cathedral at, say, three o'clock?'

" 'All right then. I'll be there.' "

Grushko hit the stop button and looked expectantly at Sasha and myself.

"This Tolya sounds like he could be a Ukrainian," I said. "Those slurred consonants."

"That's what I thought," said Grushko. He glanced at his notebook and then fast-forwarded the tape to a position on the machine's counter he had previous noted. "Now listen to this. The call was made on the morning of the same day that Milyukin reported his flat had been burgled."

" 'Hello.' " It was a woman's voice, and an educated one. The accent sounded local.

" 'Hi. It's Mikhail Milyukin.'

" 'It's been a long time, how are you?'

" 'Good, thanks.'

" 'What are you working on this time?'

" 'Well, I've got a little job for you, if you're interested?'

" 'Anything to help the press, you know that.'

" 'Good.'

" 'What sort of material are we talking about?'

" 'I'd rather not say on the telephone. Can I drop it round to you? How does later on this morning sound?'

" 'Fine.'

" 'See you later then.' "

"Now what," asked Grushko, "was all that about?"

He moved the tape on a second time.

"And then there's this," he said. "Our Ukrainian friend calling back on the day that Milyukin was murdered."

" 'Mikhail Milyukin, hello.'

" 'It's me, Tolya.'

" 'Tolya, where have you been? I was worried something might have happened to you.'

" 'Yeah well, something did happen. I got drunk last night.'

" 'What again? You shouldn't drink so much. It's not good for you.'

" 'What else is there to do? Besides it takes my mind off the other business.'

" 'You don't sound too good. It must be some kind of hangover you've got there.'

" 'Yes. It is. Look, I was wondering if we could meet again? There's something important that I haven't told you about yet.'

" 'Sure. Where?'

" 'The Peter and Paul again. You know the restaurant there?'

" 'The Poltava? Yes, I know it.'

" 'I've booked a table for 8:30, in the name of Beria.'

" 'Beria?' " Milyukin chuckled. " 'Couldn't you have chosen a different name?' "

There was a moment's silence.

" 'Why, what's wrong with it?'

" 'Nothing. Forget it. Are you sure you're all right, Tolya?'

" 'It's just a hangover. Really. See you there. OK?'

" 'OK.' "

"Well?" said Grushko.

"Tolya—he sounded nervous that time," said Sasha.

"Very," agreed Grushko.

"Now we know who Milyukin was waiting for," I said.

"Imagine not knowing who Beria was," said Grushko. "Was that just ignorance? A false name Tolya just plucked out of the air? Or was it something else? A sign that Milyukin should be careful maybe?"

"A sign which he failed to spot," I said.

"I wonder," said Grushko. "Could this be our friend from the morgue this afternoon? It sounds as if Tolya might have been the owner of that liver we all enjoyed so much."

"If that's so," I said, "then whoever tortured him might have wanted him to bring Milyukin to them. Maybe they had a gun pointed at his head when he made that last telephone call. So it could be that he's not so much ill as worried. Worried that they're going to blow his brains out when he's finished making the call. And I suspect that's exactly what happened." I paused, waiting to see if Grushko agreed.

"Go on," he said.

"They let Milyukin sit in the restaurant and then pick him up as he's leaving. It's nice and quiet in the fortress at night, so there's no fuss. Persuading him to get into the car shouldn't be too much of a problem. By that time they'd already grabbed Vaja Ordzhonikidze, so it was probably his car they were driving. Then they drive them both to the forest and shoot them."

Grushko nodded. "Yes," he said, "I think that's it. Sasha, get Andrei to ring round all the local bus and freight companies. Tell him to find out if there's one of them which employs a Ukrainian driver called Tolya who might not have turned up for work in the last week or two."

He noted the expression of doubt on Sasha's face and shook his head.

"I know that's a pretty tall order, absenteeism being what it is these days, but we have to find out who this character was and what he was up to. Once we've discovered that we'll know why Milyukin was murdered. Ordzhonikidze too, I expect."

For another ten minutes or so, we discussed a few speculative theories as to what Tolya might have wanted to tell Milyukin. Nothing seemed particularly likely. At the same time I was impressed with the democratic way Grushko was handling this inquiry. There is an old Russian saying, "If I am a boss then you are a fool; and if you are a boss then I am a fool." It was not a sentiment that Grushko would have had much time for.

Nikolai came into the office. He was carrying some photographs.

"Dmitri just brought in the snaps of the Georgian's funeral, sir," he said and laid them on the desk in front of Grushko. There was one in particular he seemed eager to draw to Grushko's attention. It was a picture of Dzhumber Gankrelidze, the Georgian gang boss.

"Handsome bastard, isn't he?" said Grushko.

"Funny thing," said Nikolai. "While I was interviewing Chazov just now, I knocked these onto the floor. He caught a good look at that one of Dzhumber, sir, and I swear it scared the hell out of him."

"Chazov's restaurant is only a short way off Nevsky Prospekt," he said thoughtfully. "When was that firebomb actually reported?"

"About 10:50 p.m.," I said.

"Ten minutes later the State Automobile Inspectorate report Dzhumber's green Merc on Nevsky. So he and a few of the boys could have been driving away from Chazov's after giving him the squeeze."

Grushko got up from his chair and went over to his

cupboard. He opened the door and started to wash his hands in the little sink.

"You know," he said, "if we were to pick the Georgians up to help us with out inquiries into the arson attack—" he paused as he dried his hands on the towel that was hanging inside the door—"we might manage to help keep Sultan Khadziyev alive for a while. At least until we find him."

His eyes met mine with a question for which I already had the answer.

"I think that if Nikolai were to show me his papers, then an arrest protocol could probably be issued. But remember, you'll only be able to hold them for three days."

Grushko shrugged. "Perhaps our friend Chazov will be more inclined to cooperate once he finds that we've got the Georgians in custody. And we might actually get to charge them before our three days are up."

He put on his jacket and straightened his tie.

"Are you ready?" he said to me.

I nodded and followed him to the door.

"You're in for a treat," he said. "Sometimes I think that I married the Winston Churchill of cooking. To do so much with so little . . ."

CHAPTER

THIRTEEN

★ Grushko lived modestly, I thought. Too modestly, it seemed, for someone who could have been having his paw stroked. The colour television set was an old one, but not as old as the record-player. There were more books than I had expected, although many of them were medical text-books. The sofa and armchairs were made of plastic-vinyl and in need of respringing, while the linoleum in the tiny hallway was worn in places. About the only thing that looked new was a radio-cassette player in the kitchen and a rather gaudy set of wine-glasses that still had the labels on their bases. Of course Grushko might have been the type who was patient of spending any corruptly received money. Maybe he was hoarding dollar bills underneath his mattress for a holiday abroad or, police pensions being as miserable as they were, for the day when he retired. I wondered how I might get a chance to go in his bedroom and make a quick search.

But he had not exaggerated his wife's abilities in the kitchen. We ate a delicious cabbage soup, followed by some deep-fried cheese with mushrooms and potatoes and then a scoop of ice-cream. We drank some of Grushko's home-made whisky, which was a lot stronger than it seemed, a discovery I was only to make the following morning.

With the exception of Tanya, Grushko's daughter, they were a fairly typical family: the old mother who drank just a little too much of the Georgian wine I brought with me; her daughter Lena, small and neatly dressed, who ate less so that her guest could eat more and who seemed hardly old enough to have a twenty-four-year-old daughter of her own; and Grushko himself, whose strength of character and obvious authority counted for nothing in this, the most matriarchal of Russian institutions, for Lena ran the home and he knew it.

Tanya was a different flock of sheep: young, beautiful and intelligent, she looked like one of these people who can travel—more like a musician or a ballet dancer than a doctor at the Vreden Casualty Institute. Of course the fact that she was so well-groomed I learned was due not at all to Grushko but to her boyfriend, Boris, who seemed to have unlimited access to foreign goods, or so Grushko told me later. She was also a rather capricious young woman, for I can think of no other explanation to account for why she should have chosen the occasion of my being there to announce that she and Boris were planning to get married. Unless it was simply that she knew Grushko was less likely to lose his temper about it with me being there. Or perhaps it was some sort of revenge for all the times he must have embarrassed her with his obvious dislike of Boris. Neither one of the explanations appeared to me to be particularly satisfactory. But then I am a lawyer.

On hearing the news, Lena Grushko and her old mother seemed delighted. But it was all Grushko could do not to take a bite out of his table mat. He did his best to make a show of being pleased but it wasn't much of an act and it didn't last longer than a couple of nods and a thin rictus of a smile. Still, Tanya was not about to let him get away with anything less than a complete Te Deum.

"Aren't you pleased for me, Dad?" she said.

"Well, naturally I'm pleased for you," he said with considerable difficulty. "Naturally . . ." He frowned as he tried to think of something pleasant to say. Instead he found his line of argument.

"But you have thought about where you're both going to live? I mean, you could always have this room—"

I could see that this was not an idea that held much attraction for him.

"Excuse me," I said. "Where's the . . . ?"

"Left as you go out of the door," he said.

I got up from the table, opened the lavatory door, but did not go inside. Instead I went into Grusko's bedroom. I listened to their raised voices for a second and then lifted the mattress.

"We're going to live with Boris's parents," said Tanya. "At least until we can get a place of our own."

"That could be a lot harder than you think," said Grushko. "Apartments are not so easy to come by in Petersburg."

"Boris has lots of connections," she said glibly. "He'll sort it out. You needn't worry about that."

Grushko nodded uncomfortably.

"Where do Boris's parents live?" asked Lena Grushko.

"On Decembrist's Square."

"Oh, how lovely."

There was about fifty dollars under Grushko's mattress, on his wife's side of the bed. But this meant nothing. My own wife had amassed almost two hundred dollars before I moved out. I tucked the sheets in at the corners, flushed the toilet and then returned to the dinner table.

"Not that modern block on the corner?" said Grushko.

"Yes. It's very nice."

"But those apartments were built for people who were imprisoned by the tsar, and their descendants."

"Yes," said Tanya. "That would be Boris's grandfather, Cyril."

Grushko shook his head impatiently. "What I mean to say is that those flats were for people in the Party."

"But things are different now. The Party's finished. You're always saying so."

"Maybe so, but those people who were in the Party are still enjoying their old privileges. Including a nice apartment on Decembrist's Square. Well, don't you see?"

"I haven't seen them enjoying many privileges. They still have to queue for bread like anyone else. And they don't own a car like you do."

"Living where they do, I don't suppose they need one," said Grushko. "Besides, Boris has a car. A BMW."

Grushko's wife shot him a fierce look.

"Yevgeni Ivanovich," she said stiffly. But before she could begin her reprimand the phone rang and Grushko got up to answer it.

I smiled politely at Tanya.

"Congratulations," I said lamely. "I hope you'll be very happy."

"We must ask Boris and his family to dinner," said Lena.

Tanya's eyes drifted towards the doorway and the sound of her father speaking on the telephone.

"I don't know that that's a very good idea," she said. "Besides, what could we feed them? A kilo of meat costs a week's pay."

"I have a box of English soaps," said Lena. "I could trade that."

"Oh, Mum, you can't trade that. Not your English soaps."

"Well, they're much too good ever to use."

When Grushko came back he was putting on his jacket.

"I'm afraid I have to go out," he said quietly.

"What's up?" I asked.

"Sultan Khadziyev just called Nikolai at the Big House," he explained. "Apparently he wants to talk. A chance to clear his name. He reckons he can prove that he had nothing to do with Milyukin's death."

I got up from the table.

"No need for you to leave," he said.

I glanced at Lena and her daughter and smiled.

"I'm sure you've both got a lot to discuss," I said and quickly put on my own jacket. "Thank you for a lovely dinner."

Grushko grunted indifferently but I had the feeling that he welcomed the company.

"So where are we going?" I asked him as we went down in the lift.

"He wants to meet in the open," said Grushko, looking at his watch. "I'm to be on Bank Bridge across the Griboyedev Canal in twenty minutes."

"Can you trust him?"

"We've got nothing to lose. And since there wasn't time to trace the call I really don't see any alternative."

"So you're just going to stand there and wait for him to turn up?"

"Maybe I should surround the area with militiamen and risk scaring him off: is that what you're suggesting?"

"You could wear a wire."

Grushko chuckled. "You've been watching too many movies, my friend," he said. "We've got one set of walkie-talkies for the whole department and they only work in open areas. Made in the USSR, just like this lousy lift." He thumped the side of the urinous cabin impatiently.

"About a month ago, we were going to pick this guy up in the Kutznechny Market. We had the place surrounded but the building was interfering with the walkie-talkies. So I had to get a man to keep running round the building to keep everyone informed of what was happening. How's that for a modern police force?"

"Couldn't the KGB . . ."

"We can just about twist their arms to install a few bugs for us. Like that Georgian funeral wake. But a wire, no. Not that that bug was worth the trouble. Most of the Georgians were too drunk for us to make out what they were saying."

The lift arrived on the ground floor with a lurch and we walked unsteadily outside into the late evening sunshine. These white nights took a bit of getting used to. As we drove south and then west along Nevsky, we saw so few people on the street that one might almost have thought that there had been some terrible, Chernobyl-style nuclear accident.

"You know, I never mind being called out late at this time of year," said Grushko. "It gives me a chance really to see the city. This place must have been something before the revolution. It's nights like these when you might almost imagine that the whole thing was just a bad dream, you know? That it never happened."

Passing Moscow Station we saw a group of ragged children collected in front of the station's great arched doorways. The clock on top of the short square tower said eleven-thirty.

"It's a bit late for kids to be out," I observed. "Some of them don't look more than ten years old."

"Runaways," said Grushko. "City's full of them. They prefer to move around at night, like rats, when there's less chance of being picked up by the children's militia."

We came down the side of the Griboyedev Canal and stopped a short way from a small wooden suspension bridge that looked like something out of a model village. The cables by which its short span was anchored were held in the mouths of four cast-iron gryphons.

"You stay in the car and answer the phone if it rings," Grushko told me. "And keep your head down."

He reached inside his jacket and took out an enormous

automatic. He let the gun somersault over his finger in the trigger-guard, thumbed back the catch and drew out the double magazine. Then he hammered it back up the handle with the heel of his hard hand, spun the gun back into his palm like a cowboy, and worked the slide.

"Just in case we run out of small talk," he said, and slipped the gun back into his shoulder-holster. "I hate not having the last word."

Collecting his cigarettes off the dashboard, he got out and walked across the road to the edge of the canal. When he reached the centre of the bridge I saw him light a cigarette and lean forward on the railing. Anyone seeing him there, staring down into the murky green water, might have taken him for some love-sick student contemplating suicide. I don't doubt that the evening had already given him a lot to think about and that being sick of love probably came into it somewhere. I knew a fair bit about that myself.

★   ★   ★

The time appointed for Grushko's meeting came and went and still Sultan did not appear. With a hunter's patience Grushko hardly moved on the bridge and only the occasional flare of a match lighting another cigarette signalled his continuing vigilance. It was past one o'clock when the car telephone rang. As I answered it I could see that Grushko had heard it too. He straightened stiffly and then walked slowly back towards the car.

"Sultan won't be coming," said Nikolai.

"What happened?"

"He's been shot. Get across to the Titan Cinema on Nevsky. I'll see you both outside."

When I relayed the message to Grushko he spat and took out his gun. For a brief second I thought that the death of his prime suspect was going to result in my own murder as well. However he merely removed the magazine and then worked the slide to eject the live round. He thumbed the bullet back into the magazine which he then replaced inside the grip. Grushko was quite fastidious where gun safety was concerned.

He drove us silently back up Griboyedev and on to Nevsky, slowing as we came across the Anichkov Bridge with its distinctive rearing bronze horses, and saw the blue flashing lights ahead of us. We pulled up and as we walked through the police line holding back the small crowd of onlookers which had gathered, I spotted Georgi Zverkov and a film crew. He shouted something after Grushko and was ignored.

Surrounding a red Zhiguli was a group of the Central Board's scientific experts. Two of them were holding a tape-measure through the driver's window and measuring the distance between two imaginary points: the gun which had been fired and the head it had been aimed at. This was Militia Section 59's precinct and Lieutenant Khodyrev was on hand to provide a first report of what had happened.

"Three shots in the face, point blank," she said, "fired from another stationary vehicle. We've got a witness who claims he saw the whole thing."

She turned and pointed to a small boy who was standing nervously between two militiamen.

Grushko waited until the two officers were finished with their tape-measure and then ducked through the car's open window. When he had seen all he wanted to see I took a look myself.

Sultan Khadziyev lay across the gearstick, his face hardly distinguishable from the blood-soaked passenger seat. The passenger door was open and one of the experts was carefully searching the floor and door upholstery for stray bullets.

I stood up, saw that Nikolai had arrived on the scene, and then looked round for Grushko. He was squatting down in front of the boy.

"What's your name, son?" I heard him ask.

The boy looked across Grushko's shoulder like a hungry dog. He was wearing a dirty denim jacket and a poloneck sweater that was several sizes too big for him. He rubbed his short-cropped, almost bald head and then his dark-shadowed eyes. I guessed him no more than twelve years old. He smelled worse than a mangy dog.

"Come on," said one of the militiamen gruffly. "You don't want us to send you to an institution, do you?"

"Hey, hey," said Grushko, "that's my star witness you've got there."

Grushko took out his cigarettes and offered the boy one. He took it, dipped the end on Grushko's gold lighter and puffed it expertly.

"Rodya," he said finally. "Rodya Gutionov."

"Well, Rodya," said Grushko. "You're a brave fellow. Most boys of your age would have run away when they saw what you saw."

The boy shrugged modestly. "Me? I wasn't scared," he bragged.

"Of course you weren't," said Grushko. "So, what did you see?" He tucked the rest of his cigarettes into the pocket of the boy's greasy jacket.

"The man who got shot had just pulled up at the traffic lights," said Rodya, "when, a few seconds later, this other car pulls up alongside it. The passenger in the front seat leaned out with a chalk and waved it, like he was after a light. So the other man, the one who got shot, winds down his window and is handing over some matches when the other man—the one with the cigarette, grabs him by the arm and starts shooting." He shook his head excitedly and mimed the action of the gunman. "Bam-bam-bam—just like that. I never heard such a noise. Well, then they drove off, fast. The car went up Nevsky a bit, towards the Admiralty building and then did a U-turn, tyres squealing like it was something out of a movie."

"What kind of car was this, Rodya?"

"Zhiguli. Beige colour. Local plate."

"And how many men were in it?"

"Three. But I think the one in the back was a woman." He shook his head. "I couldn't be sure, because the other car was in the way. And when they started shooting I was trying to keep my head down in the doorway there."

He pointed at the cinema entrance. The film was some old historical epic of the early sixties starring Anthony Quinn. His was a face not unlike Grushko's own.

"You did the right thing," said Grushko. "Tell me, Rodya, where do you live?"

"Block 1, 77 Pushkinskaya Street," replied the boy. "Flat 25."

"You're out a bit late, aren't you?"

The boy looked down at his filthy trainers. "My father's on leave from the navy," he said. "When he's on leave he likes to get drunk. And then he hits me. So I make myself scarce."

Grushko nodded. It sounded plausible. Pushkinskaya Street was only a few blocks away. The drunken father was a common enough feature in a Russian home. With mine it had been my mother.

"All right, Rodya, you can go. But be careful."

The boy grinned and walked carefully away.

"The lying little scrap," Grushko muttered. "Escaped from an institution more like, if that haircut is anything to go by."

"So why are you letting him go?" I asked.

"Because I've been in a few of these places and I wouldn't keep an animal in them. You might better ask why he risked being sent back to an institution to speak to us." He chuckled as he answered his own question. "Bravado, I suppose. So he can brag to his mates about it, I wouldn't wonder."

Grushko turned and went round the far side of the car

to inspect the contents of the dead man's pockets that had been laid out on a plastic carrier-bag. He picked up Sultan's revolver.

"Milyukin was shot with an automatic," he said, and flipped open the gun's cartridge chamber to inspect the barrel. "Not that this would have shot anyone. It's a replica."

Nikolai was examining a packet of Kosmos cigarettes.

"Russian chalks," he said and lifted one of the filter ends clear of the foil wrapping. "And opened from the right end of the packet."

Grushko unfolded Sultan's wallet. He tossed a wad of dollars onto the carrier bag, then some food coupons, a condom, a railway warrant and a cutting from *Novy Mir* about Milyukin's death. One thing seemed to interest him. It was a small piece of paper with an official-looking rubber-stamp on it.

"Well, well, well," he said quietly.

"What is it?" I asked.

"Sultan's alibi," said Grushko. "I imagine this is what he wanted to talk to me about. It's a release form, from the Petrogradsky Region Militia. According to this piece of paper, Sultan Khadziyev spent the night of Mikhail Milyukin's murder drunk in the local LTP. That was why he felt so confident about meeting me. If this is genuine and he did spend that night in the drying-out tank, then he would have been in the clear."

Grushko handed Nikolai the document.

"You'd best check this out in the morning," he said. "Just to make sure."

He sighed and stared up at the purpling sky. It would soon be dark, if only for about fifty minutes.

"And that is that."

"So why buy him a ticket upstairs?" said Nikolai.

"The Georgians put two and two together and made five," said Grushko. "Just like we did." He shrugged. "Or that's what they want us to think. Either way we're back where we started."

"Still want us to pick the Georgians up tomorrow?"

Grushko looked at his watch. "You mean today, don't you?" he murmured wearily. "Yes, I do. More than ever."

"There is some good news, sir," announced Lieutenant Khodyrev.

"Well, don't make us beg for it," said Grushko.

"We've found your burglar. One of my men picked him up this evening. At Autova Market. He was trying to sell Mr. Milyukin's Gold Calf."

"Who is he?"

"His name is Valentin Bogomolov," she replied. "He's a juvenile offender, lives with his parents in the same building as Milyukin."

Grushko nodded appreciatively at her. "Well done, Lieutenant," he said. "And Lieutenant?"

"Sir?"

"Sorry . . . sorry for biting your head off like that. It's been a long day."

"That's all right, sir."

"First thing in the morning, Nikolai, I want you and the lieutenant here to interview him."

"What about the Georgians, sir?"

"You can leave them to Sasha and the OMON squad boys. I want to hear this little punk singing before lunchtime. Got that?"

"Sir."

By now Zverkov and his crew had succeeded in getting past the militia line. The cameraman was as close to Sultan's dead body as his lens permitted. Zverkov stood beside him describing the scene into the microphone he was holding. There was a bright, intense sort of look on his face and he was grinning wildly, as if he was excited by what he saw. He reminded me of the small runaway boy, Rodya, who was still hovering near the scene. Once again

Zverkov called out to Grushko and followed us as we walked back to the car.

"Colonel Grushko? Can you tell us what happened here please? For St. Petersburg Television." Zverkov covered the microphone. "Come on, Grushko. You're not going to sulk about what happened the other night, are you? I was just doing my job. Same as now. Trying to find out what happened here. Was it a Mafia killing?"

Grushko stopped and looked at Zverkov with undisguised loathing. His lip wrinkled and for a second I thought he would punch the man. Instead he nodded towards the car and Sultan's body.

"Why don't you ask him?" he said.

CHAPTER
FOURTEEN

★ The OMON squad was a special-purpose unit, a sort of militia-commando outfit. They wore military-style uniforms with helmets, blue flak-jackets and carried machine pistols and AK47s. While awaiting the order to move they sat in a large room in the Big House and watched an Arnold Schwarzenegger video, their weapons cradled in their strong arms like schoolboys emulating their screen hero. The film, *Predator,* was in English, but only the action seemed to matter. Most of the squad's members were in their twenties. Good-humoured and slightly nervous, they seemed more like a team of footballers trying to relax a little before a big match than a dedicated group of police gunmen. But there was nothing sporting about the way they tackled criminals and it was rare that anyone was inclined to offer these ruthless young men more than a token resistance.

Grushko put his head round the door and spoke to a man with a moustache who was smoking a cigarette and seemed less interested in the film than the others.

"Pavel Pavlovich," he said, "a word, if you please."

Lieutenant Pavel Pavlovich Klobuyev, who was the unit's commander, stubbed out his cigarette and followed Grushko into the corridor.

"Have you got a Georgi Rodionov in your squad, Pavel?" Grushko asked him.

"Not any more. He took a bullet in the leg about a year ago. D'you remember? It was when we hit Kumarin and his gang."

Grushko nodded vaguely.

"Anyway, he was invalided out of OMON. He's now a firearms instructor at the Police Training Centre in Pushkin. Best shot with a handgun I ever saw."

"Do you think he's the sort who might handle a little private security work?"

Klobuyev turned and looked back into the room. His men cheered as Arnie let rip with a heavy machine-gun.

"Sir, half my squad is doing some kind of moonlighting." He shrugged. "It's a fact of life, salaries being what they are. At 225 roubles a month I wouldn't blame any of them if they were male models during their off-duty periods. The man you mentioned, Rodionov, do you know how much his compensation was when he got shot? Nothing. Nothing at all."

"Like I always say," said Grushko. "There's nothing more expensive than a cheap police force."

★ ★ ★

I met Grushko on the stairs, under the watchful eye of Iron Felix.

"Have you seen Pushkin yet?" he asked.

I told him I hadn't.

"You Muscovites," he said, shaking his head with pity. "You've got nothing to compare with it. I'll show you the Catherine Palace on the way to the Police Academy."

He explained about Georgi Rodionov when we were in the car.

"Does he know we're coming?"

"God, no," said Grushko. "It'll be a nice surprise for him, eh?" He chuckled sadistically.

Pushkin is about twenty-five kilometers south of St. Petersburg and so named, since 1937, after the famous poet. For Stalin the best poets were always the ones who had been dead for a century. It was a quiet, leafy little place with some beautiful parks and not one but two royal palaces.

The Pushkin Police Academy stood only a short way east of the Catherine Palace and yet it would have been hard to have found two more contrasting buildings in the whole of Russia: the palace with its 300-metre-long façade of blue and white stucco, its gold cupolas and its gilded wrought-iron gates; and the crumbling brown brick of the Academy, with its potholed courtyard, its leaking roof and its peeling paintwork.

I was no Communist, but you didn't have to be Lenin to see that a dynasty that could have built some palaces for themselves while peasants went hungry was headed for serious trouble. Yet I was glad that such places still existed: without these magnificent reminders of our former glories it would have been hard to see ourselves as anything but a third-world banana republic. With an acute shortage of bananas.

The Director of the Academy was a big ox of a man with a full, dark moustache you could have steered a motorcycle with. He had a friendly smile of the kind that is supposed to be lucky and, I was soon to suspect, a nose for making money that smelt in his Academy as many business opportunities as there were gaps between his teeth.

His office was big and gloomy, unremarkably Soviet in every way save only for the strange pictures that hung on the yellowing walls; when the telephone rang, I took a closer look at them.

Although they were expensively framed, none of the oil-pastel drawings looked particularly well rendered. But then lack of talent never stopped anyone from making a living as an artist in Russia. At the same time, what had been drawn was easily recognisable, even familiar, to anyone who has seen a science-fiction comic. There were four pictures in all and they formed a sequence that told the story of a man driving a car at night whose journey was interrupted by the arrival of an alien spaceship and who was engaged in conversation by one of these strange beings prior to being taken away in the flying saucer on a day-trip to a strange planet. UFOs were a common enough interest among people: UFOs, faith-healers, spiritualism, Nostradamus, pyramid power and Satanism. When it was a matter of believing in the impossible we are a most credulous people. Maybe that's not such a surprise. After all, we have had more than seventy years of practise.

I turned and found Grushko standing at my shoulder. He nodded with polite appreciation as the director replaced the telephone.

"You've certainly picked a busy day to come and see us," said the director. "After the local priest has finished blessing our new canteen, the newspapers are coming here to photograph those pictures and to interview me about my UFO experience."

I felt my jaw slacken with surprise.

"I imagine that's where we'll find Georgi Rodionov," he said.

"What?" I heard myself say. "In a UFO?"

The director chuckled. "No, in the canteen. You'll stay to lunch, of course?"

"Well—" Grushko glanced at his watch.

"But I insist. Our canteen is excellent. You won't find a better one. Not anywhere. To be honest, we put a lot of cooperative restaurants to shame. You and Georgi can have your little chat in the officers' dining-room."

Grushko was still too surprised to disagree with him.

"Er, fine," he said, and we followed the director into the corridor.

"He's not in any trouble, I hope. Georgi's a good man. Best weapons instructor I've ever had."

We hurried by some women who were busy replastering a wall.

"We just want to ask him a few questions," said Grushko. "About an old inquiry."

The director stopped abruptly and flung open a door. Several cadets looked up from the gym equipment they were exercising on.

"Carry on," he yelled at them. Then he looked at the two of us and grinned. "What do you think? I got a couple of metal workers to copy some American Nautilus equipment. Otherwise we could never have afforded a gym like this. In the evening this place is a health and fitness club for the local community. Leastways for those who are prepared to pay the membership fee. All the money is ploughed back into the Academy. Not bad, eh?"

Grushko and I conceded that he had done well. The director was starting to interest me in a way I had not expected.

We moved on down the corridor and once again he stopped and flung open another door. This time it was a large lecture theatre with a cinema screen.

"At the weekend," he said without any sign of embarrassment, "this is the town cinema. Schwarzenegger, Stallone, Madonna—anything. For just two roubles a head."

"You seem to have thought of everything," I said.

"To run a place like this, you have to be a good businessman. The new canteen cost 50,000 roubles. The money has to come from somewhere. It certainly doesn't come from the Ministry." He laughed bitterly. "You find it any way you know how. And it's lucky I know how."

I wondered how much the UFO story was likely to raise. The pictures had been a shrewd addition: they would probably double the price. I began to like the director. He didn't care what people thought of him just so long as it brought in the money to improve the facilities for his cadets. At the same time I saw how the success of his UFO story depended on his never admitting the truth to anyone. The man wasn't corrupt, he was a genius. He ought to have been put in charge of the entire militia budget. He could probably have dreamed up a way of doubling that too.

In the new canteen nearly three hundred cadets were already seated at their refectory tables. Like their senior officers and the dinner-ladies they were awaiting the arrival of the black priest. With any Russian ceremony there is always a lot of waiting around. Grushko and I followed the director into the centre of the room and then suddenly, as if by magic, the priest and his acolyte were among us.

The priest was a young man of about thirty who stood a head taller than anyone else in the canteen so that his sharp blue eyes seemed to be on everyone. He was bearded and, as was traditional, he wore his hair long and tied in a tail behind his head. He was clothed in a voluminous black cassock with wide mandarin sleeves, a long white silk-brocade tippet, and a large cross on a silver chain. Handsome, and younger than most of the priests I had ever seen, he was also a dead ringer for Rasputin.

His acolyte was altogether less distinguished, being younger, fatter, clean-shaven, and rather sleepy-looking, as if he had just rolled out of a warm, greasy bed.

The director barked something at the cadets who, as one man, stood to attention. They were not entirely silent and I heard a few remarks and corresponding guffaws as the priest, taking it all in good part, addressed a short sermon to his strange flock.

Especially by the standards of the Russian Orthodox Church, this was not a long sermon, lasting only three or four minutes; and the blessing, with sung responses from the nasal-sounding acolyte and which lasted perhaps six or seven minutes, was not a long blessing. But since the lunch of soup and sausage was already cooling on the tables, the priest's little service seemed interminable.

Finally, as if to make quite certain that the food was cold, the two of them walked solemnly round the whole canteen, liberally dousing cadets, tables, walls and food with lashings of holy water. A light murmur of discomfort turned louder with amusement and the director took advantage of the stir to find Georgi Rodionov and then usher the three of us into an annexe to the main canteen that was the officers' dining room. He sat us down at his own table and hospitably served us himself with three plates of soup. But he did not join us, claiming, not implausibly, that he was on a strict diet.

"Quite a character," observed Grushko when the director had left us.

"Isn't he?" said Rodionov, and sipped his soup noisily.

"Is he serious? About the UFO thing?"

"Oh yes." Rodionov looked up from his bowl and shrugged philosophically. "These days we all of us have to do some pretty strange things in the way of making a living."

While Grushko asked his questions, I studied the Academy's weapons-instructor. Rodionov was a strong-looking man with fair hair, blue eyes, a broad nose and thick sensual lips. But for the height of his cheekbones, he might have passed for a German or a Pole. It was a distinguished, dreamy sort of face, as might have better suited a poet rather than a policeman.

"So tell me about it," said Grushko, and drank some soup.

Rodionov scratched his nose self-consciously and looked from side to side. He was about to answer when Grushko interrupted him.

"Why didn't you come forward?" he said quietly. "You knew that we would want to speak to everyone who had any contact with Mikhail Milyukin in the time leading up to his death. So what's your excuse, mister?"

Rodionov's appetite was gone. He sat back on his chair and folded his arms defensively.

"If it appeared on a report that I was moonlighting, then I could lose this job." He spoke sullenly, like a schoolboy who had been caught stealing fruit. "I've already lost any real prospect of getting on in the militia. I suppose you know I was invalided out of the OMON squad with no compensation?"

"I know it," said Grushko.

"I've got a wife and family, and I can't afford to lose this job. I need the money. And any extra that I can earn." He lit a cigarette. "Besides, it's not as if there's much to tell."

"Why don't you let me be the judge of that?"

"All right." Rodionov poured himself some apple juice from the jug on the table. Really it was little more than water with a few slices of apple core floating in it.

"I head up a small syndicate of militiamen offering private security to people. You know the kind of thing I'm talking about. Mostly it's shop owners, cooperative restaurants, and joint-ventures—people trying to make an honest living who find themselves coming up against the Mafia. Occasionally we get an individual client. Like Mikhail Milyukin.

"He contacted me. Said that he'd been threatened by some people. At first I assumed he was talking about the Mafia, but it later transpired that it was some people in the Department who had him really spooked. He didn't say what they wanted from him, just that they were trying to intimidate him. Apparently there was some Mafioso, a pimp whom Milyukin had helped to send to the zone, and these KGB people had told him they were going to see to it that this fellow obtained an early release. Milyukin was worried that if he did get out, then he might come looking for him.

"Well, I went to his apartment and we talked. I worked out a plan and a price for him but he said that it was too much. He offered me fifty roubles in cash, on account—and I turned it down." Rodionov shrugged. "Simple as that, sir."

"When was this?"

"A couple of days before he was shot."

"Morning or afternoon?"

Rodionov thought for a moment. "Morning. Between nine and ten o'clock."

"It must have been just before the burglary," I said.

Rodionov looked surprised.

"Burglary? The papers didn't mention any burglary." His surprise turned into a frown. "Come to think of it though, there was something . . ."

"Let's have it," said Grushko.

"It was when I was on my way out of the building where Milyukin lived. I saw this face. Fellow with a long record for petty thieving. Mainly a pickpocket, but he's done a bit of burglary in his time. Name of Pyotr Mogilnikov. Anyway, he was talking to these two characters in a car parked right outside. But I didn't think anything about it at the time. I mean, Milyukin was worried about being killed, not ripped off."

"Can you describe the two men in the car?"

"I didn't get much more than a glance at them, sir. But they were dark and one of them was smoking American cigarettes. I remember him throwing a pack out of the car."

"Brand?"

Rodionov shrugged and shook his head.

"What make of car was it?"

"Er . . . an old Zim. Black. Red upholstery. A nice clean car." He stubbed his cigarette out with some ferocity.

"You know sir, for what it's worth, I'm not very proud of myself—considering what happened to Mr. Milyukin. I mean, he was a nice fellow. But fifty roubles, it just wasn't enough, for a syndicate."

Grushko nodded sombrely. He wiped his soup bowl with a piece of black bread and then ate it.

"Then we'll say no more about it, this time," he said and, because I had also finished eating, he stood up from the table. At the same moment one of the dinner-ladies arrived bearing three plates of steaming sausage.

"Thank you for the soup," said Grushko, "but we have to get back now."

"Here, what about your sausage?" said Rodionov.

"You eat it," said Grushko. "With two jobs, you probably need it."

CHAPTER

FIFTEEN

★ When we returned to the Big House we found the corridor outside Grushko's office busy with OMON squad militia and the Georgians they had arrested in the gym at the Pribaltskaya. We saw Sasha still wearing one of the new flak jackets that had just been supplied to the Criminal Services Department, and Grushko waved him towards us.

"Any trouble?" he asked.

"One of them gave us the slip, sir," admitted Sasha. "But we'll pick him up."

"See that you do."

We watched the gang being led into the interrogation-room. They were attracting quite a bit of attention with their dark good-looks, their smart clothes and their macho swagger. Georgians always do. Seeing Dzhumber Gankrelidze, Grushko added, "I'll want a word with that one. He's got some explaining to do."

Sasha nodded.

"Is Nikolai Vladimirovich back yet?" asked Grushko.

"In the office. He's got Lieutenant Khodyrev with him. And some kid."

We retreated down the corridor. The door to the detectives' room was open. Catching sight of Grushko, Andrei, still pursuing his telephone inquiry, stood up nervously, as if expecting to be yelled at once again.

"Still nothing to report, sir," he said awkwardly.

Grushko grunted, his interest apparently reserved for the youth sitting in front of Nikolai and Khodyrev, his left hand manacled to a statue of Lenin. He wore a black leather jacket with a painting of the Buddha on the back and several earrings. His hair was fashionably quiffed and he looked as if he had been crying. He was reading through the statement he had given to Nikolai.

"If you're happy with what's written there, then sign it," said Nikolai, and handed him a pen.

The youth nodded and then sniffed unhappily. He took the pen, wet the end on his yellowish tongue, laid the statement on the desk and signed it carefully. Nikolai collected the statement, inspected it to see if Mickey Mouse had given him his autograph and, seeing Grushko, stood up and came towards us.

"Is this the kid who washed Milyukin's Golden Calf?"

"That's right, sir. His name is Valentin Bogomolov. He's a rope-swallower."

Grushko frowned. Before he had joined Grushko's team, Nikolai had spent several years with the drugs squad. His knowledge of drug-users' slang was second to none.

"I mean, he smokes a bit of hash."

"Thank you," growled Grushko.

"He lives with his mum and dad in the flat upstairs from Milyukin."

"So what's his story?"

Nikolai handed Grushko Bogomolov's statement. The older man glanced over it and then nodded.

"Perhaps I'd better hear this for myself," he said and perching himself on the corner of Nikolai's desk, picked up the Golden Calf, nodded at Khodyrev and then faced the youth sternly.

Nikolai took out his cigarettes and shoved one in Bogomolov's mouth as if he had been feeding a baby.

"This is Colonel Grushko," he explained, and lit the cigarette. "I want you to tell him what you've been telling us. Let's start from where you first saw these men outside Milyukin's door."

Bogomolov took an unsteady chestful of smoke and nodded meekly.

"Well, I was on my way downstairs when I saw them," he said tremulously. "These three men. At first I thought they might be plainclothes militiamen or something. I mean, they didn't look like thieves, but I knew they didn't live in that flat. Plus the fact that they had keys. Two of them let themselves in the door while the third one stayed outside. He looked like he was keeping watch, and I guess then I knew they were up to something. Actually, he seemed less well-dressed than the other two who went in, and more like a thief, if you know what I mean."

He sighed profoundly and placed the cigarette in the corner of his mouth. With the leather jacket he looked quite like James Dean. But if there had been any cool bravado, it was long gone.

"Go on," said Grushko.

"I was watching to see what happened. You see, it was quite dark on the stairs, so they didn't know I was watching them. Anyway, I suppose they were in there for ten or fifteen minutes, and when they came out again they had a few papers as well as some stuff in a carrier bag. . . ."

"What stuff?" said Grushko.

"I don't know. Probably more papers. One of them said something funny—something about 'going back to the seagull.'"

"The seagull?" Grushko looked at Nikolai. "Fans of Chekhov, were they?"

"I'm sure that was it," said Bogomolov. "Even though it didn't make any sense to me."

" 'Seagull' is army slang for a car, sir," explained Nikolai.

"That's interesting," murmured Grushko. "But it's also one of those old copies of American cars that Zim or Zil used to turn out. A Seagull was a Buick copy, I think. We'd better check it out." Grushko glanced down at Bogomolov and frowned.

"Well? What happened next?"

"They cleared off, leaving the front door open. Well, that was my chance. I thought I'd just duck in and see if there was anything valuable lying around. There was some money on the table—about fifty roubles—and that golden cow thing. I had that and the money and ran out."

He clutched at Grushko's sleeve with a hand that was covered with eczema. Grushko's nose wrinkled with distaste.

"That's the honest truth, sir, I swear. I was going to sell the cow to buy some wheels, but I don't know anything about a murder, sir. Please, sir, please tell her that, will you?" He nodded fearfully at Lieutenant Khodyrev. "She's been saying all kinds of things, but they're not true, sir."

Grushko nodded and detached the youth's scrofulous hand from his sleeve. He pushed himself off the desk and walked through the doorway where I was standing. Nikolai followed.

"Think he's telling the truth?" said Grushko.

"After the stick Olga waved at him, I'm sure of it."

"Olga?" Grushko smiled.

"Lieutenant Khodyrev. She's a first-class cop, sir. Threatened the kid with the whole bunch of flowers. Murder, theft of state property—"

"What state property is that?" I asked.

"The Golden Calf," said Nikolai. "It is an important literary award. You see, at first he claimed he'd just found it lying on the road, but Lieutenant Khodyrev, she . . ."

"We get the picture, Nikolai," said Grushko. "You don't

have to give her the Order of Lenin." He looked back into the room.

"Keep him here for a minute," he said, and then went back into his own office. He picked up the phone and asked the Big House operator to put him through to the Criminal Records Department.

★ ★ ★

"Is this one of the men you saw?"

Bogomolov stared at the photograph Grushko had removed from the file and placed in front of him.

"It was dark," he said, "but I think he was the one who had the keys: the one who stayed outside and kept a lookout for the other two."

"The one who looked like a thief, you said."

Bogomolov nodded and Grushko smiled.

"Good boy," he said. "Now then, how do you feel about seeing if you can identify these two other men you saw? I'm talking about an identity parade."

Bogomolov shrugged. " 'S fine by me," he said. "But look, what's going to happen to me when all this is over?"

Grushko looked over at Lieutenant Khodyrev.

"Have the papers gone to an investigator yet?" he asked.

"No, sir," she said, "not yet."

"Then what do you think?"

"You mean if he's helping us with our inquiry, sir? Under the circumstances, I should be inclined not to press charges."

"You hear that?" Grushko said to Bogomolov. "You can go home after you've had a look at these men. But take a good look at them, mind. And don't say it's them just because you want to be helpful. Understand?"

Bogomolov nodded.

We returned to Grushko's office.

"We'll see if he recognises any of our handsome Georgian friends," explained Grushko.

"Want me to organise the protocol?" I offered.

"Please."

"Nikolai took a look at the man in the photograph whom Bogomolov had positively identified.

"Who's the face, sir?"

"Fellow called Pyotr Mogilnikov," said Grushko. "A pickpocket. Georgi Rodionov saw him hanging around outside Milyukin's apartment building on the day of the burglary. He was with two men in a black Volga. My guess is that these two characters paid him to lift Milyukin's keys from his pocket. Probably bumped into him on the street or something like that. And while he was out they simply let themselves in through the front door." He glanced over Bogomolov's statement once more.

"I reckon one of these characters was our careful Winston smoker," suggested Nikolai. "You know, the one who takes his chalks from the wrong end of the packet."

"Rodionov did say that one of the two men in the Volga was smoking American cigarettes," I said.

Grushko's forefinger tapped the photograph in Nikolai's hand.

"Then you'd better get that circulated," he said. "I don't want this *zek* going the same way as Sultan Khadziyev. We have to burn him out, and soon." He smacked his fist into his palm. "Right then. Let's sort these Dzhugashvilis."

★ ★ ★

Georgian men enjoy a not undeserved reputation with women, being hot-blooded, passionate characters and having a cynical eye for the main chance. Any joke or story involving sexual excess usually has a Georgian as its hero. There are two other things most people knew about Georgia. One is that the region produces an excellent cognac.

The other is that it was the birthplace of Joseph Stalin. Only then he called himself Josef Dzhugashvili. It used to be people also knew Georgia to be a nice place to go for a holiday. But since the collapse of the Soviet Union it is only the mercenaries who are much inclined to go there.

Once, many years ago, when I was a small boy, my parents took me to Georgia for a holiday by the Black Sea. I remember how hot it had been and the kindness of the people with whom we had stayed. Now, as I looked at the truculent faces of the men who had been brought to the Big House, it seemed almost impossible to associate them with the warm and distant land that I remembered from my childhood; and all too easy to associate them with the violent struggle for power in Georgia that followed the end of Communism. But for all their black looks and weary yawns, the Georgian Mafiosi conducted themselves with dignity; and treating Grushko's men with courtesy they found that their courtesy was returned.

It was, I realised, a relationship born of mutual respect. The Georgians knew that the men of the Central Board were not the kind of militia that people were inclined to make jokes about—the kind that you could see strutting on the streets, blowing whistles, waggling batons and extracting fines for fictitious offences in order to supplement their wages. At the same time, the men of the Central Board knew that these Mafiosi were hard men, many of them having spent time in the labour-camp system that, despite the provisions of the Corrective Labour Code, treated men little better than animals. Having survived that dehumanising experience, most Mafiosi were sufficiently resourceful to make them hard to convict.

There were seven Georgians in custody and since the police rules regarding identity parades only required that a suspect be placed in a line with two other persons, this meant that fourteen members of the public were now required. Grushko explained that in order to make what was an admittedly crude procedure as fair as possible they had often gone to the blackmarkets at Autovo and Deviatkino in order to recruit suitably swarthy citizens; there was among these, however, an understandable lack of enthusiasm to go anywhere near the Big House and, as a result, all of the men who now volunteered to take part in Central Board identity parades were cadets from the local army barracks.

Not that there was even much of a parade: the suspect waited in a room with two of the volunteers and several militiamen: all three were asked to stand; the witness was brought into the room; and then he was asked if he recognised any of the three men standing before him. It was as simple as that.

Valentin Bogomolov looked at all seven Georgians in this way. He took his time and there was not pressure exerted on him to pick out a face. And seven times he shook his head. With the last of the Georgians, their boss Dzhumber Gankrelidze, Grushko asked Bogomolov if he was absolutely sure and Bogomolov said that he was.

"All right," said Grushko and Nikolai ushered Bogomolov out of the room.

When both of the army cadets taking part in the parade had left, Dzhumber lit a cigarette and smiled.

"So, what's this all about, officer?" he asked.

With nothing to connect the Georgians with the burglary of Mikhail Milyukin's apartment Grushko decided to return to an earlier line of inquiry.

"You told my men that on the night Vaja Ordzhonikidze was killed, you spent the whole evening at the Pribaltskaya Hotel."

Dzhumber shrugged. "Did I? I don't remember."

"But you were at the Pushkin Restaurant."

Dzhumber pointed at the door that had closed behind Valentin Bogomolov.

"Not according to Elvis," he said.

Grushko did not bother to correct the Georgian's misapprehension of the identity parade's purpose.

"You didn't get to the Pribaltskaya until well after you said," he said. "Your car was seen driving along Nevsky just a few minutes before eleven."

"You had your Kodak at Vaja's funeral, didn't you?" sighed Dzhumber. "You saw the send-off we gave him. Now why should we do that if we killed him, eh?" He was keeping away from the subject of the Pushkin Restaurant and the firebomb.

"I don't know," said Grushko. "Not yet, anyway. But say one thing, do another, that's the Georgian way, isn't it? Stalin, Beria, they were both from your part of the world."

Dzhumber smiled his expensive gold smile and shook his head.

"You sound just like the newspapers," he said. "Knocking Stalin is just another way you Russians have of knocking Georgia."

"You're a naturally contrary lot," persisted Grushko. "Everyone knows that. Even your word 'mama' mean father. Doubletalk and deceit are part of the Georgian psychology."

"So who are you: the police psychiatrist?"

"You know what I think?"

"Go ahead. Surprise me."

"I think this whole thing has been cooked up as a pretext for you to settle a turf war with the Chechens. You kill Vaja and then go after them for it."

I didn't think much of this theory. I wasn't sure that Grushko thought much of it himself: he seemed to want to provoke Dzhumber somehow. Perhaps that was part of this whole strategy of interrogation. But Dzhumber didn't think much more of Grushko's idea than I did.

"You've got an active imagination," he said. "For a Russian."

"We had the same thought ourselves for a while. About

the Chechens. Sultan Khadziyev looked like a pretty good suspect. Only he couldn't possibly have murdered Vaja. He spent the night of the murder in an LTP after a two-day bender."

"So now you've come back to us, is that it?" Dzhumber gazed wearily out of the window and then back at Grushko.

"Hey, Sultan Khadziyev wasn't the only Chechen in St. Petersburg, you know. Maybe you're right: maybe he wasn't the one who shot Vaja. Maybe it was one of the others. Those stinking caftans don't need much of an excuse to come after Georgians. Ever since the Central Board cleared out the Armenians, those Muslim bastards have been looking to fill the vacuum."

"Our success brings its own problems," shrugged Grushko.

"So you miss one Muhammad, I say look for another. Sultan couldn't have done it you say? Fine. Then it was another Chechen."

"I'll bear it in mind."

"You do that."

"Maybe we're wrong about this firebombing, too," said Grushko. "I don't know. The owner, a Mr. Chazov, he's not helping us very much, so it's hard to know what to think."

"Go ahead. Tell me your problems."

"You had nothing to do with that either, right?"

"Right. We were nowhere near the Pushkin Restaurant."

"Who said anything about the Pushkin Restaurant?"

"You did," said Dzhumber, frowning. "Just now."

"No, I was talking about a firebombing." He shook his head. "I didn't say that had anything to do with the Pushkin Restaurant. It was you who connected the Pushkin with Mr. Chazov, not me."

Dzhumber's jaw shifted uncomfortably. He wasn't sure

if Grushko had trapped him into saying something incriminating or not.

"I want to see my lawyer," he said.

"Maybe in the morning," said Grushko. "But tonight—you're our guests."

★ ★ ★

Katerina was watching television by herself when finally I returned home to the apartment on Ochtinsky Prospekt. I found the tinned meat and spaghetti she had left out for me and then joined her sitting on the sofa, although I was ready to unfold the thing and go straight to sleep. She noticed my stifled yawn.

"Tired?"

"Like I've been listening to Gorbachev. What's this you're watching?"

"Hamlet."

Hamlet was making a good job of ravishing Ophelia, or his mother, I wasn't exactly sure which. Either way it was Pasternak's translation, the famous Moscow Arts Theatre version and just the sort of thing that Katerina, who worked for Lenfilm on Kirovsky Prospekt, was only able to watch when Porfiry was away on one of his frequent business trips aboard. Porfiry preferred to watch videos of the kind that were also enjoyed by the OMON squad.

"When's he back?" I asked.

"Sometime tomorrow." She shrugged and I had a fine view of her plunging cleavage.

"I have to go back to Moscow tomorrow evening," I said. "To pick up my car. They've sent the part I was waiting for. I'm catching the overnight train."

"When you're there, maybe you can find some aspirin," she said. "There's none in any of the local pharmacies."

"Anything else?"

"Well, we could always use some light-bulbs, live or dead. Even the duds are getting hard to find."

It was an old dodge: people would swap the duds with functioning bulbs at their place of work.

"I'm not so sure about that," I joked. "They used to call that 'wrecking' under Article 69."

"What it is to have a cop around the house," she laughed. "All right. I'll watch breakfast television and see what the latest shortages are. But really, with Porfiry away so much, it *is* nice to have you here. There are so many robberies around here these days."

"Maybe if the corridors weren't so dark," I said pointedly, "muggers would get less of a chance. But with people taking the lightbulbs . . ."

We talked for a while longer until finally Katerina said good-night and I was at last able to unfold the sofa bed. This wasn't particularly comfortable but I slept well enough, which was more than Grushko could have said. The next morning, on my return to the Big House, I could see that he hadn't been to bed at all. Not long after returning home Grushko had received a call from Sasha informing him that a militiaman on duty at the Moskva Hotel had spotted Pyotr Mogilnikov in the lobby.

CHAPTER

SIXTEEN

★ Two stops on the metro west of the city centre and overlooking the Alexander Nevsky Monastery, the Moskow Hotel has the shape and character of a communal-sized nuclear bomb-shelter. With nothing to distinguish the place architecturally, it is chiefly remarkable for the number of hard-currency prostitutes hanging around the doorway and the lobby, as well as for the Finnish drinking parties that arrive on the ferry from Helsinki every weekend. The prostitutes and the drunken Finns often end up together and it is commonly held that they deserve each other.

Grushko regarded the Moskow and its attendant dollar-hungry girls with obvious distaste. Like many men with grown-up daughters, albeit one who earlier that same evening had announced her intention to emigrate to America, Grushko had been shocked at a recent survey conducted among teenage Russian girls that revealed that being a hard-currency prostitute was regarded as one of the most attractive professions open to a girl.

Grushko and Sasha shoved their way past the vixen-pack waiting patiently between the hotel's double doors and entered the huge lobby, looking around for the militia-man who had summoned them. They spotted him crossing the marble floor, half-saluting as he came towards them, his thick, sinewy neck bulging over the blue collar of his uniform's shirt.

"Your suspect was in the restaurant when I phoned," explained the militiaman, who was a sergeant. "But now he's gone into the amusement arcade. One of my lads is keeping an eye on him. I'd have arrested him myself, but I thought I should speak to you first."

The three of them started towards an open flight of stairs that led up to the huge dining-hall and, beyond, the slot-machines.

What had sounded like the band at a circus was now revealed as the cabaret orchestra. On a brightly lit stage a troupe of dancing girls, wearing only G-strings under short Circassian-style red shirts, were going through their paces with all the artistic grace of a detachment of soldiers guarding Lenin's tomb. Waiters hurried to ignore their troublesome, often paralytically drunk customers, while pimps shifted between tables, finding clients and recovering percentages from prostitutes before returning to the Vegas-style amusement arcade.

To Grushko's tired eyes, it seemed a millenially decadent sight and he would not have been much surprised to have seen a hand appear in the smoky air to write the words of some prophecy on the strobe-lit wall. What bothered him most was the sight of so much food, with much of it going to waste, disregarded or rejected by those who had ordered it with hardly a second thought for whether they were actually hungry or not, while outside in the city at large the shops were empty and people queued hours to buy a loaf of bread.

"Look at this swamp," he muttered. "God knows we need the hard currency, but we shouldn't have to sell our souls for it."

"This way, sir," said Sasha.

The amusement arcade was full of people, most of

them Russian, and all of them frantically feeding tokens into machines as if they too had seen the writing on the wall. They came from all over the old Soviet Union. There were agricultural engineers from Kharkov, steel workers from Magnitogorsk, timber merchants from Novosibirsk, miners from Irkutsk and teachers from Habarovsk: Siberians, Ukrainians, Tazaks, Armenians and Uzbeks—Intourist travellers paying their first and only visit to the cultural and historical capital, pilgrims come to see the treasures of the Hermitage and the tombs of the tsars. But mostly they came to peer through Peter's grimy window on the West and to grab a two-week ersatz version of it for themselves.

The militia sergeant accompanying Grushko and Sasha caught his colleague's eye, followed it to a bank of fruit machines, and then drew Grushko's attention to a man sitting on a stool who was pumping coins into the slot from a paper cup that was resting in his lap. He was wearing jeans, a blue track-suit top and he had a pale, sharp-looking face. A cigarette hung like a referee's whistle on the man's grey and pendulous lower lip. It was Pyotr Mogilnikov.

As Grushko started forward he saw the second man. Or rather he saw the light catch on the knife that the man was holding close to his thigh. His was a darker-looking face with heavy brows, a long broad nose and a full Stalin-style moustache. The man advanced steadily on Mogilnikov's back and as the knife began its deadly ascent, Grushko drew his gun.

"Drop that feather," he yelled.

The man with the knife turned and saw the huge Makarov automatic in Grushko's hand. Mogilnikov turned on his stool and saw the Georgian with the knife at the very same moment that the machine he had been feeding so assiduously hit the jackpot. It was just enough distraction to enable Mogilnikov to make his getaway. He shoved the Georgian backwards and bolted towards the restaurant.

Seeing the shower of descending coins deserted by their winner, other gamblers struggled to get their hands on the payout and, in the ensuing mêlée, the Georgian made for the back door. Grushko did not dare to fire. It was not that he worried about missing the Georgian, so much as he knew a .45 calibre bullet might pass straight through the man's body and hit an innocent bystander. Sasha had already chased after Mogilnikov and that left Grushko struggling to get through the crowd of gamblers and then the back door in pursuit of the man with the knife.

Arriving outside he glanced north along the side of the river, and then across the bridge. There was no sign of the Georgian and so he started to run round the front of the hotel. Still holding the big gun in his hand, he jogged carefully through the taxi rank, checking between the cars as he came and scanning the other side of the square and the gate of the monastery. At the corner of Nevksy Prospekt he stopped and, still seeing no sign of the Georgian, he began to retrace his steps. There was only the Metro station left to try.

Grushko came through the heavy glass doors and stopped by a busker who was collecting up the few roubles and copecks he had found in his guitar case.

"Did you see a man run in here just now?" he said.

The busker caught sight of the gun in Grushko's hand and for several seconds he was too scared to do anything but open and close his mouth soundlessly.

"What sort of man?" he finally stammered.

Grushko shook his head impatiently, vaulted the barrier and then jogged to the top of the huge and empty escalators. A wind stirred his hair and cooled his face pleasantly as he stopped there to decide his next move. With no one coming up, he doubted that a train could have come and gone. If the Georgian had gone into the Metro, he was probably still down there.

He stepped onto the escalator and started his descent,

all the time keeping an ear out for the loudspeaker-voice that would announced the arrival of the next train. Then, at the bottom of the ascending escalator, he saw another man start back as if something had dissuaded him from going up, and Grushko knew that his quarry was lying low on the other moving stair. The Georgian must have heard him questioning the busker and climbed on the up escalator in the hope that he could get past Grushko coming down.

Grushko turned and started to climb against the downward motion of the wooden stairway. For a moment or two he succeeded only in keeping pace with it and had to climb harder in order to make his ascent. On reaching ground level again he kept low until he got to the barrier. He jumped silently over it and, seeing the busker once more, he put his finger to his lips and quietly took the guitar with him. Pressing himself into the wall, he started to tune one of the strings.

He heard the footsteps and then saw the gun. The next moment he swung the guitar by its neck and caught the Georgian full in the face. The man's gun clattered to the ground as he fell. Grushko moved quickly forward and kicked it away. Then he returned the still-ringing instrument to the busker.

"Nice tone," he said.

As the Georgian sat up and wiped the blood from his mouth, he found himself expertly handcuffed.

"Come on, you," said Grushko. "On your feet. You've got some more music to face."

He frog-marched the Georgian back to the hotel's front door, where a small crowd was gathering near Sasha.

"Don't say you lost him."

Sasha pointed at Grushko's car. Pyotr Mogilnikov was sitting in the back seat with his forearms covering his face.

"Is he all right?" Grushko asked solicitously.

"He's all right," said Sasha. "I had to hit him, that's all. He's just a bit winded."

"What about me?" mumbled the Georgian as he tried to stanch the copious flow of blood from his nose and mouth. "I need a doctor."

"You need a lawyer more," said Grushko and shoved him towards the militia sergeant as a black police van sped towards them with its blue light flashing.

"Stick him in the raven, and bring him down to the Big House," he said. "I'd take him myself only I don't want to get any blood on my upholstery."

"Right you are, sir," said the sergeant and, taking hold of the Georgian's blood-stained shirt collar, he shoved him towards the van as it pulled up beside them.

★ ★ ★

It was after two o'clock by the time they got back to the Big House. The Georgian, whose name was Ilya Chavchavadze, was not saying a thing, so they locked him up in the old police gaol underneath the Big House and turned their attention to Pyotr Mogilnikov. Sasha unlocked his handcuffs and sat him down on a chair in front of Grushko.

"You know," he said, lighting the man a cigarette, "another few seconds and that Georgian would have had you." He tipped his own cigarette towards the lighter.

"My lucky day, isn't it?"

"I'd say so. I don't suppose you have any idea why he wanted to kill you?"

Mogilnikov pushed his chair back onto two legs and rocked with insolent nonchalance.

"Who knows what goes through that sort of sick mind?" he said.

"How about if you were to hazard a guess?"

"Your guess is as good as mine."

"Better, I shouldn't wonder," said Grushko.

Mogilnikov smirked.

"So why are you asking me?"

"Oh, I just thought that almost being murdered might have helped you to see your priorities."

Mogilnikov tugged the cigarette from his lips and stayed silent.

"So tell me, why did you make a run for it?"

"I thought you were with the other guy, of course. How was I to know you guys were the fairies?"

He let the chair down on all four legs, reached forward and flicked his cigarette ash at the tin lid on the desk. Grushko caught his wrist and whistled loudly.

"Now that's a very nice watch," he said, "eh, Sasha?"

"Looks expensive, sir."

Grushko scrutinised the brand name on the watch face.

"Rolex. Is it a real one?"

"Nah, of course not," said Mogilnikov. "It's one of those fakes. From Hong Kong. How could I afford a real one?"

"How indeed?" Grushko unbuckled the gold and stainless-steel strap. "Do you mind if I have a closer look?"

Mogilnikov shrugged uncertainly and then drew his hand out of the bracelet. Grushko turned the watch over and inspected the underside of the case.

"Amazing," he said. "I'll bet that only an expert could tell them apart." He pursed his lips and nodded. "You know, I've just thought of something. Maybe that's why the Georgian wanted to knife you: to get his hands on this watch. Those Georgians, they like flashy looking stuff like this."

"You don't say."

"What do you think, Sasha?" Grushko tossed him the watch.

"Hey," protested Mogilnikov, "be careful."

"Sorry," smiled Grushko. "But after all, it is a fake."

"Fake or not, it still cost money."

"Nice, very nice," said Sasha, nodding appreciatively. "Looks too good to be home-made."

"So who are you?" frowned Mogilnikov. "The militia's resident watchmaker?"

"No, but he will give you a pledge," said Grushko.

"Oh? And what might that be?"

"That it was you who fingered Vaja Ordzhonikidze."

"Vaja who? Look, what are you talking about?"

Sasha tossed Grushko the watch. Mogilnikov sighed and shook his head.

"You phoned him up," said Grushko. "You offered to sell him this watch." He dangled it in the air as if he had been teasing a catch with a piece of fish.

"You've been sitting on someone's needle."

"You told Ordzhonikidze that you'd washed this off some foreign tourist's arm, didn't you?"

"I never heard of the guy. And I didn't steal that watch."

"That's the real reason you were booked on the midnight plane from Georgia," declared Grushko. "You set Vaja up to get murdered."

Mogilnikov continued to shake his scrawny head.

"Just like it was you who helped to turn over Mikhail Milyukin's place," added Sasha.

"Mikhail who?"

"Maybe you helped to shoot them both," said Grushko. "Either way you're looking at the maximum fifteen years in the zone, strict regime. Felling timber in Perm . . ."

"Freezing winters," said Sasha, "blazing hot summers, miles away from anywhere. Even the guards don't want to go there, it's so remote. The camp there covers thirty-eight whole regions of the country. The place is vast and so empty that you might think the world had forgotten all about you."

"You don't scare me," said Mogilnikov.

"Good-looking fellow like you—make some *zek* a nice boy-girl," said Grushko with malicious pleasure. "If the mosquitoes don't drive you mad, or TB doesn't kill you first."

"You bastards," snarled Mogilnikov.

"Of course, the chances are," added Grushko, "that you may never even get there—now that the Georgians have marked you down for the top tower. You could be in sit at Kresti and they might still tickle your ribs, son. Isn't that so, Sasha?"

"Nothing easier. Those Georgians have got friends in every gaol in Peter. Price of killing a man when he's in sit is a couple of bags of scratch. Or maybe a loan of some-one's boy-girl for an afternoon."

Sweat started on Mogilnikov's pale forehead. He rubbed it away with his hand and then tore the cigarette from the corner of his trembling mouth. Ash fell unnoticed onto his trousers.

"Who put you up to it?" Grushko's voice sounded harsh and impatient. It was early in the morning and he wanted to go home.

"Nobody—"

"Who were the two men you went to Milyukin's flat with?"

"I—I don't know what you're talking about."

"Why did you kill Milyukin?"

"I never killed anyone.

Grushko sighed wearily and leaned back on his chair. He held the butt of his cigarette to another one and then screwed it out in the ashtray.

"You know, your life isn't worth five copecks unless you start talking to me, son."

Mogilnikov smiled a nervous, sarcastic sort of smile.

"And if I do? How much will it be worth then? Maybe less than that. It could be I am in danger, but I'm dead meat for sure the minute I open my mouth to you bastards."

Grushko shrugged, looked at the Rolex and then put it into his desk drawer.

"Hey, give that back," said Mogilnikov.

He was starting to stand until he met Grushko's hand, which pushed him back down onto his chair.

"Stay where you are," he said. "You'll get it back when I say. But only if you're a good boy."

Mogilnikov shook his head impatiently.

"I've got no time for your games," he said.

Grushko laughed harshly.

"Son," he said, "you've got nothing *but* time."

★　★　★

It was nine o'clock in the morning and they had just taken Pyotr Mogilnikov down to the lock-up when I arrived. Grushko explained the night's events while he shaved with an ancient electric razor. It looked like it had been designed to shear sheep.

"We'll transfer him across the river to Kresti later this morning," he announced. "Perhaps a stretch on remand will persuade him to change his mind. Organise it, will you, Sasha? But let's have someone keeping an eye on him. I don't want any accidents. And if we do manage to charge those Georgians we'd better make sure they're remanded somewhere else: Shpalerny or Nizhegorodsky, anywhere but Kresti."

He glanced round at me and grinned.

"Talking about Georgians, that reminds me. You've got a visitor."

CHAPTER

SEVENTEEN

★ Semyon Sergeyevich Luzhin was a brisk, small man, bald on top, with a short sandy-coloured beard and thick black-framed glasses, more like a university professor than the Mafia's favourite lawyer. He wore a checked short-sleeved shirt, grey flannel trousers, and was smoking a small cigar. I guessed him to be about fifty. I found him waiting in my office. He was reading some international law journal that was written in English but I decided that he probably did that just to impress me.

"Ah, there you are," he said and stood up politely.

We did not bother to shake hands, and although I knew exactly why Luzhin was there, I decided to let him earn his fee. So I sat down behind my desk and reached for my cigarettes. Luzhin offered me a cigar from the tin he had laid open on top of his papers, but by then I had already had the cigarette alight. I said nothing and watched him get ready to make his move.

He shuffled his papers, disposed of the cigar, glanced at me over the top of his glasses and finally spoke in a firm baritone, his manner brisk and businesslike.

"Now I understand that you are holding my clients," he said and proceeded to name every one of the seven Georgians, patronymics included, and all without consulting any of his notes.

That did impress me. Some of those Georgian names were a mouthful.

"You seem to know them very well," I said. "And you're very well-informed. We've only just picked them up."

"I'm on a permanent retainer with Mr. Gankrelidze and his colleagues," Luzhin said without a hint of embarrassment. "A friend of Mr. Gankrelidze contacted me late last night and informed me that they'd been arrested. I thought it best that I come straight here this morning." He paused and waited for me to say something, but when I merely shrugged at him, he smiled politely and added:

"I presumed that at some stage during the day you would observe the normal protocol whereby the suspects are reacquainted with the charges that are facing them, in the presence of their advocate. Well, I am here and I am at your disposal."

"Thank you, Mr. Luzhin, that's very helpful of you," I said. "But I'm not sure we'll be doing that until I've asked the State Prosecutor's Office for a search protocol."

"May one inquire what you are looking for?"

"I'm afraid not."

The fact of the matter was, I hadn't much of a clue what we could look for that was specifically related to the firebombing of the Pushkin Restaurant. I could hardly have asked Voznosensky for permission to search for some empty vodka bottles, some assorted rags, a can of gasoline, oil and a box of matches. The whole idea of a search protocol was simply a delaying tactic. I knew it. He knew it.

"And when will you be going to see the State Prosecutor?"

"Sometime today," I said vaguely.

He made a note with his gold pen and lit another of his

small cigars with a slimline gold lighter. I noticed that it was the same kind of lighter that Grushko had. Then I saw the gold watch and the gold wedding ring to match. Maybe he had a sensitive skin, I said to myself: one that could not bear the touch of any metal except gold.

"And what are the charges facing my clients?"

"Racketeering, extortion, arson and murder."

"Can you be more specific?"

"Not without compromising our witnesses. But I'll certainly keep you informed, Mr. Luzhin."

"Please do," he said, and taking out his crocodile leather wallet he handed me his business card. It was printed on both sides, in Russian and in English.

"Now then. I understand my clients were arrested early yesterday afternoon," he said. "That gives you fifty-three—well, let's be generous, say fifty-five—hours before you must either bring charges against my clients or release them."

"No, let's just say fifty-three," I said coolly. I didn't want any favours from this snake.

"Fifty-three it is then," he said, without sounding insulted, and made another note. "Naturally if my clients are charged I shall be applying for bail."

"Which I will oppose."

He smiled patiently.

"Might I see the interrogation protocols? I merely wish to ascertain that my clients' rights under Article 51 have been observed."

I opened my drawer and took out the file.

"Sometimes these fellows in Criminal Services can get a little carried away," he added by way of an apology.

"Not in this particular case," I said, handing him a sheaf of paper. "One protocol for each of the seven dwarves. I think you'll find everything's in order, Mr. Luzhin."

"Thank you," he said and inspected them carefully.

When he was satisfied he returned them to me and puffed several times at his cigar, almost as if he had been about to light a length of fuse.

"You're not from St. Petersburg, are you?"

"Moscow."

"You'll like it here," he said confidently. "It's a very civilised sort of city."

I thought of the firebomb sailing through the window of the Pushkin Restaurant, the bodies at the monument to the Heroes of Leningrad and outside the cinema on Nevsky, and nodded politely.

"Much friendlier than Moscow. Let me know if I can be of service to you."

He collected up his papers and placed them inside a smart black leather attaché case. Then he lingered as if there was something else he wished to tell me.

"It's several years since I went to Moscow," he announced. "The last time was in 1987. Margaret Thatcher was on a visit to the Soviet Union. I saw her when she was walking round the city."

I smiled. Luzhin just wanted to be able to talk to another lawyer, someone who wasn't a criminal at least. I wondered if Thatcher's trip to Moscow had also been the occasion of Mikhail Milyukin meeting her.

"That's a very great lady," he said. "A very great lady indeed."

This was not an uncommon view. Most Russians were of the opinion that "little Maggie," as she was affectionately known, would have made a great Russian premier.

"Yes," I said, "but don't forget: the British had the same opinion of Gorbachev."

★ ★ ★

Grushko had disappeared when I returned to his office. Nor was there any sign of Nikolai or Sasha. But Andrei was in his usual seat, staring at the telephone; however, on this occasion he was looking rather pleased with himself.

"Where's Grushko?" I asked.

"Gone out with Nikolai," he said. "They're checking out a lead." He grinned proudly. "Something I turned up with that telephone inquiry."

"Well done," I said. "What was it?"

"You remember that body they found the other day—Tolya?"

"The one with the electric-iron burns? I could hardly forget it."

"Turns out he worked for one of those Anglo-Russian joint-venture companies. An outfit called Anglo-Soyuzatom Transit. One of their truck-drivers apparently. They're in the nuclear-waste-disposal business."

"Grushko told me they just dumped the stuff in the ocean. I guess he must have meant the low-level stuff."

"You mean there's more than one type?"

"Low-level, intermediate and high-level. You need a proper disposal programme for the intermediate and high-level stuff."

"Sounds like you know something about it, sir."

"Only what I read in the papers, and see on TV."

"Then maybe you can tell me," he said, consulting his notebook. "Radio-biology: is that anything to do with nuclear?"

I shrugged.

"Haven't we got a dictionary round here?"

Andrei laughed and shook his head. "We haven't even got a telephone directory."

"Well, isn't there a library in this building?"

"Not that I know about."

I picked up the phone and asked the operator to put me through to Colonel Shelaeva's office in Scientific Research. When at last I was connected I explained my problem to her.

"Radio-biology?" she said. "It's a branch of biology that is concerned with the effects of radioactive substances on living organisms. Why do you ask?"

I looked at Andrei.

"Why do you want to know?"

"Well it might just be a coincidence," he explained, "what with this Tolya fellow working for Anglo-Soyuzatom Transit, but there's a Dr. Sobchak in Mikhail Milyukin's address book. She works at the Pavlov—the Medical University here in Peter. Well, when I rang up to speak to her they told me that she was away on holiday. And so I asked what kind of a doctor she was and they said a radio-biologist."

"Did you hear that?" I said to Shelaeva.

"More or less," she said. "And you can tell that detective something important from me. Tell him that it's always a mistake to dismiss things as a coincidence in a criminal investigation. Coincidence is what this business is all about."

With that advice she rang off.

"What did she say?"

"Radio-biology: it's to do with the effects of radiation on living organisms. And she says to tell you that coincidence is what this business is all about."

Andrei pulled a face.

"Bitch," he said. "Now you know why I didn't phone her myself. You risk a bloody lecture every time you ask for a lousy fingerprint. Reckon it's worth calling Grushko on the car phone and telling him? I mean about Dr. Sobchak."

"Why not?" I said. "Maybe the people at Anglo-Soyuz will have heard of her."

I lit a cigarette and watched Andrei write down the definition as provided by Colonel Shelaeva.

"Where is this joint-venture anyway?" I asked.

"About seventy-five kilometres west of here, along the coast on the road to Sosnovy Bor."

I glanced at my watch.

"Then I may be gone by the time they're back," I said. "Look, I've got to go to Moscow this afternoon. To pick up my car. Perhaps you wouldn't mind telling Grushko that I'll be back tomorrow, mid-morning with any luck."

"Sure," said Andrei. He lit a cigarette and gave me a sideways sort of look, as if trying to gauge what kind of character I was. "Mind if I ask you a question?"

"Go ahead."

"Do you like the ballet?"

"When I can afford it."

"We've got a pretty good one here in Peter. I'm a close friend of the director. Maybe I could get you some free tickets."

I wondered what someone like Andrei could possibly have done for the director of the Kirov.

"I get it. Do a favour for a good man, right?"

"Something like that," he said.

"So what is it you want?"

"Well, when you're in Moscow, if you happen to see any music tapes—but especially the new Michael Jackson album ..." He took out his wallet and handed me two greasy five-dollar bills. "For my son's birthday," he added quickly.

I pocketed his ten dollars.

"Kids," I muttered. "They've got a lot to answer for."

★　★　★

Andrei called Grushko after I had left and told him about Dr. Sobchak.

"So where's she gone on holiday?" he asked.

"A friend's *dacha*. The secretary wasn't exactly sure where that was."

"So you'd better find out, hadn't you?"

Then Andrei remembered to pass on my message.

"Has he gone yet?"

"About ten minutes ago."

"Damn," said Grushko. "I wanted him to get me some chocolate."

★ ★ ★

With the exception of the high wire fence that marked its perimeter, Anglo-Soyuzatom Transit, situated in a remote birch forest on the shores of the Gulf of Finland, did not look like the kind of place that had anything to do with Russia's nuclear-power industry. There were no tall towers or bubble-shaped reactors. No security guards and no dog patrol. The small collections of buildings that comprised the Russian headquarters of the joint-venture company were all pre-Revolutionary in their construction with the largest a well-restored *dacha* that might have belonged to some Finnish aristocrat in the days before that part of the coast came to be Russian. Built of white brick with grey pointing and a grey roof, it had a small Palladian-style portico and so many different shapes and sizes of window that Grushko was tempted to suppose that the original architect must have had some private deal with a local glazier.

The battered Zhiguli carrying the two detectives drew up alongside a smart new BMW. They got out, admired the other car briefly and then walked up the steps to the front door.

The building's interior was no less impressive to Grushko and Nikolai than the exterior: wall-to-wall thick wool carpets and expensive hardwood furniture. Near the door was a polished walnut desk on top of which was a computer. Peering at the four-colour monitor were an extremely attractive-looking girl of about twenty and, behind her, an academic-looking type with rimless glasses and a strong line in aftershave. The man straightened when he saw the two detectives.

"Can I help you?" he said.

"This is Anglo-Soyuzatom?" Grushko sounded uncertain. He hadn't been expecting anything like this.

"That's right. I'm Yuri Gidaspov, transit controller here."

Grushko produced his identity card and gave the man a long look at it.

"Colonel Grushko, from the Criminal Services Department, sir," he said. "And this is Major Vladimirov."

Nikolai's eyes were busy with the secretary's thighs, easily visible under the remnant of skirt that she was wearing.

"It's about Tolya," Grushko explained. "Anatoly Boldyrev. I understand he worked here."

Gidaspov's face registered a fleeting look of discomfort.

"Ah yes," he said hesitantly. "I spoke to your lieutenant earlier this morning, didn't I? Look er ... why don't we go into my office and discuss this."

"No calls, Katya," he said to the girl on the desk, and ushered them towards a shiny pine door.

Grushko's eyes crossed the ceiling and the walls.

"We're not what you imagined, eh, Colonel?" said Gidaspov, opening his office door.

"No indeed, sir."

"The place used to belong to a member of the Politburo. As a matter of fact, he's still here, in one of the smaller guest-sized *dachi* on the estate. We can't get rid of him unless we can prove he came to live here illegally, but there's no documentary evidence to prove anything either way."

"Evidence can be tricky stuff," Grushko observed.

"Not that he gives us any trouble. Keeping his head down, I shouldn't wonder. Still, he knew how to live well,

I'll say that for him. There's a sauna, a billiard-room, an indoor swimming pool, a movie theatre—we use it as a lecture theatre—and six tennis courts. The tennis courts are where we park our trucks for the moment. ASA bought the place from the Russian government for $2 million."

"Is that all?" said Grushko.

Nikolai whistled quietly. Gidaspov closed the door behind them. Grushko silently crossed the wide expanse of carpet and came round the mausoleum-sized desk to the picture window. In front of a row of trees he could see the tennis courts and on one of them was parked the most futuristic-looking truck Grushko had ever seen. It looked like one of the UFOs dreamed up by the Director of the Police Academy.

"You seem to want for nothing, sir," he said. "Is that one of your trucks there?"

"Yes. Quite something isn't it. Cost $1 million, and there are four more the same as that one." He picked a packet of Winstons off the desk and offered one to Grushko.

Grushko seemed about to accept one, but changed his mind. He had only wished to take a closer look at the packet—to see from which end the packet had been opened.

"No, thanks, sir," he said, taking out his own pack of Astra, "I'll stick to my own. It's best that I'm not reminded of how bad they taste in comparison with yours." He pointed towards the truck again.

"Did Tolya drive one of those?"

"Yes, he did. Tolya was one of our best drivers actually. He was with us since the beginning, about ten months ago. Before that he worked for SOTRA, driving to Afghanistan, India and Iran for Irantransit and then for Yuzhtransit. He came highly recommended, like all our drivers. Well, you can imagine what our vetting procedures are like. Ingostrakh, the state insurance organisation, was very strict about the kind of men we could employ: only the best drivers with absolutely clean licences.

"Anyway, about a month ago Tolya started to become unreliable. Family problems of one sort or another. He started drinking rather a lot. There was never any question of him driving under the influence, you understand, but it meant that he was late on a number of occasions. I'm afraid I had been intending to dismiss him, Colonel. But before that happened he just stopped coming to work altogether. That's why we've one vehicle still here instead of on convoy.

"Of course I had no idea that something had happened to him. I tried telephoning him. I even went round to his address once." Gidaspov shrugged. "To be honest with you, I assumed his drinking had got the better of him, and that he was probably out on a bender." He sighed and shook his head. "Poor Tolya. Have you any idea how he died?"

"He was murdered, sir," said Grushko. "Shot through the head. But only after someone had tortured him with an electric iron."

"Good God," breathed Gidaspov. "But why . . . ?"

"That's what we're trying to find out, sir," said Grushko. "It might help if you could tell us a little more about your work here."

"You don't think it might be connected, do you, Colonel?" Grushko sucked nervously at his cigarette. "Oh, I'm sure it wasn't."

"We're investigating all the possibilities, sir," said Grushko. "No matter how remote."

Gidaspov nodded and then remembered Grushko's request for an outline of the company's operation.

"Well, Colonel, as you may or may not know, there are four reactors working at Sosnovy Bor, and reactors produce waste. Our past record in the matter of waste disposal has not been a good one in this country. And many of the

RBMKs operating in Russia, Lithuania and the Ukraine are in poor condition. At the same time they also provide half of the former Soviet Union's nuclear electricity. So you can see how important they are.

"In order to qualify for certain international loans to help us modernise these plants, Russia has agreed to cooperate with the International Atomic Energy Authority in the matter of nuclear-waste disposal. In the short term we are dealing only with intermediate-level waste from the local facility and the Lithuanian reactor at Ignalina. But when St. Petersburg becomes a free economic zone it is hoped that it will become an entrepôt for the whole of northern Europe's nuclear waste.

"The waste itself is sealed inside steel drums and loaded onto our part-refrigerated vehicles. As you can see they're even part armoured in case of accident. The British led the field in this particular area and they have provided the technical know-how, and the trucks themselves, of course. The trucks then take the barrels to our long-term encapsulation plant."

"In other words," said Grushko, "the West is helping us to modernise our own nuclear reactors in return for letting them dump their waste with us."

"That's about the size of it, Colonel, yes. Of course it's not just waste that needs to be dealt with. There is also the matter of transporting nuclear warheads to destruction sites. There are already plans afoot for us to operate another specially designed fleet of trucks to cope with that problem as well."

"But why transport all this stuff by road?" asked Nikolai. "Surely rail would be a lot safer?"

"Forgive me, Major, but anywhere else and I might agree with you. Here in Russia, however, most people don't own a car and when they travel any distance at all they go by train. Passengers take priority on the railways. That makes rail freight slow and unreliable. You can't afford any delays where the transport of radioactive material is involved."

"I'm sure you've investigated all the feasibilities with an operation like this," said Grushko. "But I would like a chance to speak to some of your other drivers. Men who knew Tolya. Ones he may have got drunk with, maybe. Perhaps they can help to shed some light on his death." He shook his head vaguely. "He may have said something to someone."

"By all means, Colonel, only you'll have to wait for a few days. At least until the convoy returns from the disposal site."

"And where is that, sir?"

"Didn't I say? It's in southern Byelorussia, on the Ukrainian border. Near Pripyat."

"But that's close to Chernobyl, isn't it, sir?" said Nikolai.

"Three kilometres away, to be precise."

"I thought there was some sort of exclusion zone in operation around the whole area." Nikolai was frowning now. He didn't much care for the nuclear industry. Nobody did in St. Petersburg. Not since the leak of radioactive iodine gas from the reactor at Sosnovy Bor.

"You're right, there is," said Gidaspov. "A hundred-kilometre exclusion zone, enforced by the KGB. But the zone does not apply to nuclear-industrial personnel. After all, three of the four reactors in Chernobyl are still in operation."

"Three still operating? I didn't know that," said Nikolai.

Gidaspov tried to look reassuring.

"I can assure you that this is all perfectly in order, gentlemen," he said smoothly. "The whole programme has the full blessing of our own Ministry of Atomic Energy and the IAEA, not to mention the new Nuclear Power Plant Operating Directorate of the Russian Federation. Why, just last week we had a team over from the SKE—that's the Swedish nuclear-installations inspectorate.

"And after all, the waste does have to go somewhere. The exclusion zone at Pripyat already has 800 separate burial sites containing 500 million cubic metres of radioactive scrap and debris from the accident at the Chernobyl reactor." He shrugged. "That's land that will never be reclaimed. Can you think of a better place for a nuclear-waste-disposal facility than somewhere that is already impossibly contaminated?"

"No, I guess not," admitted Grushko. "It makes a change from just dumping it into the ocean, I suppose." He paused and lit another cigarette.

"You said you undertook vetting procedures for all your drivers, sir: does that mean you keep personnel files on them?"

"Nothing wrong with that, is there?"

"No, of course not. I just wondered if you might let me have Tolya Boldyrev's file. There might be something in his background that is relevant to our inquiry."

"Yes, I'm sorry. I didn't mean to sound defensive."

Gidaspov unlocked a filing-cabinet and pulled out a drawer. He sorted through the contents and then took our a file that he handed to Grushko.

"You'll find everything in there," he said. "Address, passport number, medical report, employment records, everything right back to when he was in the Young Pioneers."

"Thank you, sir." Grushko handed Gidaspov his card. "When the convoy does return, I'd be grateful if you could give me a ring."

Nikolai followed Grushko to the door.

"One more thing, Mr. Gidaspov," said Grushko. "Are you at all familiar with a Dr. Sobchak?"

"No, I don't think I've heard of him."

Grushko nodded. He did not bother to correct

Gidaspov's assumption that Sobchak was a man. It seemed only to confirm that his answer had been an honest one. Instead he thanked him for his time, once again complimented Gidaspov on the excellence of the facilities at ASA and then left.

He and Nikolai then spent the remainder of a hot and sticky afternoon fruitlessly inquiring into the particulars of Tolya Boldyrev's life.

CHAPTER

EIGHTEEN

★ I came out of Leningrad Railway Station (Muscovites continued to call the station that served travellers to St. Petersburg by its old name) and caught a trolley bus going south. It was good to be back in Moscow and, even at that early hour of the morning, the place felt more affluent, more like a big city than Petersburg. People moved with more of a spring in their step. The traffic moved faster. There were already more of the gold-coloured aluminum kiosks housing privately owned shops than I remembered from before; and it seemed that there was more food about than in St. Petersburg. But the prices were hard to believe. How could people afford to buy things?

I got off the bus and walked west along the Boulevard Ring to the Militia Headquarters that was located just north of the Ring, at Number 38 Petrovka, close to the old Hermitage Gardens. From the outside the Moscow Big House was very different from its St. Petersburg counterpart: the neoclassical frontage looked on to an attractive garden with flower beds, herbaceous borders and a marble monument of the militia insignia's sword. But inside the place was more or less identical.

I went through the security turnstile, walked through the garden to the front door and rode the lift up to the second floor. Shaverdova's secretary, Irina, was making tea. She did not look surprised to see me.

"Is he free?" I asked her.

"Yes," she said.

I knocked at the door and went in. Vladimir Shaverdova, the Chief of Moscow's Organized Crime Department, was on the telephone. He waved me towards him and started writing something on a piece of paper. I sat down and lit a cigarette while I waited for him to finish his call. The only pictures in his office were the ones of his wife and family that lay under the sheet of glass on his desk.

Shaverdova was a tall, dark man, with one of those heads that looked as if it had grown through his hair, and a rather sulky, childish sort of mouth. He wore a claret-coloured three-piece suit, a light-grey shirt and a black tie.

Irina came through the door with his tea. Shaverdova replaced the receiver and collected the cup and saucer from her.

"You want some tea?" he asked me.

"Thanks, I could use one."

Irina nodded and went out again.

Shaverdova nodded at the telephone.

"Guess what?" he said. "That was Khasbulatov."

Khasbulatov was the Moscow State Prosecutor.

"We just charged Batsunov with accepting bribes."

"You're joking."

Arkady Batsunov was the Assistant State Prosecutor who had been responsible for the majority of the prosecutions involving the Organised Crime Division. Most of my investigative life in Moscow had been spent in preparing cases for him. Arkady Batsunov had also been my friend.

"It's true," said Shaverdova. "He's admitted it. Well he could hardly do anything else. We caught him red-handed, taking a twenty-thousand-rouble bribe from a Dazhakstani.

We found over a hundred thousand roubles at his apartment."

Irina returned with my tea and I sipped it thoughtfully while Shaverdova took another call. Arkady Batsunov, corrupt. It seemed incredible. I wondered if they imagined that I might also be corrupt. Guilt by association.

Shaverdova finished the call and lit a cigarette.

"I'd never have believed it," I said.

Shaverdova shrugged silently. "So how are things going in St. Petersburg?" he asked. "What have you found?"

"Nothing," I said. "Not a damn thing. And you know me—I've got a nose for corruption. Well, if they are bent, I can't spot it."

"You've looked in all the usual places?"

"Of course. You know me. I'm nothing if not thorough. Shit, I've even looked under Grushko's mattress. If you ask me they're clean. Most honest bunch of cops I've seen in a long time. I can't imagine why Kornilov ordered this investigation."

Shaverdova shrugged.

"It's up to him. It's his department."

"Besides, I'm pretty sure Grushko knows what I'm up to. He wasn't much impressed by all that crap about intercity liaison, and finding out about the way they handle things in St. Petersburg."

"Grushko's not stupid." He flicked some ash towards the ashtray. "So what's he doing with you? Is he playing things close to his chest? Or what?"

"He couldn't be more open. I've even been to his home."

"So I gathered. Well, that's good. If he were bent he wouldn't have let you through the door. So what's the story?"

"They need a new carpet, and the colour TV's on the blink. The wife was planning to trade some English soaps in order to get hold of a piece of beef. If there's any extra money around it isn't coming from Grushko. The daughter's a doctor. She's seeing a yuppie who makes plenty of money on the local exchange. Could be he's some kind of crook, but you can hardly hold that against Grushko. Besides, he hates the boy's guts."

"What about the others?"

"Like I say, they seem clean enough."

"Well, 'seem' isn't 'is.' After all, we all thought Batsunov was on the side of the angels, didn't we? And look what happened to him. So just keep at it for a while longer, will you? I know it's a lousy job but it has to be done. Well, I don't have to tell you that. You've done this sort of thing before. If they're straight then they've got nothing to worry about. Besides, it's not like you're not trying to catch them out; you're just trying to prove that they're on the level, right?"

I nodded gloomily.

"Right."

★ ★ ★

Emerging from the Big House I walked south down Petrovka and into the large square that was the downhill end of the shopping street of Kuznetsky Most, which still retained a faded echo of its grander, pre-Revolutionary days. To the left of the Bolshoi Theatre was a modern glass building called TSUM, the Central Universal Store, and it was there that I found a hard-currency music shop that sold Andrei's Michael Jackson tape. It was depressing to see just how many shops now had signs in their windows declaring themselves "Hard Currency Only." It would soon be impossible to buy anything with the rouble.

I went down into the underground passageway that led to the Metro. It was full of beggars: gypsy women with children, an old woman who was busking with an accordion to pay for an operation, a teenage war-veteran both of whose legs had been blown off just above the knee, and yet more drunks. There were people selling pornographic newspapers, and others offering to trade whatever small surplus they had: a bottle of vodka, a packet of American cigarettes, a pair of boots, chocolate, and a set of bed-sheets.

I bought a couple of tokens and boarded a northbound Metro. Even the price of a token had quadrupled in price.

My apartment was just off Mira Prospekt, in Duboyava Roshcha. From the bedroom window you could just see the soaring obelisk that marked the Memorial Museum of Cosmonautics, a pompous and wholly unrealistic celebration of Soviet scientific and technological achievement. I rode the lift up to the sixth floor and knocked at the front door. When after a minute or two there was no reply, I found my keys and let myself in. I was surprised to see there was nobody at home, although it was not quite nine o'clock. I was not sorry that my wife and her lover were out of the apartment. But I almost missed seeing my daughter. Then I found a note that explained that they had gone away for a few days to our *dacha* in the country. I had been planning to go there myself on my journey back to St. Petersburg to pick up a few of my books. But now I was more inclined to give the place a wide berth. Still, I wasn't about to let my wife acquire the *dacha* as well as our apartment, and I told myself that she would have to ask permission to use it in future. My father had built that *dacha* and I intended to keep it.

I put the piece of cheese I had bought for her in the fridge and helped myself to some breakfast. There was some chocolate so I took that too. Then, having found my head gasket waiting for me on the dining table, I put on my overalls, collected my tools and went down to the locked compound where I had left my car. It wasn't a complicated job and I had it fixed within a couple of hours. By eleven I had washed and was on the road.

★ ★ ★

I'll admit it was not a very professional thing that I did. Especially for an investigator. Detectives have more leeway in these matters. For example, a detective is allowed to have an informer, but an investigator is not. But when you've spent several hours on the M10 from Moscow—a journey of over 500 kilometres—you're not always thinking straight. That's half of my excuse anyway. The other half? I expect I was feeling sorry for myself.

So there I was, coming along Nevsky at just around three o'clock that same afternoon when I saw her.

Nina Milyukin was standing at a tram stop in front of the House of Books, reputedly the largest bookshop in the city. In pre-Revolutionary days the building had belonged to the Singer Sewing-Machine Company, but it might just as well have belonged to them still for all the books they sold in there now. The line for the tram was enormous and I didn't think she would be getting on one for a while. She looked as sad as ever, her arms folded in front of her in that way women have when they're waiting for something that isn't going to arrive. But she was just as beautiful as I remembered. She was wearing a light black and white print dress with a wide lacy collar and in her hand was an empty shopping bag.

I pulled up next to the line, leaned across the passenger seat and wound down the car window.

"Nina Romanovna," I called to her.

At first she did not recognise me, but then slowly she came forward.

"Can I offer you a lift somewhere?"

She seemed inclined to refuse, but straightening up she took another look at the number of people who were waiting for a tram. The day was already a hot one and even the shortest tram journey was likely to prove uncomfortable. For a moment the car window framed the swell of her belly against the thin material of her dress, and I thought of that photograph on Mikhail Milyukin's pinboard. Not much of a sex life when you think about it, but at the time it seemed better than nothing.

"I don't think I'll be going your way," she said leaning in the car window again. "I'm going to the television centre to pick up some of my husband's things."

"Then hop in."

"Well, if you're sure it's no trouble."

"It's no trouble," I said, although it was considerably out of my way, "no trouble at all."

When she got in I pulled out into a space in the traffic and headed west.

"You'll have to direct me when we get across the Neva," I told her. "I'm still not all that familiar with the streets here."

She smiled politely and nodded.

"Is this your car?" she asked after a moment or two.

"Yes. I've just driven it up from Moscow."

"It's nice."

"It belonged to my father," I explained. "When it goes, it goes very well, but the spares are a problem. And the tyres are very worn. I wouldn't like to drive it in winter."

"I'd say that's when you need a car most."

"My wife used to think the same."

"And now she agrees with you?" She sounded surprised.

"Now it really doesn't matter what she thinks. She's living with my daughter's music teacher. Or rather, he's living with her."

Nina laughed, the first time that I had ever heard her amused by something.

"I'm sorry," she said, stifling it with the back of her hand. "It's not funny."

"There's a funny side to it. She's only interested in his money."

"Now you really are joking," she said. "Teachers don't make money."

"Music teachers do," I insisted. "Especially when they've studied at a top piano school. Around 25,000 roubles a month, some of them. Anyway, my wife thinks he's one of those."

"And he isn't?"

"No."

She laughed. "Twenty-five thousand," she said. "That's more than a surgeon."

"It's more than a government minister. What you have to bear in mind is that most families will make any amount of sacrifices for their children. Especially when it comes to music. Especially when the teacher tells the parents that their child is gifted."

"And your daughter? Is she gifted?"

I laughed. "My daughter is as tone deaf as her mother. He just told us she was gifted in order to justify the tuition fees. You can't say he's not trying hard to make as much as the best of them."

We went past the Hermitage and across the Palace Bridge on to the eastern point of Vasilyostrovsky Island, with the two red Rostral columns to our right, before crossing the river once more. In front of the walls of the Peter and Paul Fortress some of the city's more zealous sun-worshippers were trying to catch the afternoon rays. They stood flat against the grey granite, as if held there by gravitational force, their bodies almost colourless from many months of wearing winter clothing.

"You're not at all like that other policeman," she said. "Colonel Grushko. He's made of stone, that one."

"Grushko's all right," I told her. "But he takes this investigation very seriously."

"I don't think he likes me very much."

"That's nonsense. Why on earth should he dislike you?"

She shrugged and was apparently unwilling to offer a reason.

"Grushko gets impatient," I added. "He wants to know everything right away. He can't seem to understand that you might need a little more time before you can talk about Mikhail Mikhailovich. But he means well. I'm sure of it."

"It won't bring Mikhail back," she said, the sadness returning to her face. "So what good is it if he does mean well?" She sighed and looked out of the window. "Even if you do catch the men who killed him, it won't make any difference. 'I think I can summon up words, as pristine as those in your song, but if I don't, I won't give a damn, I don't care if I'm wrong.' "

Nina glanced over at me, her face reddening a little with embarrassment.

"You're going to think me such a fraud, quoting poetry at you like this," she said, smiling gently. "I'm always doing it. I did it with your Colonel Grushko when he told me . . . I don't think he cared very much for it. Still, I was quite surprised at him knowing Pasternak like that."

"Grushko's not the only cop who can quote poetry," I said.

"Yes, but with him it's done with a reason. I'm only guessing, mind, but he strikes me as the kind of person who would read a poem in order to learn something—something that might help him to understand a man's soul for example—and not for its own sake. In other words he does it like a policeman—to gain an insight into a man's soul."

"I think you're being a bit unfair," I said. "You make Grushko sound rather terrifying."

"Oh, but he is," she insisted. "He terrifies me, anyway. He's like one of those people who used to work for the NKVD. Ruthless, single-minded and utterly dedicated to what they do. No room for shades of meaning. Just black and white. Right and wrong."

"You couldn't be more wrong," I said. "He's a democrat. He was one of the first men in the Central Board to come out against the Party."

"You don't understand," she said. "I wasn't speaking politically. I was talking about the Man. And I don't know that being one of the first men in your department to come out against the Party counts for very much anyway. Except to say that he must be more dangerous than I thought."

I shook my head and smiled. "I'm not sure I understand that either," I said.

"Never mind," she said and smiled back.

By the time we reached the TV station I realized that I simply had to see her again.

"Look," I said, remembering the Michael Jackson tape I had brought for Andrei. "I have a friend who's offered me two tickets for the Kirov. I was wondering—?"

"I don't think I'd be very good company," she said, getting out of the car. "Besides, I'm not sure your Colonel Grushko would approve."

"I can't imagine why he would object."

"No, perhaps not. Even so, there are some things which he might find it hard to understand."

She closed the door and leaned in through the window.

"You're very kind," she said. "Please don't think me proud or ungrateful. I'm just not ready yet."

"Of course. I understand. It was stupid of me."

"Look, when you know all there is to know about what happened, when all this is over, if you still want to ask me, then give me a ring."

"All right."

"Promise?"

"Yes."

But things didn't work out that way. Nothing ever

works out as it should. Not these days. Not in the New Commonwealth of Independent States.

★ ★ ★

Grushko was in a sombre mood when I saw him again. He had spent the morning attending the execution of Gerassim "the Butcher," a notorious Mafioso who had killed four members of a rival gang with a meat cleaver and then fed their dismembered limbs to his pet dogs. It's always a problem, feeding pets in Russia.

All the same it is not very often that a murderer actually faces a firing squad. There are perhaps no more than fifteen to twenty executions a year and a death sentence is frequently commuted to fifteen years' "strict regime." Only the most bestial murderers such as serial killers and child murderers are shot. But the courts have a special abhorrence of cases that have some anthropophagous aspect, such as the Black Sea Widow case or the infamous Chakatilo who lived to eat his victims' genitals. Perhaps this had something to do with the fact that real meat is such a valuable commodity. Or maybe it is because people want to forget that cannibalism had actually taken place during the famines that Stalin had inflicted on the Ukraine during the 1930s. Whatever the reason, feeding a man to your dogs is considered almost as terrible as eating him yourself, and Gerassim had found himself subject to the full force of the law.

Grushko nodded grimly as he recalled the circumstances of the man's execution. I knew that he approved of the death sentence, and although it was not the first time he had been obliged to attend an execution it was clear that he had been deeply affected by this morning's experience. But I had no doubt that it would not have altered his opinion about capital punishment.

"He died like a man," Grushko said with some admiration. With a careless shrug he added: "I had to have a word with him first, mind you: to tell him to hold his head up. But he died OK. You know what he said when they tied him to the post? He said, 'You can't shoot us all.' " He uttered a short laugh. "How about that, eh? 'You can't shoot us all.' "

"Supposing we did," I said. "You and I would be out of a job."

Grushko shrugged. "Might be worth it at that."

There was something in the way he said this that made me think he might almost be serious, and I was reminded of what Nina Milyukin had said about him: that he was the kind of man for whom there was only right and wrong and nothing in between.

I told him that I had seen her, although I said nothing about my having invited her to the ballet. I hoped he might say something to confound the opinion she held of him but instead he just shook his head, as if somehow he remained disappointed in her.

"She thinks you don't much like her," I said.

He raised his eyebrows with surprise.

"Do you think it's that obvious?"

I shrugged. "Is it true?"

"As a matter of fact, I don't like her at all," he said flatly.

"Why on earth not?"

"I have my reasons."

He regarded my obvious exasperation closely and seemed somehow to guess at what I had left unsaid. His eyes narrowed.

"Let me give you some advice, my friend," he said darkly. "If you are thinking of seeing—that woman—"

He paused as if it had occurred to him that he might have overstepped that mark.

"Not that I could stop you, mind. She's a good-looking woman and what you do is your own affair. But you and I, we ought to be friends as well as colleagues. And as someone who wishes to be your friend I should tell you that you would be best advised to leave Nina Milyukin alone."

"Is she under any kind of suspicion?"

"No. She's done nothing illegal."

"Then what?"

"I'm afraid I can't tell you. There's a matter of some confidentiality here. A matter that I have to speak to her about. It would be unfair if I were to discuss it with you first. But trust me when I ask you to keep away from her."

For a moment he held my perplexed stare.

"It was just a thought," I said. "Something that came into my mind. You're right. I do find her attractive." I nodded with slow acquiescence and then shrugged. "All right. I'll leave her alone. On one condition."

"What's that?"

"That you'll explain when you think you're able."

"Very well," said Grushko. "When this case is closed, perhaps. Ask me then."

"You know, it's funny," I remarked, "but that's exactly what she said."

For a little while after this I sat in my office and tried to guess at what Grushko had been alluding to. But before I had time to think of anything we had a call from the governor of Kresti Prison, to say that Pyotr Mogilnikov had changed his mind. It seemed that he now wished to cooperate with our investigation after all.

CHAPTER

NINETEEN

★ Remand Centre IZ 45/1 at Kresti, also known as "Crosses," was just across the Neva from the Big House and a stone's throw from the famous *Aurora* cruiser, which fired the shot that signalled the storming of the Winter Palace in 1917. It was the loudest shot in history.

Built in the time of Catherine the Great, Crosses takes its name from the red-brick Byzantine cross that adorns the front of the panopticon shape. Once it had been a model of Russian penology, holding up to 800 inmates. Two hundred years after Catherine, Crosses holds 7,000 men and is an example of everything that is verminous and dehumanising about the Russian prison system.

We collected our visiting numbers at the main door and then, escorted by a prison wardress of Olympic shot-putting proportions, we made our way, one at a time, through the arrangement of locked doors and turnstiles until we reached the interview-room. Beside this was a concrete isolation cell that was the size and proportions of a safe in a large bank. The wardress selected a key from the bunch on her enormous leather belt, opened the isolation cell's massive steel door and barked an order at the man who was seated inside.

Pyotr Mogilnikov rose unsteadily to his feet and then

followed us into the interview-room, which was itself not much bigger than a sauna bath.

The wardress left the three of us alone and we sat down on opposite sides of a table that had been screwed very firmly to the floor. Grushko tossed his cigarettes across the table and sniffed the air suspiciously.

"What is that smell?" he said.

Mogilnikov grimaced. "One of the guys in the cell," he explained unhappily; "his pet cat pissed on me."

"Is that what persuaded you to talk to us?" Grushko chuckled.

"Funny," snarled Mogilnikov and lit a cigarette. "You knew, didn't you? You knew they'd try and nail me in here."

"You mean someone's tried already."

"Not as such, no." Mogilnikov trembled as he spoke. "But when I walked into my cell there was this guy, see? Razumikhin. They called him the Undertaker. He knew my name, like he'd been expecting me. And I knew, I just knew, that someone had got me into that particular cell so that Razumikhin could kill me. It didn't matter that I hadn't talked. They still want me dead."

"They're more organised than I thought," said Grushko. "They certainly didn't waste any time. Those Georgians must want you out of the way badly. Lucky for you that we were keeping an eye on you."

Mogilnikov frowned. "Who said anything about the Georgians?" He took a deep, agitated drag at his cigarette.

"Maybe you've forgotten the other night," I said.

"This isn't the Georgians," he said. "Not this time."

"Who then: the Chechens?"

Mogilnikov snorted with contempt.

"You really don't know much do you?" He shook his head with pity. "Look, Grushko, I want a deal."

"There are no loans for the naked. Not in my book." Grushko was beginning to look impatient. His fists were clenched so tight that his fingers were turning white and his mouth was a narrow, angry slit.

"Come on Grushko. I'm good for it."

"You won't be good for propping up a fence if you're dead," said Grushko.

Mogilnikov sighed and lit another cigarette.

"I'm not an informer," he said. "But if they think I've pinched them then—"

Grushko leaned swiftly across the table and caught Mogilnikov by his shirt collar. He twisted it hard and then yanked the man's head down sharply against the table top with a loud bang. He did it again for good measure.

"You're just what I say you are and nothing more, you little shitbag," he growled. "If I tell you to write me an essay on your mother's sex life, you'll do it and enjoy it, or I'll toss you back on the bunk where you belong. Understand?"

"All right, all right." Mogilnikov pulled Grushko's hand away from his collar and then rubbed his head unhappily. "Take it easy, will you?"

Grushko sat back on his chair and tugged the sleeve of his jacket down over his shirt-cuff. He picked up his cigarettes and lit one. Smoking it he seemed to recover some of his composure.

"If what I hear sounds useful," he said, "then maybe—just maybe—we can do a deal. My word on it. And most of the *zeks* in here will tell you you can't cut my word with an axe. All right?"

Mogilnikov nodded sullenly and retrieved his own cigarette from where it had fallen on the floor.

"Let's start with the burglary, shall we?" said Grushko. "Who handed you the apple?"

"It was some Ukrainians."

Grushko shot me a look of surprise.

"I don't know their names. But from what they said,

they'd spent some time in the zone. Maybe if I were to look at some photographs . . ."

"Not so fast," said Grushko. "Before we get to look at pictures we need to hear some more story."

"It was a job to order, just like you said. I was in the bar at the Leningradskaya Hotel and these two foreheads just came up and started talking. They bought some vodka and said they'd heard of me and wanted me to do a little job for them. All I had to do was wash some keys out a guy's pocket and then keep an eye while they turned his flat over. They told me there was a thing in it for me. Five hundred then and 500 when the job was done.

"So the next day we waited in their car outside this address on Griboyedev."

"What kind of a car?" said Grushko.

"An old Seagull," said Mogilnikov. "You know, one of those Buick copies."

Grushko nodded. He liked to tie up all the loose ends.

"Go on," he said.

"Well first, we saw this old couple who shared the flat leave, and then this younger couple. They had a chat for a minute and then went their separate ways. I let him get a bit up the street and then bumped into him, accidental like. While I was helping him to his feet, I dipped his pocket. Simple as that."

The thief allowed himself a small smile of professional satisfaction.

"He didn't even know they were gone," he said. "It was a neat bit of work even though I say so myself."

"Then what happened?"

"We went upstairs to the flat and they turned it over like they said. But carefully, you know? They weren't hooligans. They seemed to know exactly what they were looking for. Just some papers, they said. That worried me a bit, I don't mind telling you. You see, I had the idea that these must have been important papers—the sort you might want to hide, because when I stuck my head round the door to see how they were getting on they were even looking in the fridge." He shrugged. "Well, what sort of papers do you keep in the fridge? Except the ones that maybe you're not supposed to have anyway."

"How long were they in there?"

"About twenty minutes. They found what they were looking for all right. They were very pleased with themselves. And then we were off."

Grushko regarded his nicotine-stained thumbnail thoughtfully for a moment and then bit it. Pointing it at Mogilnikov he said: "So where does Vaja Ordzhonikidze fit into this?"

"Look, I wanted nothing to do with that, right? I want to get that straight right from the start. They threatened me. They said they'd break my legs if I didn't help them."

"When was this?"

"A couple of days after we broke into the flat. They said that they'd heard Vaja liked fancy watches and they knew I had the one I'd washed off some Japanese tourist's arm. The Rolex. All they wanted me to do was ring him up and offer the watch for sale. So I did. I rang him up and arranged a meet in front of the Admiralty building. Vaja came straight down in his car, just like these two Cossacks said he would. He pulled up and I went over with the watch. When he saw it the poor bastard looked like he thought it was Christmas.

"He was so busy looking at it that he didn't even notice one of the Cossacks come up on the other side of the car. The Cossack got into the passenger seat and stuck a gun in the Georgian's ribs. He was pretty sick about it I can tell you. Anyway the Cossack told him to drive somewhere and the other followed them in his car. That was the last I saw of them, and of Vaja."

"But I still don't understand why they wanted him dead," said Grushko.

Mogilnikov paused for a moment as if he was wondering what to say. When he spoke again the explanation offered more than either Grushko or I could ever have imagined.

"It was Mikhail Milyukin they most wanted dead, right? Even though they'd had those papers off him they still figured he knew too much about what they'd been up to. Whatever that was. But they thought that if they killed Vaja at the same time and in the way that they did—you know, a couple of olives in the bread hole—your lot would think that it was the Georgians silencing an informer. While at the same time the Georgians would naturally think that it was their old enemies the Chechens. And when a gang war broke out between them . . ."

"The Ukrainians could sit back and enjoy the cabaret," Grushko added. "Yes, I can see it now. When the two of them were finished fighting it out, the Cossacks would come along and move into both their territories. It's clever."

"It's the honest truth, Grushko, I swear."

"In court?"

Mogilnikov shrugged philosophically.

"Like my mother used to say: there's no point in worrying about your hair if they've chopped your head off. Do I have a choice?"

"Frankly, no," said Grushko. "You said photographs."

"You just show me the family album."

"You'd better hope we've got their ugly mugs. Because if you can't pick some lonely-hearts you can be sure I won't think twice about throwing you back in here and then you'll be dead meat for sure."

The thief glanced up at me and smiled bitterly.

"I knew I could count on him," he said. "He's got a kind face."

★ ★ ★

What next took place I didn't get from Grushko but from Nikolai a few days afterwards as I reconstructed the chain of events that had such tragic consequences. Now I can excuse Grushko's actions. Not only was he under a great deal of pressure from General Kornilov to make an arrest, but things were not very easy for him at home either.

Grushko's daughter Tanya had reaffirmed her intention to apply for emigration papers and this had caused another bitter argument between them. He had been especially surprised to discover that emigrating to America had not been Boris's idea, as Grushko had suspected, but Tanya's, although Boris was happy to go along with it. Grushko had a low opinion of anyone who was prepared, as he saw it, to desert his or her country in its hour of greatest need. Especially someone who was a doctor. And despite what Tanya had said about going to America being her idea, Grushko held Boris responsible. Grushko's wife was rather more sanguine about the prospect of her only daughter leaving Russia. She just wanted her to be happy and, as Tanya had argued, and indeed was almost irrefutable, there was little chance of that happening in Russia. Lena's immediate concern was the dinner party she had planned to celebrate Tanya's engagement, and it must have been around this time that she managed to buy a joint of beef at the Kutznechny cooperative food market. What this would have cost I am not sure, but probably a couple of hundred roubles and, even if she had managed to sell some fine soaps to help pay for it, I did not think that Grushko would have approved of the extravagance any more than he approved of shopping on the black market.

CHAPTER

TWENTY

★ A detective is obliged to work at all hours of the day. I tend to work fairly set hours, and this might have been thought an advantage except that people like Luzhin, the advocate acting for the Georgians whom we were still holding in the police cells, worked the same sort of schedule.

On the morning of the Georgians' third day in custody, the day after Pyotr Mogilnikov decided to spill the corn about the Ukrainians, I had yet another telephone call from Luzhin regarding his clients. He reminded me that without a charge we would be obliged to release them that same afternoon. I told him to be patient and that I would call him back before lunch to let him know what was happening. But even a cursory glance at the papers in the case would have told me what I already knew: that it would not have been possible to have charged them with much more than a few minor currency violations.

The case of Ilya Chavchavadze was different. He had already been charged with the attempted murder of Pyotr Mogilnikov, and, thanks to the hard work of the ballistics department, the murder of Sultan Khadziyev. All attempts to connect the rest of the gang with these murders had so far come to nothing. Chavchavadze was adamant that these had been personal scores that he had been obliged to settle and were nothing to do with anyone else. It went without saying that he had no knowledge of a Georgian Mafia gang.

I rang Vladimir Voznosensky at the State Prosecutor's Office and explained that we needed more time to gather evidence.

"We've got a witness for the arson attack," I said, "albeit a reluctant one." That was understating it by a long way. "The man who owns the restaurant. Only he's a bit scared to give evidence."

"What about this Chavchavadze character? Can't you prove he's part of the gang?"

"He was photographed at the Georgian funeral," I said. "And Nikolai and Sasha saw him at a gym with other members of the gang."

"I see. It's not enough to charge the rest of them with complicity in Sultan's murder," he said. "The best I can do is get you another twenty-four hours' custody. To do that I'll have to go before the Kallinin District Court. You'll need to get Sasha and Nikolai to make statements that they believe Chavchavadze was acting in concert with the rest of them."

"Thanks, Volodya," I said. "I'd best call Luzhin and give him the news. He'll want to argue it with the judge."

Voznosensky laughed. "He can certainly try."

★ ★ ★

While I was busy organising this extended period of custody for the Georgians, Grushko had gone to the apartment building on Griboyedev. But not to see Nina Milyukin again. This time he wanted to speak to her flatmate, Mrs. Poliakov.

He met her as she was on her way out to the baker's shop on Nevksy. Mrs. Poliakov had wanted to invite him inside but Grushko said that he could ask his questions while they walked.

"I'm not sure that I can tell you anything," she said meekly. "As my husband explained, we don't notice very much you know, the other day it was on the TV news that someone abandoned a baby on the corner here and I think I must have walked straight past it. Can you imagine doing such a dreadful thing? Abandoning a baby. What is the country coming to? And I didn't notice."

"Well," said Grushko patiently, "mothers were abandoning babies in Russia before you and I were born. That's how Rome got started."

"Yes, and look what happened to them."

They came around the corner on to Nevsky Prospekt and joined the early-morning queue for bread. As usual the talk among the people waiting patiently in line, most of them women, was of rising food prices. A loaf of bread, Grushko was shocked to discover—for he rarely queued for anything except vodka—cost five roubles.

"Do you remember when I told you that Mikhail Milyukin had been murdered?" he said, avoiding the fact that the Poliakovs had eavesdropped on his conversation with Nina Milyukin. "You mentioned something about him stealing food from your fridge—"

Mrs. Poliakov looked embarrassed.

"Please," she said, colouring a little under her blue satin headscarf, "can we forget all about that? I was upset. He wasn't a bad man at all. I was just being silly."

"No, I don't think so. Can you remember what was taken?"

"Remember it?" She nodded. "I haven't stopped thinking about it. That bit of beef—just a small piece you understand—it cost over a hundred roubles."

"Beef?" said Grushko.

"You're surprised that we can afford it, eh? Well, let

me tell you, we saved up for that little bit of meat. To help us celebrate our fortieth wedding anniversary."

Grushko shook his head with puzzlement.

"No, it's just that I expected something else. Something more important."

"What's more important than that?"

"I see what you mean," he smiled ruefully. "But you see I thought you might have mentioned something else. A packet. A carton. Something that could have been used as a container for something else. Was anything else taken perhaps?"

"Just the beef," she sighed. Noticing Grushko's disappointment, she added, "I'm sorry I can't be more help."

"Well, thanks anyway."

He nodded politely and tried to extricate himself from the quickly growing line of people.

"What's the matter?" snarled one old woman behind him as he pushed his way past her. "Can't you make up your mind?"

"No," cackled another. "He's like most men. No idea of what his wife buys. He's going to fetch his wife to buy their bread."

"She'll be lucky," added a third woman. "Haven't you heard? The bread's run out."

Grushko walked quickly away.

★ ★ ★

It was generally held that we were in for a heatwave. Even through the dust on the windows the sun felt like a coal fire and I wondered whether the radiator-hose on my car could take it.

When Grushko arrived at the Big House wearing his usual dark worsted suit he looked as if he had stepped out of an oven.

"Christ, it's hot," he gasped, picking the shirt off his

chest and then swatting a mosquito away from his sweat-covered face. "It's a real *churki*'s summer, this."

I explained about the Georgians and the State Prosecutor's Office.

"Maybe something'll turn up," he said optimistically. "I sure hope it does. I don't fancy having to tell the general that we had to let those bastards just walk out of here. How would that look on Zverkov's television programme?"

Nikolai and Andrei were hanging around, waiting to speak to Grushko. He glanced up at the big man.

"Any luck with Mogilnikov?"

"He's picked one of the faces." He handed Grushko two photographs. "Stepan Starovyd. The Wrestler. And a maybe on the other one. Kazimir Cherep, the Little Cossack."

"Better find out where they're hanging out."

"Sasha's gone to have a word with his pincher, sir," said Nikolai. "Reckons he might get a tip."

"Andrei?"

"Dr. Sobchak. I've found the *dacha* where she's staying. It's near Lomonosov. The address is here, sir." He handed Grushko a sheet of paper.

"Nikolai," said Grushko, "what do you say to a little drive in the country?"

"I'd say you've picked a nice day for it." He collected his jacket off the back of his chair.

Grushko signed the papers I had presented for Voznosensky and wished me luck. He started down the corridor but stopped before he had gone five paces.

"Anyone know where we can get some petrol?"

★ ★ ★

Lomonosov is a small town about forty kilometres west of Petersburg. Like nearby Petrodvorets it is the location of yet another imperial summer palace. It took Grushko and

Nikolai a while to find the place they were looking for, even though Nikolai and Sasha had built themselves a smaller *dacha* only a few kilometres away. Residents paid a small tax on the land where the *dacha* was situated but otherwise were free to build on a plot as they wished. There were no addresses as such, just plot numbers.

As with most Russian *dachi*, this one was little more than a wooden cabin on a large allotment of similarly gimcrack-looking constructions. Built on two storeys, the *dacha* was painted blue with a high, corrugated-iron roof and surrounded with a small picket fence. On the dirt track outside the gate was parked an old white Zhiguli. As they knocked on the door, Nikolai sniffed the air with distaste.

"That septic tank wants emptying," he said.

"It's just the heat," said Grushko, and then the door opened.

She was a lean, hard woman of around forty with pale blue eyes and the kind of face that was no stranger to drink.

"Dr. Helen Sobchak?"

"Yes?"

Grushko showed her his ID.

"I wonder if we might ask you a few questions?"

"What about?"

"Mikhail Milyukin. It won't take very long."

She shrugged and stood to one side.

The room was barely furnished, with a wooden floor and a big cast-iron stove. Books covered the walls and a cigarette was burning in the ashtray next to a bottle of vodka. On the floor was an open briefcase.

"I'm not sure I can tell you anything," she said, closing the door behind them.

"You'd be surprised how often people say that," said Grushko. "And then they manage to help us after all."

Dr. Sobchak picked up the cigarette and puffed it back into life.

"This is very pleasant. Are you on holiday?"

"A working holiday. I'm catching up with some paperwork."

Grushko eyed the bottle and then the briefcase. There was something about her voice . . .

"So I see," he said. "Well, you've certainly picked a fine week for it." He loosened his shirt collar. "The city is like a furnace. I couldn't trouble you for a glass of water, could I? It's a long drive out here."

"Yes," she said reluctantly, "or there's lemonade if you'd prefer." She raised an eyebrow at Nikolai.

"Thank you very much," he said.

Dr. Sobchak stepped into the tiny kitchen to fetch the lemonade. Grushko picked a book from off the shelf and started idly to flick through it.

"Are you any relation?" he called to her. "To the mayor?"

"No," she said, returning with two glasses and watched as the two men drained the glasses thirstily.

"You mentioned Mikhail Milyukin," she said, prompting them impatiently.

"Yes, I did. We're investigating his murder. Your name was in his address book."

He handed his empty glass to her and returned to his perusal of her book.

"Yes, well, it would be," she said. "I once provided him with a few facts and figures for an article he was writing."

"When was this?"

She shrugged vaguely.

"A couple of years ago."

"These would have been—" he brandished the book he was holding—"radio-biological facts and figures, am I right?"

"That's right, yes."

"You understand, we have to check out everyone who

knew Milyukin," he said. "But this article he was writing: have you any idea what it was about?"

"It was something to do with the Chernobyl accident, I believe."

"It may just be a coincidence, but there was another name in Milyukin's address book who is also associated with the nuclear industry: Anatoly Boldyrev. Have you ever heard of him, Dr. Sobchak?"

"No, I can't say I have."

"He was murdered too," Grushko said bluntly.

The doctor's blue eyes widened a little. She took a deep breath.

"Good gracious me," she said. "Well, Colonel, I don't know that you could exactly describe me as someone who is involved in the nuclear industry. Strictly speaking I'm a biologist. At the First Medical. My work is concerned with the use of radioactive tracers to study metabolic processes."

"When was the last time you spoke to Mikhail Milyukin, Doctor?"

"It was a couple of years ago, as I think I said earlier."

"So you did, so you did." He replaced the book on the shelf. "Then you wouldn't know if he had been planning to write another piece, or make another film about the nuclear industry? You see we found some notes he had made about the beta emitters that might be present in the atmosphere around St. Petersburg: plutonium, polonium, americium—that kind of thing?"

"No," she said, beginning to sound rather irritated. "I keep telling you, I knew nothing about what he was up to."

Grushko walked over to the window and peered out at the patchwork quilt of different-coloured *dachi*. He took a deep breath and then nodded. "This really is very pleasant. Yours?"

"No, it belongs to a friend of mine." After a pause she

added: "Well, if that's all, I'm expecting some friends any moment now, as a matter of fact—"

"Yes, that's all."

They walked back up the track to where they had left the car.

"Well, that's that," said Nikolai.

"Not quite."

Grushko drove a short way along the track and then turned off to park behind a line of trees. They could just see the *dacha* and Dr. Sobchak's car parked out front. Grushko wound down the window, opened the glove box and started to sort through his cassettes.

Nikolai regarded him with puzzlement. It seemed an odd time to stop and listen to music.

"Keep an eye on the *dacha* will you?" said Grushko, throwing cassettes over his shoulder and onto the back seat.

"You reckon she was lying, sir?"

"Those beta emitters you heard me describing? They're alpha emitters."

Nikolai looked impressed. "Where did you learn that?"

"From that book I was looking at when we were in there. No, Dr. Helen Sobchak was very keen for us to leave, otherwise she would have corrected me, don't you think?"

He found the tape he was searching for and pushed it into the car's cassette-player.

"Still, this should tell us for sure."

It was the KGB recording of Mikhail Milyukin's telephone conversations. Grushko had played it many times and knew the tape virtually by heart. He listened for only a second and then pressed the fast-forward button on the machine until he found the excerpt that he was interested in now:

" 'I've got a little job for you, if you're interested.'

" 'What sort of material are we talking about?' "

Dr. Sobchak's voice was unmistakable. Grushko smiled with some satisfaction.

"I knew I'd heard that voice before," he said, and, winding the tape back a little, he played this small section of dialogue again.

"Mikhail Milyukin spoke to Dr. Sobchak three days before he was murdered," he said, reminding himself.

"Why don't we just go back in there and confront her with it?" said Nikolai.

Grushko shook his head. "It might yet come to that. First let's see if there was a reason she wanted to be rid of us." He stuck his face in the way of the sun and closed his eyes. "Besides, it's a lovely day for a spot of surveillance."

Fifteen minutes passed and Grushko sighed contentedly. No harm in waiting a little while longer, he thought. The name of the game was patience. Then an engine started and Nikolai tapped him on the leg.

"So much for her guests," he said.

They ducked down as the white Zhiguli came laboriously up the track and past the line of trees that screened them.

Grushko started his own car and, after a decent interval, followed her. At the top of the track she stopped and then turned onto the main road, heading east in the direction of the city.

Grushko was an old hand at traffic surveillance. He knew that on a country road you could hang well back and allow four or five cars in between. Dr. Sobchak was not a very quick driver and he could afford to give her some space. But he was suspicious when quite soon afterwards she turned off the main road and drove into Petrodvorets.

"Maybe she's going to drive around and see if she's being followed," he said.

"Maybe she's going sightseeing," Nikolai suggested.

Petrodvorets was certainly worth a look, with its lovely

palaces, extensive gardens and numerous fountains. But Grushko was not impressed by this idea.

"No, we spooked her back there at the *dacha* and no mistake," he said. "She's not out for the drive. She's going somewhere specific, I'll bet my pension on it."

They followed the white Zhiguli along Krasney Prospekt until it pulled up by the railway station and Dr. Sobchak got out. For a moment Grushko thought she was going to board a train for the city but then she crossed the road and went in the entrance to the main park.

The two detectives left their car and, in an effort to blend in with the tourists, they removed their jackets and rolled up their sleeves before following. By this stage Grushko was intrigued.

"What's she up to?" he said as they meandered through the trees, trying to look inconspicuous.

"Maybe you're right, sir," said Nikolai. "Maybe she is trying to cover her tracks."

"Is that what they teach people in radio-biology?" mused Grushko. "Perhaps we should have stuck a radioactive tracer on her ourselves."

As they came round the front of the Great Palace of Peter the Great and walked along the sea canal that split the park from north to south they were suddenly aware that Dr. Sobchak's leisurely pace had become something more urgent.

"She can't have seen us," grumbled Nikolai as they broke into a gentle trot.

It was then that they saw the hydrofoil.

Dr. Sobchak mounted the gangway and the very next minute the white craft started to draw away from the landing point. Grushko swore loudly.

"Of course," he said. "It's only thirty minutes from here to the city centre. I should have realized. Why waste petrol when she can go in and out for a couple of roubles?"

They turned and started to run back towards the station. It was several minutes before they reached the car again. As Grushko started the Zhiguli's small engine Nikolai was looking at his watch.

"Can we do it?" he puffed. It had been an effort keeping up with the smaller, lighter man.

"Just about," said Grushko. "But even if we don't, I think I know where she's going."

★ ★ ★

They watched the hydrofoil dock at the pier in front of the Hermitage from a safe distance. It was mostly foreign tourists getting off, their pockets stuffed with dollars and black-market roubles, but even among so many people Dr. Sobchak was easy to spot in her comparatively shabby clothes. It always amused Grushko how even Russian-speaking foreigners could imagine they might escape identification. Once he had confounded an Englishman, a fluent Russian-speaking friend of Tanya's who had bought all his clothes in Russian stores, by identifying him within only a few seconds and without one word exchanged. Grushko had explained to the man that what had given him away was the smile on his face: there was, he said, little for any Russian to smile about as he walked along the street.

Dr. Sobchak stepped off the hydrofoil and turned north up Dvorkovaya towards the Lenin Museum. But she wasn't smiling.

"What now?" said Nikolai as they observed her walking away in the opposite direction.

Grushko found first gear and slipped the clutch. As they drove past Dr. Sobchak Nikolai knew better than to look back.

"My guess is that she's going to take a tram across the bridge," said Grushko. "A Number 2, I should think."

He stopped the car on Suvorov Square and lit a cigarette.

"Are you going to tell me?" said Nikolai.

"Well, can't you guess? The First Medical Pavlov University. That's where she's going."

As Grushko had predicted she caught a Number 2 bound for Petrogradsky Region. The Kirov was the longest bridge in the city, with four lanes of traffic north and south, and the tram ran along on a track in the central reservation. They followed it across the bridge and then along Kubyseva Street.

"It must be nice to be right all the time," grumbled Nikolai.

The tram terminated on Kapayeva Street right in front of the modern red-brick building that was the University Hospital. Dr. Sobchak got off and walked across the front lawn and into the entrance.

Grushko and Nikolai got out of the car and walked up to the hospital. They showed their identity cards to the security guard who met them inside the door.

"The lady who just came in," said Grushko. "Dr. Sobchak."

The security guard nodded.

"Where did she go?"

"Up to her laboratory. That's on the second floor and along the corridor to your right as you come up the stairs. Room 236."

"Thanks."

"Want me to call her up for you?"

Grushko smiled and shook his head. "No, we'll announce ourselves."

They climbed two flights of stairs and went along the corridor until they came to the open door of Dr. Sobchak's laboratory. They said nothing as they watched her remove something that was frozen hard and wrapped in several layers of plastic from the fridge-freezer where Grushko guessed she kept the organic samples she used in her work.

"I'll take that, Dr. Sobchak," he said, advancing into the laboratory. "If you don't mind."

She squealed with fright and dropped the package. It sounded like a rock dropping on the linoleum floor. Recovering her composure she stared malevolently at Grushko.

"What the hell do you mean by following me like this?" she snarled.

He had to hand it to her. She had plenty of nerve.

"Don't make it worse than it already is," he said and picked the cold package from off the floor.

Dr. Sobchak sighed and then sat down heavily on a laboratory stool. She lit a cigarette and tried to steady her nerves.

"Well, what is it?" Nikolai said impatiently.

Grushko sniffed the package and then laid it down on the work bench.

"It's a piece of meat," he said and went over to the sink where he started to wash his hands carefully. "It's the material Mikhail Milyukin wanted analysed by a radio-biologist."

Nikolai moved forward to pick it up and inspect it more closely.

"No, don't touch it," said Grushko. He shook his hands free of water and dried them on a towel that was hanging beside the sink.

"Just how radioactive is it, Doctor?" he asked.

She blew a column of smoke at the ceiling and then looked for a handkerchief. Wiping her eyes, she said, "It has a tissue burden of plutonium that's approximately one thousand times higher than a control sample."

Grushko lit a cigarette and flicked a match at the piece of frozen meat.

"And if I were to eat this . . . ?"

"Assuming you were able to consume 150 grams of that meat every day for a month—imagine, meat every day for a month, in Russia—" She laughed out loud at the very idea of such a thing.

"Just the figures please," said Grushko. "There's a good doctor."

"Why, then you'd ingest about twice your annual maximum safe dose of radiation." She shrugged. "You add that to your normal background levels of radiation and it starts to get really serious."

"Where did Milyukin get this?"

"I've really no idea. He didn't say and I didn't ask. By the time I'd completed the analysis, he was dead."

"So why didn't you come forward, Dr. Sobchak? And why all the lies now?"

She pursed her lips and shook her head sadly.

"I didn't want to get involved, I guess. On the TV they said that the Mafia was probably behind Milyukin's death: that he'd been killed for speaking out against them. I got scared. So I decided to go away for a while. And then when you turned up and said that someone else was dead as well, I suppose I must have panicked. I thought I had better get rid of the meat, before someone found out I had it, and they got rid of me too."

"What were you going to do with it?"

"Put it in the hospital incinerator. With all the human tissue." She took a halting drag of her cigarette and shrugged. "Sorry," she said. "It was stupid of me. I don't know what I could have been thinking of." She paused and then added: "Will I go to prison?"

"That all depends," said Grushko, "on whether or not you help us now. You can start by explaining how meat becomes as radioactive as this."

"I've been asking myself the same question," she said. "My own conclusion was that there must have been some sort of accident at the Sosnovy Bor Reactor."

"Well, we've just had one," said Grushko. "There was that escape of radioactive iodine gas only a few weeks ago."

Dr. Sobchak shook her head.

"No, to get into the food chain like this, the lead would have to have been some time ago. At least six months."

"Is that possible?" said Nikolai. "Without anyone having been informed?"

"There were two major accidents at Sosnovy Bor during the mid-seventies," she said. "Nobody heard about either of those for years."

"You're suggesting that there's been some sort of cover-up?" said Grushko. "Like at Chernobyl?" He shook his head slowly. "No, I don't buy that. Things are different now that we've got rid of the Party. Not only that but we're trying to put our nuclear house in order. Another cover-up might jeopardise our chances of screwing some money out of the Western atomic-energy people."

"You seem to know more about this than I do," said Dr. Sobchak.

"Besides," he continued, "where's the percentage for the Mafia in a cover-up? Unless ... Doctor, do you have a Geiger counter?"

"I have a radiometer," she said, unlocking a cupboard and removing a device that resembled a photographer's light meter. "It's more sensitive than a Geiger counter."

She held the device over the sample of frozen meat and drew Grushko's attention to the dial.

"On the highest range setting the needle picks up hardly anything at all." She turned the setting knob through 180 degrees. "But on the lower range you can easily see that this material is registering significantly. About 500 milliroentgens per hour."

Grushko held the radiometer and tried it himself. Then he looked at the underside of the instrument.

"Astron," he said, reading the name of the manufacturer. "Well, what do you know? Made in the USSR, and it works."

Twenty minutes later the two detectives stood outside the Pushkin Restaurant on Fontanka and rang the doorbell.

A glazier was replacing the window that had been broken when the restaurant was firebombed. It was only now that he had been able to obtain a sheet of glass to size.

Chazov's face fell when he saw Nikolai and Grushko.

"What is this?" he whined. "I've spent all week answering your questions. Can't you people just leave us alone?"

Nikolai placed a large hand against Chazov's chest and moved him gently out of the way.

"This is harassment. That's what I call it. I'm going to write to the city council about this."

"You do that, Comrade," said Grushko, and made his way through the restaurant and into the kitchens. A cockroach scuttled quickly out of his path and Grushko looked at it as he might have looked on an old friend.

"Is this some kind of pet?" he said. "I'm sure that roach was here the last time we came."

The chef was a big man, almost as big as Nikolai, with large, Cossack-style moustaches and a dirty, blood-stained apron. He was busy chopping cucumbers with a butcher's knife, but when he saw the two detectives he stopped and regarded them with deliberate menace.

"And where do you think you're going?" he said, pointing the large knife at Grushko's chest.

"It's the militia, Yeroshka," said Chazov. "Best put the knife down, eh? We don't want any trouble."

"That's right, sir," said Grushko. "Do as he says."

The chef wiped the sweat from his broad face with the sleeve of what had once been a white jacket.

"Nobody comes into my kitchens without my permission," he growled belligerently. "Militia or not."

Grushko noted the bottle of vodka that stood open beside the basin of cucumbers. You had to be careful how you handled a man of Yeroshka's size when he'd been drinking heavily. He could have done with a drink himself.

"I don't think you were here the last time we came in here," he said, and put down the radiometer.

"Lucky for you I wasn't," said Yeroshka. "Otherwise I might have trimmed your ears for you and given them to you in a bag." He picked up the bottle and took an enormous swig.

This was Grushko's cue. He grabbed Yeroshka's elbow and pressed the hand holding the knife against the joint and towards the shoulder. Done expertly it was an effective and immensely painful method of dealing with a man who was armed with what the militia called a cold weapon. Yeroshka bellowed with pain and dropped both knife and bottle onto the floor. In the same instant Nikolai sprang forward and quickly handcuffed the man.

"Now sit down and shut up," said Grushko and collected the radiometer from the worktop.

Yeroshka sat down on a case of Russian champagne and dropped his head onto his chest. Chazov placed an avuncular hand on his chef's broad shoulders.

"It's all right," he said. "Take it easy."

Nikolai hauled the fridge door open and reviewed the contents with quiet appreciation, as if he had been looking at a favourite painting.

"Look, I've told you," said Chazov. "I get all my meat from a legitimate supplier."

Grushko stepped inside the fridge and switched on the radiometer. He pointed the instrument at a carton of meat and watched the needle move from one end of the scale to the other.

"What is that thing?" said Chazov. "I'm afraid I'll have to ask you to come out of there. This is all very unhygienic."

"It certainly is," said Grushko. "Did you know that this meat is radioactive?"

"Radioactive?" Chazov laughed. "Oh, I get it. This is your way of persuading me to give evidence against those bastards who firebombed me. You're as bad as they are. Well I'm not falling for it—d'you hear?"

Grushko pointed to the flickering needle on the radiometer dial.

"You might be right. Except for this. It's a radiometer. Like a Geiger counter only more sensitive. According to this little machine you could power a small town with what's coming off this meat of yours, Chazov. And that means this place will be closed."

"You can't do that."

"You're right, I can't. But when the officials from the Department of Health and the Department of Radio-biological Security get here, they will close you. Whether you're ever allowed to reopen again depends on you telling us where this meat came from."

Chazov shook his head.

"You must think I came down the river on a hay barge," he sneered.

Grushko shrugged and then looked at his watch. He took out a bottle of orange pills and handed two to Nikolai.

"Here—it's time we were taking our potassium iodide tablets," he said and swallowed two himself.

"What's that for?" Chazov asked suspiciously.

"Potassium iodine? It stops the build-up of radioactive iodine 131 in the thyroid gland," said Grushko. "That's the most sensitive human organ where radiation is concerned. Just standing next to this meat is hazardous."

Chazov frowned and then felt at his throat.

"God forbid that anyone should actually eat any," added Nikolai.

Chazov's hand descended to his stomach. He rubbed it uncomfortably and then gulped.

"I don't feel too good," he said, eyeing the meat in his fridge with suspicion. "Look, I'm getting out of here."

Nikolai stood in his way.

"Not so fast," he said.

Grushko smiled and pointed the radiometer at Chazov's throat suggestively. He looked at the dial and shook his head grimly.

"What is it?" said Chazov. "What's it say? Please, you've got to let me have some of those tablets."

Grushko held the bottle of orange pills in front of Chazov's eyes.

"These?" he said. "They're very expensive. And I don't know that there's enough for you."

Chazov snatched desperately at the pills and found his hand held in Nikolai's big paw.

"Well, maybe," said Grushko, "but not until you've told us where all your meat comes from."

"All right, all right." Chazov sighed exhaustedly. "His name is Volodimir Khmara. He comes in about once a week and sells me as much meat as I want. Mutton, pork, but mostly beef. Hundred roubles a kilo. All of it top-grade too. Or at least I thought it was." He rolled his eyes at Grushko. "Now will you give me those pills?"

"And where does he get it, this Volodimir Khmara?"

"There's a consignment, from southern Byelorussia, a couple of times a month. Khmara's part of a Cossack mob from Kiev. About three months ago they hijacked a whole load of EEC food-aid and they've been selling it here and in Moscow."

Grushko's eyes met Nikolai's. "I've got this horrible idea about how they're bringing it into Petersburg," he said.

"Me too," said Nikolai.

"Now give me some tablets," groaned Chazov. "Please."

"After you've made a statement down at the Big House," said Grushko. He handed Nikolai the bottle. "And while you're at it, you can make a statement about those Georgians too. That should tidy things up nicely."

Nikolai glanced at the bottle, pocketed it and then leaned towards Grushko.

"What are they?" he murmured.

"Indigestion tablets," said Grushko. "Tanya gets them from the hospital for me." He shrugged dismissively. "Well, there's not much demand for them. Not these days. Not unless you're a cop."

He grinned amiably.

"Take care of Chazov, will you?"

"Where are you going?"

"I think I'll pay another little visit to Anglo-Soyuzatom Transit."

CHAPTER
TWENTY-ONE

★ Grushko's journey to Anglo-Soyuzatom Transit took him south-west through Leninsky Region and along Gaza Prospekt, past Petersburg's 8th Cold Store. Grushko had often driven by it and seen lorries from the Uryupin meat-processing plant unloading tons of meat under the close supervision of the local militia: without this security, much of the meat would simply have disappeared. The State Meat Board was the only wholesale meat consumer in the country, supplying all the state meat markets and, seeing the Uryupin truck, it occurred to Grushko that while he had Dr. Sobchak's radiometer it would be a good idea if he checked the meat in one of the city's main cold stores for signs of radioactive contamination. The manager of the 8th Cold Store, Oleg Pryakhin, was quite used to the ingenious methods used by people trying to get their hands on the meat in his refrigerators, not to mention the many threats and bribes he had been offered. His predecessor had once sabotaged the cold-store generator in order to sell a con-signment of "spoiled" smoked sausage on the local black market. So he listened to Grushko's strange request with-out much surprise, although he had his doubts. At the same time he saw no particular harm in letting him use the radiometer, if that was what it was. But then it was not as if he would be allowing the grey-haired Colonel of Internal Affairs to remove any meat from the premises. And if there was something wrong with it then he would pass the problem on to the food and light-industry department in the Petersburg People's Inspectorate and let them sort it out.

But he was a little surprised, even disappointed when, having waved his little machine over a one-ton delivery of Doctor's salami, the colonel told him that there was nothing at all the matter with it.

Grushko drove along the road he had taken to Dr. Sobchak's *dacha* near Lomonosov. This was turning into quite a day. But at least now he was getting somewhere. And he was almost looking forward to seeing the look on Gidaspov's face when he told him about the use to which the Mafia was putting his expensive foreign trucks.

When he arrived at ASA, Gidaspov looked pained to see him again. Well, Grushko was used to that.

"I did say I'd call," said Gidaspov, "when the convoy got back. They're still *en route*."

"I wonder if I might take a closer look at Tolya's truck, sir," he said.

Gidaspov led him out to where the huge vehicle was parked on the *dacha*'s tennis courts.

"Here she is," he said proudly. "Originally built for the British army, it's an eight-tonne wheel chassis with an on-board crane to lift the barrels of waste into the container. The interior is part-refrigerated to help keep them cool. The armoured louvres on the windscreen are to prevent anyone taking a shot at the driver in the event of a terrorist attack."

Grushko climbed into the cab and sat in the driver's seat. It felt more like a limousine than a truck. He looked at all the instrumentation and nodded appreciatively. It was certainly an impressive-looking vehicle.

"That's your fire-suppression system there," said Gidaspov. "And this controls the temperature inside the container."

"What about communications between the trucks?" Grushko asked. "I don't see any short-wave radios."

"Er well ... the British seem to be having a problem with them," he said. "You see, it would appear that all short-wave frequencies are owned by the state-security apparatus. We've been trying to get our own frequency for some time now." He shrugged. "But until we do, there are no radios. It's been several months."

"I know the feeling," said Grushko. This was the bit he was looking forward to. "What happens to the trucks once the waste is removed?"

Gidaspov pointed to another switch on the dashboard.

"This operates a special decontamination process. The truck cleans its own interior automatically. Then, when the truck reaches the edge of the exclusion zone, the driver uses an on-board hose to spray the exterior with decontaminant as well."

"And how efficient is that?"

"The radiation levels are considered acceptable, I believe. But I'm afraid it's not my field. You'd have to speak to Chichikov to get the exact levels. He's the scientific controller here."

Grushko smiled and showed him the radiometer.

"Mind if I check it myself?"

Gidaspov frowned. Grushko was beginning to worry him.

"No," he said reluctantly. "Why should I mind? We've got nothing to hide. But do you mind telling me—"

"All in good time, Mr. Gidaspov. All in good time." He pointed at the dashboard. "We operate the container doors from in here, do we?"

Gidaspov nodded and flicked the switch. They stepped

down from the cab and went round to the back of the truck. When the big doors were open Grushko climbed into the back and, with the radiometer switched on, he walked the length of the container and back again. Even after having been sprayed with decontaminant the truck's interior was registering 800 milliroentgens, which was more than the meat in Dr. Sobchak's laboratory. Grushko turned the machine off and jumped down beside Gidaspov.

"And then they're just driven back here empty?"

Gidaspov was looking distinctly unhappy.

"Well yes, of course. What else would you want to put inside them?"

"What else indeed?" Grushko lit a cigarette and regarded the truck with quiet distaste.

"Tell me," he asked. "Have you ever heard of black haulage?"

Gidaspov bridled.

"Of course I have. I have had many years experience of managing freight, Colonel. But I can't see that anyone would want to put any sort of illegal cargo inside one of these trucks. After three or four days in this sort of environment, any cargo would show traces of some contamination. Even after spraying with decontaminants."

"Do your drivers know that?"

"I would have thought so, yes." But Gidaspov sounded vague.

"But you're not sure?"

"Well, not absolutely sure. But common sense would seem to indicate that—"

"Either way it probably doesn't really matter," said Grushko. "Not to the Mafia, anyway. They're not particularly fastidious about things like contamination. Not when there are such large profits to be made."

"I think it's about time you told me exactly what's going on here, Colonel, don't you?"

"Yes, you're right," said Grushko. Experimentally he

ran the radiometer over his own person. It showed a small reading that he hoped wasn't enough to worry about.

"A Mafia gang has been using your trucks to transport supplies of frozen meat to cooperative restaurants here in St. Petersburg," he said. "EC food aid that was destined for the people of Kiev."

Gidaspov's mouth slackened like a deflating tyre.

"You can't be serious, Colonel," he said.

"Oh, but I am. What better way for them to avoid the attentions of customs officials and militiamen on the look-out for illicit food supplies? After all, nobody feels much inclined to go near anything nuclear these days. Not since Chernobyl."

"But what you're suggesting, it's monstrous," spluttered Gidaspov. "And I can't see how—I mean, I'm sure our drivers would have had nothing do with such a thing."

"The Mafia have their ways of persuading people to do what they're told," shrugged Grushko. "All the same, I shall want to see your personnel files. There may be a weak link, despite your admirable security precautions."

Gidaspov was still finding it hard to take in. He lit one of his American cigarettes nervously.

"But the meat," he repeated dumbly. "It would be hopelessly contaminated."

"Yes, you're right," agreed Grushko. "But like I said, I doubt that would worry the Mafia. After all, contamination's not something you can actually see. Just the same I think it must have worried Tolya. Perhaps that's why he became a vegetarian. Anyway, he decided to take his story to Mikhail Milyukin. He even took along a sample of the meat."

Grushko watched the colour drain from Gidaspov's well-fed face.

"I'm not exactly sure what happened next," Grushko admitted, "but somehow the Mafia—a gang of Ukrainians it would seem—well, they discovered that Tolya had told someone. Perhaps Tolya was foolish enough to have confided his doubts to one of the other drivers. If so, then it cost him his life. The Ukrainians grabbed him, tortured him and found that the person Tolya had told was an investigative journalist. *Ogonyok, Krokodil*—it would have made good copy wherever it appeared. But with the sort of money involved, the Mafia couldn't afford to let that happen. There were twenty tonnes of beef on that plane from Britain. At today's black-market prices that's worth about five million roubles—as much as any narcotic. So they killed them both."

"But why transport the meat here?" said Gidaspov. "Why not just sell it in Kiev?"

"Have you been in a cooperative restaurant in St. Petersburg?" said Grushko. "The prices they charge are many times higher than those people could be expected to pay in Kiev. Because of the tourists. And however badly off for food the Ukraine thinks it is, it's still a lot better off than we are in Petersburg. After all, the Ukraine is, or at least used to be, Russia's bread-basket."

Gidaspov had steadied himself against the truck. He was looking distinctly green.

"Exactly where are the trucks right now, Mr. Gidaspov?"

"You'd better come inside," he said.

They went back to Gidaspov's office where he showed Grushko the convoy's position on a map.

"They'll aim to be here, in Pskov, by this evening," he said. "And all being well, they should be back in St. Petersburg sometime tomorrow night."

"Good," said Grushko. "That gives us time to prepare a welcome for them. With any luck we'll catch them redhanded."

He looked at Gidaspov and wondered whether or not he could trust him. The man seemed genuinely shocked by what Grushko had told him, but there was no way to be absolutely sure that, left at liberty, he would not try and warn someone. Grushko knew he had little alternative but to take Gidaspov into custody until the arrests had been made.

CHAPTER
TWENTY-TWO

★ That night, an elk came running through the streets of St. Petersburg. Someone told me that it was usually about this time of year that they started to migrate and that instinct led them to take the same route that their ancestors had taken before Peter the Great had even thought of founding his city. For a while I sat at a window in the Big House and watched the huge bewildered beast gallop up and down Liteiny Prospekt. It made a pleasant diversion from hours spent dealing with the Georgians.

"I wish I had my rifle," said Nikolai. "I could put some real meat on the table." He lifted an imaginary gun to his shoulder and pretended to take aim at the animal. "And those antlers: they would look great on my living-room wall."

For my own part I preferred to think of the elk alive; as something magnificent. There was precious little dignity to be found in any other variety of Russian life. It was true the beast seemed to have no idea where it was going any more than it knew why it was going there. But probably it would get there in the end and in that there might have been a message of hope for us all.

After we had charged the Georgians and locked them up for the night Grushko spent an hour discussing the forthcoming operation with the OMON squad commander and General Kornilov. When finally he emerged from this meeting he asked me about Gidaspov and his secretary, who were still waiting in an adjoining office.

"I can't let them go," he said, "but I can't just lock them up downstairs with the rest of the scum. That's the way we did things in the old days. What do you think?"

"How about taking them to a hotel?" I suggested. "A nice room with a TV and a bathroom, but no telephone, and a militiaman outside the door."

Grushko snapped his fingers.

"I know just the place," he said. "The Smolensky on Rastrelli Square. It used to be the Party VIP hotel. Now it's mostly European television crews staying there, but the place is owned by the city, so we'll get a cheap rate."

He picked up the phone and made the arrangements. Half an hour later, Gidaspov and the girl were on their way.

"Well, that was easily solved," said Grushko and looked at his watch. "Now all I have to do is go home and tell the wife that I'm going to be late for this dinner she's giving for our future son-in-law and his family tomorrow night." He shook his head wearily. "Well, it's not as if I can ask the Mafia if they can reschedule their delivery for a more convenient night, is it? All the same, she's going to have my guts for breakfast. I don't suppose you've got any bright ideas on that one, have you?"

I smiled and collected my briefcase from the floor beside Grushko's desk. I took out a bar of chocolate and handed it to him.

"A present from Moscow," I said.

"You must be psychic," he breathed. "But I can't take your chocolate—"

"It's not mine," I said. "It's my wife's. I nicked it from her when I was at home." I shrugged. "The fat cow eats too much chocolate already. Her cupboards were full of it. The music teacher must have a connection somewhere."

"If you're sure," said Grushko and put the chocolate in his own briefcase. "Thanks. It'll make a useful peace-offering."

I shrugged modestly and hoped that there was nobody in Grushko's family who spoke German. The chocolate was already two years past its sell-by date. But then, even two-year-old chocolate is better than no chocolate at all.

★   ★   ★

The next morning everyone was in early to hear Grushko describe the evening's operation in the briefing-room. The OMON squad attended, as did General Kornilov, Lieutenant Khodyrev and Captain Novdyrov of the GAI—the State Automobile Inspectorate. Oleg manned the lights, Andrei the blinds and Sasha operated the slide projector. Nikolai had driven over to ASA.

"May I have your attention, please," said Grushko. "This afternoon's realisation, codename Meathook, will be commanded by me and will commence at 1600 hours."

He reached up and drew down a map of St. Petersburg and its surrounding area.

"There are two stages to this operation," he explained. "The first stage is as follows: Captain Novdyrov's GAI will take up a position about fifteen kilometres south of Gatcina on the M20 to Pskov. At the same time a unit of the OMON squad, myself and Nikolai will take up a position about five kilometres further north. Just before the airport there's a Sovinterauto service station and next to it a sort of lay-by and a line of trees.

"When the convoy passes the GAI, a patrol car will pursue it and bring the tail vehicle to a halt as close to our position as possible. We'll be parked behind the trees so they won't see us. The GAI men will ask the driver and his mate to step out of the cab and follow them to the rear of the vehicle, on the pretext of a faulty brake-light. But when they get there they'll find two OMON squad officers, myself and Nikolai waiting for them. Having persuaded them not to continue with their journey—"

Grushko paused for their laughter.

"—Nikolai and I will take their places in the truck cab. Right now he should be familiarising himself with one of the Anglo-Soyuzatom trucks that's currently off the road.

"We will then follow the rest of the convoy and, using walkie-talkies, we will direct the main force of the OMON squad to wherever they are planning to unload the stolen meat. We're not sure as to how many men the other side will be fielding; however, you can bet they'll all be well-armed and more inclined to shoot than not. But according to our informers, there are three faces we do expect to see." He nodded at Oleg. "Lights, please."

Sasha switched the projector on. The first slide was of a mug-shot from the files.

"Kazimir Cherep, also known as the Little Cossack," said Grushko. "A team leader for the Ukrainian gang here in Peter. Born Kiev, 1958. Served five years in the zone for attempted murder. And the next one, please, Sasha."

Sasha moved the second slide into the projector.

"Stepan Starovyd, born Dnepropetrovsk, 1956, also known as the Wrestler on account of his having once been the army heavyweight wrestling champion. He would have gone to the Olympics but for drug charges that earned him two years in the zone. But rope swallower or not, he's a big boy, so don't let him put his arms around you.

"These two men were almost certainly responsible for the murders of Mikhail Milyukin, Vaja Ordzhonikidze and one other man. So you can imagine how keen we are to get a hold of them. Sasha?"

Grushko's audience looked at the third face from Criminal Records.

"Volodimir Khmara. Born Zaporozje, 1955. A known

black-marketeer. One conviction for theft. This is the character who has been selling the contaminated meat to the cooperative restaurants in Peter. And the last one, please, Sasha."

The fourth and last photograph was different from the previous mug-shots. It was a longer-distance shot of an older man wearing a black leather coat and getting out of a Mercedes that was parked in front of the Maryinsky Theatre, home of the Kirov Opera and Ballet.

"Last, but by no means least, we have Viktor Bosenko. Born Dnepropetrovsk, 1946. Also known as the Black Swan because of his reputed love of the ballet. One conviction for currency offences during the late 1970s, but nothing since then. We've long suspected that Bosenko is the godfather who runs the whole Ukrainian underworld here in Peter. We don't actually know how much he's directly involved in this particular crime, but the chances are he knows about it. So take a good look at that face just in case he should put in an appearance." Grushko looked over at Andrei. "Can we have the blinds up, please?"

Sasha switched off the projector while Andrei lifted the blinds.

"Any questions?"

One of the OMON squad men raised his hand.

"Why the switch?" he said. "Wouldn't it be simpler just to follow them?"

"We can't take the chance that when the convoy reaches the city it won't be watched by the Mafia. If they see a tail then that'll be it—finished. We would use a helicopter but for the fact that the air force refused to lend us one unless we let them control the whole realisation. Which would probably mean them taking the credit."

There was a murmur of outrage and disbelief. Another hand went up.

"Won't you be recognised through the windscreen, sir?"

"No, the windscreen is protected by armoured louvres."

Another hand.

"After the realisation, what's going to happen to all that meat?"

"I'm glad you've asked me that," said Grushko. "On no account must anyone touch any of the meat."

There was a loud groan of disappointment at this particular piece of news. Grushko raised his voice.

"The meat is radioactive," he said. "Let me be quite clear about this: the meat is unfit for human consumption."

"That never stopped anyone," quipped someone.

"It may look all right," Grushko continued, "but, to quote an old saying, 'never believe what you can see with your own eyes.' I discussed the matter with General Kornilov and he agrees with me that the best thing would be if Anglo-Soyuzatom Transit were to dispose of the meat in the same way that they already dispose of other nuclear waste. So let's leave it to the experts, shall we?"

In another place, at another time, we might have been more shocked to discover the whole character of the crime that had brought about the death of Mikhail Milyukin. This cynicism is not just attributable to our low expectations of the Mafia. It is also referable to our inherent national distrust of the most ordinary commodities. For everyone except foreigners, the consumption of food and drink has become increasingly hazardous. Even something as ordinary as water is not to be relied upon: nobody is ever foolish enough to drink the tea that is laughingly called tap-water without boiling it very thoroughly. The same caution cannot be said to apply to alcohol substitutes, however, which annually claim the lives of thousands of people.

Food scares are common enough. Just before I went to St. Petersburg, Muscovite health-inspectors had found dead dogs and cats being sold as rabbit meat in the

Rozhdestvenska Street market. And most people are becoming used to the sight of reporters from national TV filming Chernobyl chickens—the radiation-mutated two-headed variety—in the state meat markets.

High levels of pesticides and nitrates mean that fruit and vegetables are no less hazardous than meat. One radio journalist has estimated that a person can commit suicide by eating fifteen cucumbers. Many shoppers carry small chemical-detection kits—strips of chemically sensitive paper that enable the housewife to take a quick toxicity reading before purchase.

Of course for many of us probably it is already too late. Our pale grey skins and red eyes, so different from those of sleek and healthy foreigners, seem to indicate as much. My own father died of cancer at the age of forty-seven. My mother is virtually crippled with bronchitis. My sister, with whom she lives, has an incurable liver disease from years of hard drinking.

At the Central Board's hospital in Moscow they told me that I have high blood pressure and advised me to give up salt. I said that I never touched the stuff: life was already quite bitter enough without adding any salt to it. Then the doctor charged with making my medical report listened to my lungs and suggested that I might try to cut down on my smoking. He had a cigarette in his mouth at the time. I had read about this thing in the West called "passive smoking" and asked him if he had heard of it. Just being around Russian cops, I told him, was probably worth about a packet of twenty a day.

Nobody thinks long-term any more. You take your pleasures where and when you can find them. As we all left the briefing-room I heard several men from the OMON squad joke that, radioactive or not, meat was still meat and that it might just be worth the risk to taste a good bit of British beef. At least I assumed they were joking.

★ ★ ★

One of the three vans that had been earmarked for the realisation was found to be completely unroadworthy, and there was no time to get a suitable replacement. Thus it was that I found myself sitting in an Intourist coach parked a short way off the M20, just south of Gatcina. Grushko didn't seem to mind. He said nobody would expect the militia to use a tourist bus to mount an operation against the Mafia.

"Besides," he added, "it's air-conditioned and we can listen to the radio. There's no telling how long we'll have to sit here."

Several times during the next hour or so I saw him look at his watch and I wondered how much his wife's dinner party was on his mind. A look at my own watch seemed to confirm that he wasn't going to be just late for dinner. He stood in danger of missing it altogether.

A policeman's lot. I thought about all the occasions on which I had let my own family down and for the first time since leaving Moscow it didn't seem so hard to see why my wife had started an affair with the music teacher. At least he would never be late for dinner. It was true what they said: sometimes the only things that made the job worthwhile were the people you did it with.

The OMON squad commander, Lieutenant Khlobuyev, stared hard at his walkie-talkie as if willing Captain Novdyrov to call in and report that the convoy was on its way to us. Nikolai smoked another cigarette and tapped his big foot in time with the music on the radio. The other three OMON squad officers, deprived of their usual comforting Schwarzenegger video, stared out of the windows of the coach. Dmitri checked the batteries for the video-recorder with which he would film the whole operation. The bus-driver dozed behind his steering wheel: to him we were just another bunch of passengers, of lesser interest than a tour-group of Americans that might have offered him some hard currency by way of a tip. Andrei looked up from cleaning his pistol and cleared his throat.

"A man goes into his local meat market and says to the butcher, 'Can you cut me some very thin slices of sausage.' And the butcher says . . ."

Several of us came back with what the butcher said, in unison: " 'Bring me the sausage and I'll cut it as thin as you like.' "

"That joke is so old," groaned Nikolai.

"You tell one then," Andrei muttered.

"I don't know any jokes," he said. "Not since I lost my memory. By a coincidence, though, it happened when I was standing outside my local meat market, just the other day. D'you know, I looked in my empty shopping bag and I swear I couldn't remember if I was about to go in the shop, or if I had just walked out of it."

Even Grushko smiled at that.

The walkie-talkie crackled in Khlobuyev's hand. But it was only Lieutenant Khodyrev to say that the Department of Health had found samples of the contaminated beef in the Kallininsky, Zverkovsky, Vasilyostrovsky and Kuznechny cooperative markets. Everyone was silent for a moment, but before the news could quite sink in Novdyrov had contacted us to say that the convoy was passing him even as he was speaking.

Grushko drew his gun.

"All right, everyone," he said. "This is it. Let's get into position."

The bus-driver sat up and operated the automatic doors and switched off the radio. Those of us, myself included, who were staying on the bus watched as Grushko, Nikolai, Khlobuyev and one of his men climbed down the steps and crept forward to the line of trees that screened us from the road. They had chosen their spot for the ambush well. Between the trees and the four-lane highway was a short area of waste ground, long enough on which to have parked not one but several trucks.

I picked up my walkie-talkie handset and called Sasha. He and two van-loads of the OMON squad were waiting somewhere on the M10 where it entered St. Petersburg parallel with the M20.

"The convoy's on its way to us," I told him. "Stand by."

We heard the siren on the GAI patrol car before we saw anything. Then the roar of the big Fodens trucks as they started to slow down. The sky between the trees was suddenly filled with the black, rectangular shapes of the first three trucks as they pulled in to the side of the road and finally drew to a halt a long way further up the lay-by, with a loud hiss of their hydraulic brakes. Behind these three, almost immediately opposite our coach, we saw the blue flashing light of the GAI car as it drew to a halt in front of the fourth Anglo-Soyuzatom truck.

Grushko's teams were running for the back of the truck even before it had quite stopped moving. This was the weakest part of his plan, for he was gambling that the eyes of the driver and his mate would be looking at the patrol car in front of them instead of what was happening in their wing-mirrors.

Minutes passed and just as I was beginning to think that something must have gone wrong, I heard the sound of the patrol-car doors closing and then saw the blue light extinguished. As the GAI car sped away, the trucks began to re-start their engines and slowly the convoy started to move again. Seconds later I heard Grushko's voice on the walkie-talkie.

"Passengers on board," he said gruffly. "I'm going to leave this channel open for a while," he added, "so you can hear what's going on."

"It's lucky we've got these armoured louvres on the

windscreen," he said to Nikolai. "If there's any shooting we might be very glad of them."

A loud bang against the side of our coach announced the return of the OMON squad men with their two prisoners. As they shoved them onto the coach I noticed that one of the crew had a bloody nose. I raised my eyebrows at Lieutenant Khlobuyev. He shrugged and said as if by way of explaining the man's injury, "I just thought it might be useful to find out if they were carrying beef on board."

"And are they?"

He nodded and pushed his man roughly down the centre aisle to the back of the coach. I called Grushko to let him know.

"See if you can persuade them to tell you where we're going," he said.

I went down to the back of the coach where both men were already handcuffed to the handrails of the seats in front. Neither of them said anything. Sunk in gloom, each man leaned forward and buried his face against his manacled forearms. I relayed Grushko's message and then walked back up the aisle to the driver.

"Right, let's get going," I told him. "Just stay on the main road until I say different."

He nodded, lit a cigarette and then started the engine. Having gunned the motor a couple of times he steered us slowly off the track and onto the M20. I sat down in my seat and looked at Andrei.

"I've been on one of these before," he said. "We went on a sightseeing tour."

"It takes all sorts to make a world," I murmured and, when Andrei went to help question the truck's two crewmen, I turned my attention back to Grushko's own travel commentary.

"We're just passing the airport," he announced.

"This is a nice truck," said Nikolai. "I hardly felt that pothole. And this seat—it's better than my old armchair.

All it needs is a few cigarette burns and I'd be right at home. Light me one, will you?"

Hearing a slap and a loud yell from the back of the coach I turned round. Lieutenant Khlobuyev had one of the crewmen by the hair and, filmed by Dmitri, he started to bang the man's head against the coach window. The driver paid no attention. It wasn't his coach, after all.

"There you go," said Grushko.

"One thing I still don't understand," said Nikolai. "Tolya gives Milyukin a sample of contaminated meat. Milyukin hands it over to Dr. Sobchak for analysis."

"Right."

"But the meat that was stolen from the flat . . . that belonged to the Petrakovs?"

"Yes. But of course the two Ukrainians had no idea that Milyukin had already taken the meat to Sobchak. They opened the Petrakov's fridge and found a piece of beef. They weren't to know it wasn't the right one. Beef is beef and, after all, it wasn't as if there was any other meat in the fridge."

"So the Petrakovs just bought it in the local market?"

I heard Grushko swear violently.

"Sasha?" he said urgently. "Sasha, are you there?"

"Where are you, sir?"

"Never mind that now. Look, call Lieutenant Khodyrev and get her to send someone round to my flat straight away. I reckon my wife's bought some of that contaminated meat from a cooperative food market. She's probably serving it up as we speak." He swore again. "Look, I don't care how she does it, but on no account must anyone eat that beef. Have you got that, Sasha?"

"Yes, sir. I'll call you as soon as we hear anything."

"Do that. And for Christ's sake, hurry."

Grushko said nothing for several minutes. Then Andrei came back up the aisle and jerked his thumb over his shoulder.

"We've got a rough location out of our friends," he said.

I handed him the walkie-talkie.

"There's a warehouse in Kirovsky Region," he told Grushko. "Somewhere off Stacek Prospekt. The two crewmen are not exactly sure where, because they usually just follow the truck in front of them. Anyway, there's this cold store that used to belong to the State Fish Board, until the Mafia paid someone hard currency for the place. They reckon it's pretty well protected too: about thirty or forty armed men on average."

Grushko grunted. Andrei shrugged and handed me back the handset.

"What's the matter with him?" he murmured.

"He's worried his wife might have bought some of that contaminated meat," I explained. "And that right now his family might be sitting down to eat it."

"Home cooking," sniffed Andrei. "It'll be the death of us all." And so saying he returned to the back of the coach and sat down.

Ten minutes passed and Grushko radioed that the convoy had reached the outer suburbs of the city on Moskovsky Prospekt. Nikolai was doing his best to distract Grushko from troubled thoughts.

"There's this old priest, right?" he said. "He's been out shopping all day and he's tired, so he stops for a minute to lean against a wall and closes his eyes. After a few minutes he opens them again and by now a queue of about fifty people has formed up behind him. A couple more minutes pass and then the Ivan standing right behind the old priest asks him what they're queuing for. And the priest explains that he'd just stopped to have a rest. 'Well, why didn't you say so?' says the man. And the priest says, 'It's not every day that you find yourself standing at the head of the queue.' " Nikolai laughed enthusiastically.

Grushko was losing his patience.

"Talk to me, Sasha," he said through clenched teeth. "What the hell is happening?"

"Just a minute, sir," said Sasha. "I'm speaking to Olga now."

There was a long, long pause during which I imagined Grushko's family seated around their dining table watching Lena carve the precious joint of meat. A loud knock summons Tanya to the door where she finds herself confronted by several men wearing radiation suits and carrying a radiometer before them like some small ark of the covenant. The guests jump up in horror as the men make their entrance and then they yell with outrage as the contaminated meat—their dinner—is thrown into a plastic bag. I almost wished I could have been there to see it myself.

"Someone's been to your house, sir," said Sasha finally. "Everything's all right. Nobody ate a thing."

"Just like any other Russian meal, then," said Nikolai.

Grushko breathed an audible sigh of relief.

"Thank you," he said quietly. "Thanks, Sasha."

"It's just as well you're wearing a flak-jacket," said Sasha. "Because your wife's going to shoot you. According to Olga she thought it was your idea of a joke. But you were right. The meat was radioactive."

There was not time for Grushko to react to this latest piece of information.

"We're turning off," said Nikolai.

Grushko waited a second and then said: "We're now heading north-west on Krasnoputilovskaya—towards Autovo."

I heard Sasha tell his driver to head west, along Taskentskaya.

"I think we're being tailed," said Nikolai. "That car's been with us since the airport."

I leaned towards the bus-driver.

"I heard," he said negligently. "Krasnoputilovskaya."

He twisted the wheel round to avoid a horse that had strayed onto the road.

"Meat, is it?" he said when we were back in lane. "There's plenty around, if you know where to look. Believe me, a man who drives this road need never go hungry."

I recalled my own car journey from Moscow to St. Petersburg. In principle the M10 was the country's most important arterial road and yet in places it was little more than a two-track highway upon which a wide variety of animals—pigs, goats, cattle and chickens—were allowed to stray. I wondered how a coachload of Americans would have reacted to the prospect of their bus-driver's lethal opportunism.

"Heading north on the M11 and Stacek Prospekt," said Grushko.

"Heading up Trefoleva," said Sasha.

By now the coach was in the outskirts of the city and, as if to underline the fact, we hit a tramline standing proud of the road surface with a loud bang.

"We have you in sight," said Sasha. "Passing the end of Trefoleva."

"He's signalling left," said Nikolai.

"Sasha, we're turning left onto—"

"—Oboronnaya," said Nikolai, prompting him.

"Drive straight across Stacek," Sasha told his driver. And then to Grushko: "We'll stay parallel with you on Trefoleva."

"This looks like it, sir," said Nikolai. "We're slowing down."

"We're here," said Grushko. "It's between Gubina Street and Sevastopol Street."

Sasha instructed the driver of the second OMON van to

turn up Sevastopol Street and then his own driver to drive on to the end of Trefoleva.

"We'll turn right on to Barrikadnaya," he announced, "and then come at them from both ends of the street."

"This is it, everyone," said Grushko. "Let's get these bastards."

CHAPTER
TWENTY-THREE

★ Grushko told me later that his first thought on seeing the first truck back into the cold store was that the militia might be outgunned. It seemed that there were gangsters everywhere, some directing the trucks, some starting to take the cartons of meat out of the containers and some just holding guns and looking out for trouble. As the second and then the third truck reversed through the steel shutters a man whistled loudly and beckoned Nikolai to drive towards him.

Nikolai slipped the clutch and followed the man's directions until he was best placed to reverse into the loading bay. Hearing another whistle from behind he glanced in his wing-mirror and saw a second man waving towards him.

"Stall it," said Grushko. "They mustn't bring that shutter down behind us or the squad won't be able to get in."

Nikolai engaged gear, took his foot off the gas and then released the clutch pedal. The big truck jerked spasmodically as the engine cut out.

He turned the key in the ignition and without touching the accelerator he made a show of trying to get started again. With a Russian-built truck he might have succeeded

DEAD MEAT ★ 263

in flooding the engine. But the Fodens had electronic ignition and started first time.

"Isn't that just great," said Nikolai. "A reliable truck."

"Where the hell's Sasha?" said Grushko.

Nikolai started to move the truck back into the cold store. When he was only halfway through the door, he stalled it again and this time he removed the keys and pocketed them.

Behind them there were shouts and someone started to beat impatiently on the side of the truck's container.

"You'd better find your party invitation," said Grushko.

Nikolai took out his automatic and worked the slide.

"Here comes our friend," he said, glancing in the mirror.

"What the hell's going on?" said a voice outside the driver's door. "C'mon. Move this thing."

Grushko and Nikolai stayed put.

Through the armoured louvres Nikolai saw the man frown and then stand back as he began to realise that something was wrong.

"The electronics have gone," Nikolai shouted. "Everything's stuck. We can't even get the door open."

But the man was already drawing his own weapon. He shouted something to another man and then levelled his gun at the driver's door.

"What do we do now?" said Nikolai.

"Sit tight," said Grushko. "Let's hope this thing is as tough as they said it was."

Nikolai leaned across the seat, out of the line of fire.

They heard a burst of automatic gunfire but nothing hit the cab. Then there was another volley of shots and some shouting.

"Either this thing is tougher than we thought, or that's Sasha," said Grushko.

Gradually a voice began to make itself heard with a loud hailer.

"This is the militia. You are surrounded. Put down your weapons. Walk into the open and lie down with your hands behind your heads. I repeat, you are surrounded. . . ."

"About time," said Grushko and reached for the door handle.

He opened the door a crack and peered out. Men were already dropping their weapons and raising their hands as, from every side of the cold store, came the men of the OMON squad.

Grushko jumped down from the cab and walked towards one of the trucks. The rear doors were open and inside the container he could see hundreds of cartons of meat, some of them still carrying the distinctive EC roundel of yellow stars on a blue background. Beside this same truck was a group of two or three men with their hands raised and among them, wearing a smart suit, his fingers studded with gold rings, was a face Grushko recognised from his own briefing. It was Viktor Bosenko. In his hand he was holding not a gun but a walletful of money.

"Well, well," smiled Grushko, "not just the caviar. We got the whole rotten sturgeon."

Behind him the OMON squad started to kick the feet away from under some of those Mafiosi who were not quick enough to lie down. Bosenko remained standing. He grinned and took a step towards Grushko and away from his own men.

"I think there's been some sort of mistake here," he said. "We thought you were the Mafia."

"That's a good one." Grushko laughed. "You thought we were the Mafia."

Sasha appeared at Grushko's shoulder, scanning the gangway near the cold store's ceiling for signs of further resistance.

Viktor Bosenko took another step forward.

"But, thank God, you're the militia," he said. "Look here, officer, I'm sure I can explain this to your satisfaction. We're just businessmen trying to protect what's ours, that's all." He shrugged as if he was trying to seem accommodating.

"Maybe we can come to some kind of an arrangement?" He lowered his hands carefully and, opening the wallet, took out a whole fistful of dollars.

"Some compensation for you and your men. For your time and trouble. And to thank you for your protection. You know, there's nearly five thousand dollars here. What's that to you and your men? Maybe two years' salary for everyone?"

Grushko looked at Bosenko with growing incredulity. Then he snatched the dollars from his hand and threw them in the Ukrainian's grinning mouth.

"To my face?" he snarled. "You'd try and bribe me to my face? In front of all my men?"

The punch came up from Grushko's waist and caught Bosenko flush underneath the jaw. As Bosenko hit the ground Grushko sprang forward to catch him by the lapels and hit him again.

Arriving on the scene it seemed to me that Sasha was moving to restrain Grushko. His yell of warning was lost in the larger sound of a gunshot and Grushko found himself supporting the man who had seemed to be holding him. He turned and saw one of Bosenko's men escaping through the back door, gun in hand. Grushko let Sasha slip onto the floor and went after him.

There was blood running out of Sasha's mouth. Nikolai dropped down on his knees and tried to turn his friend over onto his stomach in the coma position, to stop him drowning in his own blood. Sasha winced and held Nikolai's arm.

"I told you," he wheezed. "I told you—these flak jackets are no good."

Then he jerked convulsively, as if hit by a small bolt of electricity, and was dead.

★ ★ ★

Stepan Starovyd, the Wrestler, came out of the cold store on to a cobbled alleyway. Seeing a distinctive blue OMON squad uniform he fired once again, and caught his man in the leg. Then he ran towards the Yekateringofka Canal and a pier where he knew Bosenko kept a small boat. Hearing the sound of running footsteps behind him, he spun round and squeezed off a couple of wild shots. The slide locked open on the last of them.

Grushko picked himself off the street and moved towards the Ukrainian.

The Wrestler could see that it was quite useless. There were men from the OMON squad behind the man he had fired at. But instinctively he continued to back away from Grushko towards the canal. He grinned sheepishly and started to raise his hands.

He was still backing away when Grushko shot him. The .45 calibre hollowpoint hit him square in the chest and carried him across the edge of the canal. The Wrestler was dead before he hit the dirty water, with such a look of surprise on his big, strong face that it was still there when, the next day, they put him on the section table at the Bureau of Judicial Medical Examinations.

Grushko walked over to the canal's edge and looked down at the floating body. Then he spat into the water.

Nikolai met him as he walked back towards the cold store.

"Sasha?" said Grushko.

Nikolai shook his head.

"No, I thought not."

Inside the cold store the OMON squad had lined up all the Ukrainians against the wall and, filmed by Dmitri, were searching them for concealed weapons.

Grushko stood over Sasha's body, hardly caring that his feet were surrounded by a spreading red flag that was the dead man's blood. I went over to him, hoping to think of something kind to say and, finding myself speechless at the waste of it, could merely shrug and shake my head like some disappointed pensioner. But Grushko's soul was made of more extrovert stuff. He said it as he saw it and, truth to tell, at the time the words from Pushkin's epic poem, *Eugene Onegin* did not seem so affected as they do when I recall them now:

" 'The storm is over, dawn is paling, the bloom has withered on the bough; the altar flame's extinguished now.' "

Nikolai lit a couple of cigarettes and handed one to Grushko.

"Come on, sir," he said. "Let's go home. It's all over."

Grushko gave him a baleful sort of look and Nikolai shrugged philosophically.

"Well, until the next time anyway," he added.

Grushko sucked hard on the cigarette.

"Nikolai Vladimirovich," he said, "you've been reading my bloody horoscope."

CHAPTER
TWENTY-FOUR

★ Nina Milyukin had not mistaken Grushko. She had recognised him for what he was, a man of one book—the Book of the Law and Morals as he saw it, without benefit of equity, without mercy. Beware of a man of one book. That was how I began this story and now I must explain why.

A few days after we had arrested the Ukrainians he must have telephoned Nina and arranged to meet her at Mikhail's grave in Volkov Cemetery. I can't imagine that it would have been her idea to meet him there. That must have been part of his design. Did she guess what he wanted to say to her? I think she must have done. Perhaps she may even have thought that Grushko was one of them. After all, he was a Colonel of Militia. But if she did think that then she was quickly disabused of that idea.

He found her laying a single carnation—one was usually all that anyone could afford—on the bare earth covering Mikhail Milyukin's coffin. Before she knew he was there he tossed the file he had brought with him beside her flower. Nina recognised it immediately. The sword and the shield stamped on the file's buff cover were notorious. But she did not pick it up. She looked at the file almost as if it would have burned her to touch it.

"I thought that you might like to dispose of this yourself," said Grushko. "Now that he's dead it would seem that they have no further use for you."

"They?" she said pointedly.

"Oh no," said Grushko, shaking his head, "not me. I've never been part of that." He lit a cigarette and watched her as, reluctantly, she bent down to pick up the file.

"You know, I couldn't work out why you were being so reticent with us. I mean, there we were trying to find your husband's killers and you said nothing. But of course when I saw that file everything suddenly started to make sense. It's shame that makes one silent, isn't it?"

"They gave this to you?" she said angrily. "Just like that? I don't believe it."

"I had the very same thought myself," said Grushko. "How could you do it? How could you spy on your friends, on your own husband?"

"It's easy to ask that now," she said bitterly. "A lot of people can be brave in retrospect. But believe me, it wasn't so easy to say no to the KGB." Her eyes flashed. "I've had to live with the fear of them all my life. Virtually the first thing I remember being scared of were the people who arrested my father."

"That's a nice story," said Grushko, "but it doesn't explain how you came to work for them."

"You've read the file," she sighed.

"Yes, but it says you were passing them information as long ago as 1974, when you were still a student. That's a long time."

"They said that they had proof that my mother was a dissident: that she regularly passed on copies of forbidden books. You think I was going to let them send her away too?" Nina shook her head. "It wasn't unusual, what I did. You should know that."

She opened her handbag and took out a packet of cigarettes. She lit one and smoked it without much enjoyment.

"For a while after university they left me alone. I was never that useful to them. I'm not the kind of person who ever remembers what anyone has said. But then, after I married Mikhail, they contacted me again. They said they would stop him from working because he was a Jew. Well, don't you see? He could never have stood that. His work was his whole life. It was only little stuff, nothing important: foreign journalists Mikhail knew. What they were saying. Who they met. But after a year or two Mikhail noticed something, I think. He never said anything, but I'm sure he suspected something."

"That's why he became secretive with you about his work, isn't it?" said Grushko. "It wasn't because he didn't want you to worry about him. It was because he wasn't sure if he could trust you or not."

"You see?" she shrugged. "In a way, I was telling you the truth. I really didn't know anything after all."

"So then what happened?"

"If Mikhail went out, he didn't tell me where he was going, or who he was seeing. Nobody came back to the flat. I stopped being much use to them. So they went after Mikhail himself. They wanted him to spy on an English journalist, someone they suspected of having an intelligence connection. And he told them to go to hell. He said they could do what they liked. They made all sorts of threats. And of course he was scared. But Mikhail was stronger than me."

"No, not stronger," said Grushko. "Just better."

"I don't know why I'm explaining myself to you," she said. "Or why you think you're any better than those bastards in the KGB. Are your own hands really so very clean, Grushko?"

"I can still look my friends in the eye."

"Then you've been lucky." Suddenly she seemed afraid. "Does anyone else—?"

"You needn't worry," he said cutting her off. "There's just you and me and your conscience—if you have one."

"You know what I hope?" she said. "I hope that one day you find out that someone close to you has betrayed you. I wonder if you'll be more forgiving then."

"Oh, I can forgive you," said Grushko, snapping his fingers. "Just like that. But him?" He pointed at Milyukin's grave. "Well, I guess we'll never know, will we?"

Tears welled up in Nina's china blue eyes.

"You cruel bastard."

Grushko grinned. "A mind-reader as well as an informer. There's no end to your talents."

He left her standing there.

★ ★ ★

The newspapers say that suicide has become a political weapon. The conservatives in the Congress of People's Deputies were quick to associate the collapse of the old system and economic hard times with an increase in the number of people taking their own lives. It was up ten percent since 1987. If you were a democrat, would knowing that make you less inclined to kill yourself?

They also say that women are less inclined to commit suicide than men. Perhaps someone should have told Nina Milyukin. A few hours after her meeting with Grushko she drank a whole bottle of strong vinegar and died. It was a common, albeit painful method of killing yourself, if you could still find a bottle of strong vinegar in the shops. When several people telephoned Militia Station 59 to ask them where they might buy this vinegar, Lieutenant Khodyrev was forced to put out a statement saying that the bottle was an old one and had been in Nina Milyukin's cupboard for several years.

The newspapers and television agreed that grief made her do it. Of course by then I knew different.

The heatwave ended a couple of days later. A cool breeze stirred the leaves of the poplar trees in the Summer Gardens where I had taken to walking and St. Petersburg seemed like the most beautiful city on earth. It did not seem like the kind of city you would pick to commit suicide in.

When I discovered what Grushko had said to Nina Milyukin I was angry and told him I thought he had behaved abominably.

"With a woman who betrayed her husband like that?" he said. "I don't think so."

"My wife betrayed me," I said, "but it doesn't give me the right to judge her. God knows, maybe I drove her to it."

"That's different," he said. "Nina Milyukin wasn't just someone who failed in her duty as a wife. She failed in her duty as a human being. She was false. She lived the worst kind of lie."

"Where have you been?" I said scornfully. "The whole bloody country's been living a lie for the last seventy years. We have to put all of it behind us if we're ever going to make it something better. And that includes the Nina Milyukins of this world."

The more I thought about it the angrier I became.

"You know what you did? You said what Mikhail Milyukin had purposefully left unsaid. He knew she was spying on him, but he chose to stay silent. He felt it was better to have her reporting what he did to the KGB than not to have her at all."

I shook my head sadly. "You've thrown away a valuable life," I told him. "I hope you can live with that."

★ ★ ★

After that I stayed out of his way for a while, liasing with Vladimir Voznosensky at the State Prosecutor's Office and busying myself with the preparation of the numerous cases we had against the Georgians and the Ukrainians. But at Sasha's funeral he came up and took me aside for a minute.

"You were right," he said. "There was no need to say what I said. It was unforgivable."

"I wasn't right," I said, and told him how I had been planning to see more of Nina Milyukin. "But maybe we were both wrong."

They gave Sasha a burial with full honours. A militia detachment fired a salute over his grave. And the city council gave his widow a cheque for two thousand roubles. It was just four months' pay.

After the funeral several of us went back to Nikolai's house for a drink. It wasn't much of an evening. At an early stage Nikolai lifted a glass and said "Good health," and Grushko glowered at him and replied, "Are we drinking, or talking?" But gradually, as more vodka was consumed, things eased up just a bit and Grushko described how his daughter seemed determined to go and live in America.

"Why should anyone want to go and live in America?" he said. "That's what I'd like to know." Then he looked at me meaningfully and added: "At least here you can always blame someone else when something goes wrong."

C H A P T E R
TWENTY-FIVE

★ As my reverie ended, the compartment door opened with a rush of air and noise and the carriage attendant came to offer us tea from her samovar. As if to atone for my poor company I paid for two glasses and handed one carefully to my attractive travelling companion. Then the door closed, leaving us alone once again.

She smiled. "Thank you."

"Where are you from?" I asked her. For a moment she was silent, her hands cupped around her glass as she sipped the steaming hot tea.

"From Moscow. I'm a ballerina. I was with the Kirov, but now I'm going back to the Bolshoi. What about you?"

"I'm a policeman." Briefly I described my trip to St. Petersburg.

I wondered whether or not to add that I had really been sent to St. Petersburg as part of an undercover investigation, to look for any evidence of corruption in Grushko's department. Perhaps these things are best left unsaid, even today when there is so much honesty and openness in government. Some people find it hard to understand this kind of work. But with all investigations into police corruption you have to put duty ahead of personal relationships. Like the time I had to pretend to be corrupt myself in order to trap another policeman. That wasn't pleasant. The man, who lost his job and went to prison, had a wife and family. Besides, it was not as if I had found any evidence that Grushko and his men were on the take. Far from it. To me, it seemed that Kornilov had merely wished to be quite certain that his men were thoroughly honest. That was understandable. The nature of Grushko's work made him and his men vulnerable to corruption. So I had little to feel too guilty about. After all, as Grushko himself would have agreed, an honest police force was the only way that the Mafia would ever be broken. Even so, I could have wished that there had been an opportunity for more honesty between us, although right to the last I think Grushko had always suspected who I was and what I was really up to.

I shrugged. Now it was me trying to make conversation. "I would have been driving back to Moscow now, except that the head gasket went on my car again."

"Again?"

"Yes, I'd just got it back on the road after the last one went."

She laughed, shook her head and the air was filled with the smell of her perfume which was like nothing I'd ever encountered before. "That's too bad."

"Well, at least I've had the chance of meeting you."

"Oh, there's nothing much interesting about me."

"No? I should have thought being a dancer was interesting."

She grimaced. "Hard work."

"I love the ballet. Someone in Central Board offered to get me tickets for the Kirov, only I never found the time to go."

"I'll arrange some tickets for you to come and see me at the Bolshoi, if you like?"

"Just the one would be fine."

She took out a notebook and a pencil. "Tell me your address and I'll send you one."

I thought for a minute. I could always stay with my mother and my sister for a few days, but I couldn't see how I could go and live there permanently any more than I could have gone back to my wife. I explained about how my wife and I were seeking a divorce and that she had better send the ticket to the police headquarters on Petrovka.

She made a note of the address and then looked concerned.

"But where will you live?" she asked.

"I'll find somewhere I expect," I said and changed the subject. "Are you married?"

"Divorced."

"You know," she added tentatively, "if you're looking for somewhere, there's a spare room you could have."

"Really? No, I couldn't." But my thoughts were already racing ahead to something altogether more connubial. Did beautiful ballerinas ever fall for policemen outside of the movies? I thought it more likely that my tone-deaf daughter would become a concert pianist. "Could I?"

"It's not much of a place," she said. "Besides, it might be handy to have a policeman around. After all, it's not very safe these days." She showed me the air-pistol she carried in her handbag. "You know, I often come back quite late at night."

"Look, are you sure? I mean, you don't really know me. I mean, I could be absolutely anyone."

But she had convinced herself of the merit of her idea.

"Yes," she said thoughtfully. "It might be quite nice to come home and know that there was a policeman in the place."

"Well, you know what they say," I said. "It's a lot cheaper than owning a dog."

ABOUT THE AUTHOR

Philip Kerr was born in Edinburgh in 1959. He is the author of four previous novels, including *A Philosophical Investigation*, upon which a feature film by Paramount is to be based. *Dead Meat* has been filmed by the BBC as a three-part serial under the title *Grushko*. Kerr now lives in London, England.

Also by Philip Kerr

GRIDIRON

Kerr is at his best in this thriller about a "smart" building in L.A. where all the systems are controlled by one central computer which breaks down—with deadly consequences.

Praise for GRIDIRON:

"Ingeniously gruesome ... you will just love it!"
—*The London Times*

"The brainy thriller of the year!"
—*The Independent*

Available in hardcover from Doubleday Canada

A PHILOSOPHICAL INVESTIGATION

Suppose there was a simple test that could determine those with a genetic tendency toward repeated homicidal behaviour. Suppose the government kept a list of these potential serial killers. Suppose you found your name on the list ...

Praise for A PHILOSOPHICAL INVESTIGATION:

"A truly intellectual thriller that makes the brain cells as well as the hairs on the back of the neck tingle."
—*GQ magazine*

"One book that no one should miss ... intelligent, impeccably plotted."
—*The Globe and Mail*

Published in paperback from Seal Books.
Available wherever books are sold.

Doubleday

SEAL